CHASING THE DRAGON

Also by Domenic Stansberry

The Confession

Manifesto for the Dead

The Last Days of Il Duce

Exit Paradise

The Spoiler

CHASING
the
DRAGON

Domenic Stansberry

 St. Martin's Minotaur ✠ New York

www.minotaurbooks.com

Library of Congress Cataloging-in-Publication Data

Stansberry, Domenic.
    Chasing the dragon / by Domenic Stansberry.— 1st U.S. ed.
      p. cm.
    ISBN 0-312-32467-7
    EAN 978-0312-32467-4
    1. North Beach (San Francisco, Calif.)—Fiction. 2. Funeral rites and ceremonies—Fiction. 3. Undercover operations—Fiction. 4. Fathers— Death—Fiction. 5. Police, Private—Fiction. 6. Drug traffic—Fiction. I. Title.

PS3569.T3335C47 2004
813'.54—dc22

                                         2004050857

First Edition: October 2004

10 9 8 7 6 5 4 3 2 1

For Concetta and Domenic Mussolino, Vincenza Rose,
Chadwick Leroy—and all the rest

Special thanks to
Fred Hill and Kelley Ragland

CHASING THE DRAGON

PROLOGUE

O n the night he died, Giovanni Mancuso heard the floorboards creak, and he knew someone was in the house. *My murderer,* he told himself. Not that he needed anyone to finish him off. He would go on his own soon enough. Though the pain was worse now—accompanied by double vision and a loss of control in the extremities—there were consolations. The doctor had given him a medication implant under the skin, a squeeze pump full of morphine. He had visions, at times quite beautiful.

There was a creaking around the corner, down the hall, at the top of the stairs.

Giovanni Mancuso had lived in the house long enough to know that the sound he heard, those footsteps, were not his imagination. It was not the sound of the house settling.

There was someone here, he was all but sure. A shadow appeared in the mirror across from his bed. In the mirror, the shadow moved again, stepping through the slanted light that fell through the hall window from the arc lamp outside.

His heart beat more rapidly.

"What are you hiding, old man? Tell me. Where is it?"

The pain flooded him, and he reached for the remote that controlled the pump, sending morphine to a little cavity in the base of his spine. He was on a bluff, overlooking the ocean, and his wife was below him down on the shore. She was singing like she used to do, her voice carrying up from the kitchen. Rossini, maybe. Verdi. Her voice had been beautiful once. A wind moved through the pines and set the shadows in motion. The footsteps were closer, and he opened his eyes.

The shadow hovered over him, and there was a face inside that shadow.

"No," Giovanni said. "My son will track you down . . . my son, the cop, my son . . ."

His words were unrecognizable, he realized, an old man's mumbling—a sound like the fluttering of wings. The face was still in shadow. He couldn't see the features, but he felt the visitor's hands on his shoulder. It was not a gentle touch. The hands rolled him over, face into the pillow. He felt a hand on his skull, holding him in place.

He coughed, struggling for air. The pain wracked through him and he squeezed again.

There were birds, there were flowers, there were all the people he had ever known, his old buddies from Lucca and Calabria, from Genoa and Santa Lucia from all over the goddamn place, women with hawk noses, peasant dresses, here among the poppies and the oak and the madrone, here on Telegraph Hill with its shanties tumbling under skyscrapers, the wind gusting through the clothes on the line, down the alleys. But they were all gone now, the old crones and the winepresses and the fishmongers, buried under the mud, under the concrete, the passing feet.

The pressure on his head relaxed.

"Where, old man? Who do you think you're fooling?"

He couldn't answer such a question. He tasted the pillow in his mouth. He could smell the intruder's body against his own. He groped for the remote. The doctor had warned him to be careful, not to overdose.

Then he was coughing. Face into the pillow. There was blood in his throat. He squeezed again, trying to get back into the vision—then a spasm shook through him.

He had passed some boundary.

I know who you are, Mr. Shadow, he thought. *I know and I will tell my son.* But it was too late. The footsteps were already receding, growing fainter, back down the steps, the carpet, through the front door, into the streets, fainter, and for a second he could see all of North Beach below, here on the edge, on this peninsula jutting into the dark Pacific. Meanwhile the footsteps, fainter, then fainter still . . .

My heart has stopped. The stranger is gone. There is no one in this room.

And the vision. . . .

PART ONE

ONE

It was August in New Orleans, and Dante Mancuso was far from San Francisco, far from his dying father. He had taken to sleeping in the afternoon, after the daily thundershower, during that time of day when the light outside had begun to grow white again, hot, more merciless than before, and the humidity rose from the ground in vapors thick enough to see. Outside, the traffic slowed, and people sought the shadows. It usually took Dante a couple of shots to go under, but once he did he tumbled into a sleep that was sweet and dark and empty.

At the deepest point, he awoke. Since his last assignment, it often happened this way. He awoke with no transition to find himself sitting bolt upright in his bed, heart beating like a drum. His clothes were damp; the room smelled of his own sweat. The image that stayed in his head was simply one of darkness, but beneath that darkness, he knew, there had been something else.

Things had gone badly on his last assignment, in Bangkok. A young Thai girl—a professional concubine, with sweet, drug-clouded eyes—had been slashed to death, and he'd been the one to find her, bloody on the sheets.

It was time to quit, he'd told himself. To leave the company. But it wasn't so simple. He took the bottle and went out on his stoop.

The bourbon helped, but not enough. The darkness was still inside him, an emptiness he could not fill. In Bangkok he had grown used to stronger stuff. It had been part of his role: a decadent businessman gone over the edge, bingeing on liquor and opiates and sex. He'd taken it a little too far, carried away in the part, and those cravings still haunted him.

The Ninth Ward was a working-class neighborhood. Black families, Irish, Italians. They lived in bungalows like Dante's, built on swamp fill underneath the levee that held back the wide, polluted waters of the Mississippi. At twilight people came out on their stoops to chatter. The "yat" couples in their blousy clothes, mouths full of booze, out to greet the evening. Young black men walking alone, escaping the heat of the Desire projects.

Though the similarities were superficial, there were times when the streets reminded him of home—or made him long for it, anyway. For San Francisco, North Beach, the old Italian neighborhood where he had grown up: its nineteenth-century rowhouses, its concrete patios and the sound of drunks caterwauling in the midnight streets. An old man's face, maybe, glimpsed in passing; a building cornice; a woman's skirt—such things would trigger in him an unreasonable nostalgia.

But he was far away. He had been away from home seven years. The air here was heavy. Even his memories were languid, full of murk.

Inside, the phone rang. Dante hesitated, drenched in sweat,

already a little drunk, thinking about getting drunker. He let it ring three times, then meant to grab it, because he was superstitious about numbers—a trait he'd inherited from his grandmother on his mother's side, Nanna Pellicano.

It was a superstition that amused him, that he did not really take seriously, he told himself, but it stuck with him anyway.

Three. The number of the Trinity. Of flesh and spirit in union with the divine.

Nanna Pellicano had gotten truths like this from the nuns in Calabria when she was a little girl, but hers was an older Catholicism mixed with the spirits of the old country—the kind of demons that rose from the peasant landscape, informed by some pagan augury—and Dante had been drilled in it more thoroughly than he cared to admit.

There are things you should know, my grandson, Mr. Homicide Cop. The devil can't come in if you don't invite him. . . . If you wear the scapular beneath your shirt. . . . If you count the beads as you pray.

Tonight, though, he was a little bit slow and did not catch the phone until the fourth ring. When he heard the thin voice on the other end, he wished he had not picked it up at all.

"New Orleans Import?" asked the voice.

He didn't know for sure if it was the same voice that had contacted him in the past—when he thought of the voice later he could not be sure, at times, even of the gender—but either way there was a certain timbre, a reedy quality, not quite human, like that of an insect speaking through a megaphone.

Dante paused, knowing that if he didn't come back with the right phrase, the conversation might end. Part of him was tempted to foil the whole business.

"Import-export," he said.

"We have some cane furniture coming in."

"Can the routine," said Dante, breaking from the script. "Just tell me what you want me to do."

There was silence on other end. He'd violated protocol. The company liked their sequence of greetings, their routine. The business had to be played out, no matter if they had his every move monitored, likely as not. No, the company liked these conversations to proceed in a certain way. Each phrase like a number in a combination lock. And all those numbers had to line up precisely, in the right order, or the alarms went off.

Which was sweet in theory, except little the company did quite worked according to plan.

The thin voice tried again. "I said, we have some cane furniture coming in."

Dante sighed. "Good quality?"

"The highest."

"When can I see it?"

"We have a salesperson coming into town. You could meet her. If you wish."

"Name?" Dante asked.

"Name?" repeated the voice on the other end.

"Yeah, name. How do I know who I'm meeting if I don't have a name?"

"Anita."

"Anita who?"

"Anita Blonde."

It was an absurd name, of course, the kind of cover name that company people were prone to use, that called attention to itself, the exact opposite of what you'd expect.

"All right," Dante said.

The man gave him the information regarding the meeting in the backhanded way his people always did. As Dante took it down, he felt a hunger for the man he had once been—or imagined himself to have been—back in North Beach, walking the streets his father had walked, and his father before him.

What it came out to now was this: He was to meet this Anita Blonde tomorrow morning, just past ten, down at the Café Du Monde.

"Hey," the voice said. It was a kind of a whisper—a tag on the end. A direct address, strictly against protocol.

"Yeah?" said Dante.

"Go to hell, smart-ass," said the voice, and the line went dead.

TWO

The next morning, the woman called Anita Blonde sat alone outdoors at the Du Monde under the patio umbrella. There were couples on either side of her, tourists most likely, and though the men in the restaurant may have given her an appraising glance—and the women, too, for that matter—there was no reason for anyone to regard her as anything other than she appeared: a woman waiting for her companion to arrive so they might together begin to eat their strawberry croissants and drink the chicory coffee. She had a perfectly composed face, difficult to read. So it would have been impossible to tell at what point she caught a glimpse of the man crossing the square toward the Du Monde—or if indeed she had noticed him at all. A handsome man, though a bit dissipated. An odd, loping walk. A man with penetrating eyes, an aquiline nose that gave his face a certain fierceness—and whom the night before had been instructed by telephone to meet a woman in a straw hat sitting under an umbrella.

The man was Dante Mancuso and he walked up to her table without hesitation.

"I love strawberries," he said.

"Myself as well."

"Are these for me?"

"If you want them."

Dante sat down across from her and looked out over Jackson Square. The sun was not quite blinding yet, but the day was already redolent with heat. He could smell the muddy Mississippi behind him, and the flowers in the window boxes of the French Quarter, and the rats who left their droppings in the gutter at night. The stones on the café floor beneath the table were wet from a trickle of water that ran out of the vegetable stands at the other end of the Du Monde.

Dante regarded this woman from across the table, and she regarded him, and together they began to prattle, improvising, as if they were a couple on some lost weekend.

"Did you happen to see those little mints the hotel left on our pillows last night?" she asked.

"I ate mine."

"Let's have crawfish étouffée for lunch."

"I'll have oysters. And a Dixie beer."

"This town, I don't know how anyone here ever gets any rest."

"You should come for Mardi Gras. We could meet in disguise."

"You've suggested that a million times, dear. In the last two days."

"A million and one."

They laughed, ha ha, carried away with the pretense, making it up as they went. You got good at this kind of stuff after awhile with the company, and together they looked their parts. Dante wore a Hawaiian shirt. Anita Blonde was dressed in yellow, with a straw hat and sunglasses. She was a good-looking woman, somewhere in her midthirties, though a little tired around her eyes, like maybe she'd played a few too many roles herself. He'd never seen her before and figured after today he'd never see her again.

"Let's go sit in the square," she said and smiled at him a little bit.

He imagined for a moment that they were the couple they appeared to be. Maybe stayed last night in the Cornstalk Hotel on Royal, her up from Biloxi for the weekend, a divorcée and a traveling man who'd met in a bar a few weeks back and now here they were in the Big Easy for some illicit fun, some fucking on starched sheets. He took her hand as they went across the street, and there was a kind of a cool pleasure in taking on this role, an escape from the heat.

"We want you to go to San Francisco," she said.

He was taken aback and for a second the blue haze of New Orleans thickened around him as if he were in some narcotic dream—and through that haze he imagined the spires of the Cathedral of Saints Peter and Paul, back in Washington Square.

"When?"

"Tomorrow. First flight out."

"You got a name for me? A history?"

She shook her head. "Take a room in North Beach."

"I grew up there. People know me."

"That's why we want you. Go under your real name. Go as Dante Mancuso."

"Why?"

"It's coincidence. It works out well. The company needs someone in San Francisco. And you have reason to be there."

"What's my reason?"

She looked away for a moment. When she spoke, her voice was deadpan. "A funeral," she said. "Your father died in his sleep. Evening before last."

He met her eyes. He'd known the old man was ill. He'd met with him in Houston, a reconciliation of sorts, when his father had gone to see the specialist there. *It's a slow grower, this cancer. The doctor says it's nothing. I'm going to live forever.* His old man had been full of bravado, but his eyes had betrayed him, and it had seemed there was something more he'd wanted to tell Dante. So Dante had expected the worst, but not so soon. And he hadn't expected to hear of it from the company.

"What kind of assignment is this?"

Her expression changed. He didn't catch why at first.

"How quaint!"

The exclamation came from behind him. Tourists, he realized, enchanted with the square, with New Orleans.

"You like Marlon Brando?" Anita Blonde asked suddenly, loud enough for the tourists to hear. "He lives in Tahiti, you know."

"I like him okay," Dante said. She'd changed the conversation, he understood, in case the tourists were not what they seemed and should manage to overhear.

"I've always thought you look like him, just a little." Anita paused, amused with herself. "Before he was such a fat pig, of course."

The tourists were wandering away now, out of earshot almost, but not quite. "Should we go there for our next vacation, do you think? To Tahiti?"

"Only if we stop in and say hi to Marlon," Dante said.

"Of course."

Finally, the tourists were gone. Anita moved closer to him on the bench, putting her knee up against his, playing out the routine but talking business now.

"There's a smuggling ring working out of the city," she said. "High-grade heroin. The company wants to crack it up."

"Why me?"

She ignored the question. "It's run by an old San Francisco family, the Wus."

Dante remembered the name. He'd grown up in the city and he'd spent ten years with the SFPD. The Wus headed one of the old Chinese Benevolent Associations—and their family had been around since the 1800s. The Wus also had close links with the underground tongs. With their tight kinship and their network of families and hidden relationships, the tongs in the old days had helped the Chinese survive. In legitimate ways, but not so legitimate, too—mingling smuggling and prostitution, bringing in illegal workers, drugs, and arms, and at the same time running overground businesses.

Dante remembered, when he was a kid, catching a glimpse of Love Wu, head of the Wu clan and an old man even then, standing in his blue suit in front of a door in Chinatown. He was a powerful-seeming man, Dante remembered, with a certain charisma, an expression that suggested he had a secret claim on everything he happened to glance upon and the world beyond that as well.

"I still don't see," he said, "why I get the call."

"Your Uncle Salvatore—your father's brother?"

"Yeah?"

"He has a contract with one of their holding companies. The Wus move a lot of merchandise through your family's warehouse, and, well . . ."

Anita Blonde smiled tartly, and Dante understood the implication. He'd heard it before. His uncle's warehouse these days handled shipments from China, and there were always stories about the nature of those shipments, and suggestions of dealings beneath the surface. But Dante didn't give it much credence. His uncle was a neighborhood guy—a good man, as far as Dante knew. It was hard for him to envision Uncle Salvatore playing the kind of game she was describing. The suggestion irritated him, but he let it go.

"We want you to talk to your uncle," she said. "Tell him we're putting a sting on. Get him to cooperate. If something worries him, promise him immunity—so long as he cooperates."

Dante wasn't crazy about the idea. He didn't much feel like putting the strong arm on his father's brother. Also, there was a question of cover. He'd spent seven years building a firewall between himself and his earlier life at the SFPD.

"You should get someone else," he said.

"No—your association with your uncle, the neighborhood, it gives you an advantage. You'll have access to the warehouse; it'll be natural for you to be there—and you can help set up the sting."

Dante was to connect with a man named Joe Williams, she explained. Williams was an ex-con who'd spent time for smuggling heroin. Dante's job was to get Williams and his heroin, together with Mason Wu, down at the Mancuso warehouse. Mason Wu was Love Wu's great-nephew, and the company wanted him. There was another man, too, they wanted in their net: a Black Muslim, a preacher by the name of Yusef Fakir. The company wanted Fakir and Mason Wu and Williams, all in the building, with the drugs and the money, when the DEA came swooping down.

Anita Blonde went on with it now, explaining the details. They sat in the shadow of the Old Ursuline Convent, near the center of the square, under the lurching statue of Andrew Jackson. Technically this was a DEA sting, she told him. The company wasn't supposed to work on internal police jobs, Dante knew, but it happened often enough, particularly if there was some kind of security connection.

"And, oh," said Anita Blonde, "that woman you used to know. Marilyn Visconti."

Dante felt something drop in his chest. He and Marilyn had gotten together during his last year in San Francisco, before the Strehli case had sent him packing. He didn't want to think about the Strehli case.

"What about her?"

"Pick up your relationship with her."

"Why?"

"It's part of your cover. Prodigal son, home to claim the family business. And his old girl, too."

Anita smiled. Her hair had a little flip and she had done her lips with white gloss. She kept a hand on his knee, playing it for the tourists and anyone else who was watching.

As for the truth behind the scheme and the reasons for it, Dante had no way to judge. In his experience, the company said one thing and set up another, the facts got twisted, and often you were never sure of their real intentions, or who was an agent and who wasn't, and what was the real nature of the masquerade.

When she was done talking, Anita Blonde walked with him to the edge of the square. They stopped at the corner.

"We part here," she said, and for the first time he noticed the Midwest in her voice, the broad flat part of the country gone to seed.

He looked her up and down. "I thought you wanted éttouf-fée," he said. "A little crawfish."

They stood rather close, like husband and wife, only without the easiness. The sexual tensions were there. She wore shorts and he looked her over—and in her face he saw the terrible lure of fading beauty. He had a brief impulse to take her by the hand and bring her back with him to his place. He wondered what she had done, how many people she'd left behind, from what flat part of the Midwest she had emerged.

"Do you ever have the impulse to just throw this all over? To just disappear off the books?"

She hesitated, considering. "That's heresy," she said. Her face was expressionless.

"I was only joking. I'm a loyal soldier."

"Too bad."

He was about to say something else—let's have a drink, maybe, let's get drunk and fall in the river, let's take a roll in the mud—when she raised a finger up to that white lipstick, pursing her lips, then placed that same finger into the middle of his lips, shushing him.

"Tahiti," she said. "I would love to vacation there."

Then, before he could make a move, she turned and headed away down those cobbled streets.

Though Anita Blonde stayed in Dante's mind for a moment longer—the sound of her heels on the pavement still in his ears, her scent still in his nostrils—and though it was not hard to imagine her swanning through the Rue Canal, changing directions, then changing again, engaging in all the customary dodges to make sure she was not being followed—nonetheless, his thoughts had turned to other things by the time she actually flagged down a taxi on Esplanade, then was dropped off at the Rue Sangre only to stroll through the lobby to a cab stand on the other side. She changed cabs again out in Metairie before ending up in a motel on the Airline Highway in a new outfit altogether: new pumps, hair no longer blonde but stone black, all the while with that same composure, that same coolness, so adept at hiding the feeling inside—the impending doom, the sense of everything about to go awry. It was a feeling she had known for a long time.

Wherever the company went, death followed. Sooner or later it would be her death, she knew. And Dante, alone in his cottage, had the same thought, however briefly. He might have crossed himself after the fashion of his grandmother, warding off evil, but he knew the company, and he did not think such gestures would do much good.

THREE

The Beach was in his memory again, all of a sudden, and Dante had a sensation that pulled him in two directions at once, a feeling that in some ways he had never left home. The alleys and hotel rooms of New Orleans, Bangkok, Spokane, every passage between here and there, every place he'd been, they were all somehow interconnected, part of the same town; but their streets kept metamorphosing under his feet, so he was always at home and never quite there.

Once things had been simpler. He'd been a native son, a neighborhood kid. Named for his maternal grandfather, Dante Pellicano, a fisherman from Santa Flavia who married a superstitious Calabrian and whose daughter, the beautiful Teresa, had given him a grandson.

"Oh, your nose," Marilyn Visconti had said to Dante once upon a time, petting him in his uncle's kitchen. "Your beautiful Italian nose."

And they had begun to kiss.

The Pelican.

The nickname had been his grandfather's once, but it passed to Dante, and with the name had come the whole neighborhood, he had thought, like some kind of birthright.

The phone rang. This time, he caught it on the third ring.

The voice on the other end was thick and familiar. He thought for an instant he had his father on the line—but it was Uncle Salvatore.

"Dante," he said. "I have been trying to reach you. I have some hard news. . . ."

Then Uncle Salvatore went on to tell him what he already knew: His father was dead. As he listened to his uncle, he could not help but hear his father's voice and feel again the sense of something hidden under the surface. That sense had haunted the conversation between himself and his father these last years, ever since the Strehli case and the argument that had erupted between them.

"We'll talk when you get here."

"Yes, we'll talk," said Dante.

Part of the argument with his father had had to do with Marilyn Visconti. There was a tangled history. Daughter of Alberto Visconti—with whom Dante's family had had a bitter fight a generation ago. She had been dating his cousin, but Dante had fallen for her anyway. Wholesome and forbidden both at once. Dark olive skin. Italian on one side, German on the other: German Jew. With her taut lean body and her wild hair. Wide, thick lips. A wide mouth full of laughter. Oh, Marilyn Visconti. Who did not seem so interested in Dante's cousin as his cousin was in her, and whose body fit so well against his own, there in his uncle's kitchen.

"Oh, your nose," she had moaned, her hand drifting to his belt. "Your beautiful nose."

And Dante was still thinking of her when the jet started its descent into San Francisco later that evening, and the city lay beneath him like some darkening jewel, a smear of buildings, winking palms, a wash of pastel under the fading light.

FOUR

The old men gathered at the heart of North Beach under the awning of the Diamond Mortuary. They were aware of everything, those old Italians. They watched their old buddies approach in their Cadillacs (and their enemies, too)—and they saw Dante walk around the corner in his funeral suit, *home to pay his regards*—and they made their remarks to each other, not in words, maybe, but in the language of the body: raising their eyebrows, digging their hands a little deeper into their pockets, thrusting forward with their groins, and turning their mouths up in wry smiles that suggested they knew it all. They knew every goddamn thing.

Old fishermen and restaurateurs, real estate men and plumbers, the loyal standbys, neighborhood regulars and the guys who'd sold out—for a place down in Burlingame, maybe, or San Rafael, or Richmond—and who found themselves these days back at the Diamond more often than anyone wanted to think.

All the dirty business, all the gossip. Maybe they were just old men gathered around the hive—but they knew it all.

Cavelli and Marinetti. Scarpetti and Romano. Di Nido and Pesci and Mussolino.

A car pulled into the mortuary lot, and another of the old gang crawled out. Grossi, maybe, or Anteo. Or Rossi, the Lord Mayor himself. It was a small parking lot, and a Chinese attendant commandeered the keys, directing the newcomer toward the entrance, to where the old men stood in their polyester pants, their knit shirts, and their tailored suit coats. Knock-kneed sentries. Guardians to the land of the wise.

There was a time, walking these streets, when Dante had felt all but prescient. As if he could tell at any instant what was happening anyplace in the neighborhood. How the wind had just shifted, and old man Pesci was washing out his felucca—a fishing skiff from the old days, no motor, just a sail and net—and how at the same time Gino Scaparelli was wiping down the bar at the Naked Moon, and the prostitutes were gathering under the blinking neon, and the Chinese man who everyday pushed his fish cart down Grant Street, his hair in pigtails, was just this moment turning the corner, letting out his ancient wail, the fishmonger's call.

Dante could still hear that call now, he imagined, though in fact the old peddler had been dead for years.

In the same way, once upon a time, Dante had known when something was out of whack in The Beach. *La Saggezza,* his grandmother had called that knowledge. The Wisdom. The ability to know something without knowing. To feel it in your bones.

Now, approaching the old men under the awning, he feared he had lost that wisdom. He knew nothing anymore.

Dante pitched his cigarette into the gutter and stepped off the curb. He glanced over his shoulder, scanning the alley behind, the second-story windows, a fire escape that snaked the wall. An old habit. He wore a gun holstered beneath his jacket. A .40 caliber Glock. The same as he had carried when he was with the force.

Old man Marinetti, the schoolteacher, held out his hand. "Dante Mancuso," he said. "It's good you came all this way. From New Orleans. You are a good son."

"What son would do anything different?" Dante said.

Marinetti nodded his head up and down, as if in agreement. The other men nodded, too, his father's cronies stepping closer now, lips pushed out, getting a good look at him.

"He was a *paisan,* your father," said Ernie Mollini, the butcher.

"A true Italian," said Scarpetti, the broker.

"Yes," said one of the others. They were all chiming in now.

"A Sicilian of the first class."

"You could count on him the way you can't count on any-one anymore. Where you live now, my boy—New Orleans, is that right?"

"Yes."

"What's your line of work?"

"I'm in the export business."

Dante did not elaborate. He looked up at the awning. Underneath the name of the mortuary was the name of its new proprietor: DENNIS YANG. Then a string of Chinese characters.

The old men looked up, too, following his gaze, and shrugged their shoulders.

"Gucci, the mortician, he sold out," said Mollini. "Sold his contracts with the business. All the special deals, the combination packages. So if you bought your service long time ago from Gucci, then today you get buried by the Chinese."

Meanwhile, another car pulled into the mortuary lot. An attendant helped the driver out.

Uncle Salvatore.

And along with him, Aunt Regina—using a walker now. Then cousin Gary.

"The Chinese are not so bad," said Marinetti. "They do their job. It's no disgrace."

"No. No disgrace."

A couple of the men shrugged again, big clownish gestures, lugubrious, sad—as if to say, truth be known, it was a disgrace after all, but what could you do? Men were fools. Born to be disgraced. So it was only natural to be disgraced in death, buried by strangers, because your own kind had retired to San Bruno, sold your funeral contract to the Chinese down the street.

"What difference does it make?" Cavelli said, the old bookstore owner, the philosopher of the bunch.

"No difference," responded Mollini.

"Dust to dust."

"Italian, Chinese, Jew—Lady Death, she don't care. She loves everyone all the same."

"She come into your bed at night, she give you a big kiss."

"She smooch you all up."

"That's right. A big smoocher, that lady."

"I kiss her right back," said Mollini. "Hell, I stick it right in her mouth."

Now Uncle Salvatore and his entourage were all but upon them, and at last Dante saw the light in his uncle's eyes, a fierce light that was alarmingly like his father's had been, full of some dark joy.

They embraced.

He was outgoing, his uncle, an appetitive, warm-hearted man who when Dante was young would pick him up and crush him to his chest so tightly Dante felt as if he might vanish inside him; Dante still remembered the smell of his cologne, how his white shirt was damp with sweat. Aunt Regina, though, was more reserved. She'd been a startling beauty in her day, but age had taken her beauty along with her disposition. She was palsied, and her skin was so crinkled and papery it looked as if wasps had built a nest inside.

Aunt Regina teetered on her walker. Dante moved to press his cheek against hers.

Behind him, a red Alfa Romeo turned into the mortuary lot. Dante caught it from the corner of his eye and for a second was conscious of the street, and the weight of the gun beneath his jacket.

Cousin Gary came forward, hand extended. His smile was crooked. Salvatore and Regina's only son, adopted. He and Dante had been like brothers once but that had all changed— and now Dante saw a sudden uneasiness in his cousin's eyes. The driver of the Alfa had gotten out. A well-dressed man, very sharp, close to Dante's age, but no one he recognized. He held open the passenger door and the woman who climbed from the leather seat was Marilyn Visconti.

She had the same bewildering beauty. Her eyes caught his, and he realized everyone was watching, and it occurred to him everyone knew everything that had happened between himself and Marilyn and his cousin. Or thought they knew. There were times he was not so sure himself.

Aunt Regina, hovering on her walker, cut the moment dead.

"Let's go inside," she said. "Before I fall on my face."

"Yes, yes," said Uncle Salvatore.

Behind the mortuary doors, in the viewing room, there were more people than he expected. His father's sister, a great-uncle, an old business partner—Grazzi, from the days when his father had run the grotto down at the wharf. Others, too. Judge Molinari. Gino the bartender. Max the sandwich maker. Alfonso the doorkeeper at the Naked Moon. Big shots and nobodies. Joe DiMaggio's cousin. Wendy Amato, niece of the famous film director.

And Mayor Rossi. Son-of-a-bitch. A family friend who'd been in office back during the Strehli murder—when that whole business had exploded in Dante's face—but the good mayor had done nothing to help him.

No one from his days at the SFPD was here, though. No one except Jim Wiesinski that is, the vice cop who'd left the force and gone onto to security operations in the private sector.

The Big Why, they'd called him.

Known for his love of the sleaze bars—for the open-handed way he worked the streets, questionable tactics, working both sides against the middle. Dante had run into him, oddly enough, at Mardi Gras in New Orleans, not long after he'd left town. A few days later, Dante had been recruited by the company. A coincidence, maybe, he'd never been sure.

But whatever Wiesinski's motives, or his flaws, he was here, head bowed. You could say that for him.

Dante sat down in the front row, reserved for family, next to his Uncle Salvatore. He whispered to Dante, "I want you to know your father died peacefully."

Aunt Regina coughed, then leaned over her husband.

"It's a lie," she said. "No one dies peacefully."

Father Campanella stood up now in front of the casket. In the old days, they'd dragged the caskets down the streets to the church—and people wept and wailed and threw flowers—but today the priest said his bit here in the mortuary chapel. His father had not wanted a funeral mass.

"Twenty years ago we buried Giovanni Mancuso's father," said Father Campanella. "Ten years ago, we buried his wife. Today, we bury the man himself."

The priest had a formula for such occasions, a kind of litany. He started in with the names of the deceased's ancestors, relatives beyond the pale, and as he went on he would inevitably name the streets of the neighborhood here on which the dead man had stood; events at which he had been seen; the names of friends, still living, who had once stood beside him—so that by the end everyone in the audience had been mentioned, and people were mourning not just the dead but themselves as well, and the slow disappearing of the world as they had known it.

His aunt leaned over again.

"Your father—he thought someone was trying to kill him."

"Hmm?"

"At the end, the cancer was in his brain."

"Hallucinations," his uncle said, and he put his hand on his wife's arm, as if to make her be still. She paid him no attention.

"A policeman came to the house," Aunt Regina said. "A Chinese."

It was time for the viewing of the body, the last farewells. Dante knew how it would go. The visitors would walk by, one at a time, looking down into the old man's face, verifying that it was indeed Giovanni Mancuso inside that casket, checking to see if Yang's handiwork was as good as Gucci's.

Before long it was just Dante and his uncle, the blood relatives. Father Campanella led Dante and his uncle up to the casket, and Dante knelt under the pressure of the priest's hand. Then the others left and Dante was alone with his father. He gave the old man a long look, from head to toe; then he got up himself, knowing that when he'd left the room, Yang's footmen would come out from behind the curtains—or wherever it was they waited—then close the lid on his father and wheel that heavy box down the corridor, through the padded doors, into the waiting limousine.

FIVE

Whatever wisdom there was in the world, Salvatore Mancuso didn't know anymore. He had known once maybe, or thought he knew, but he did not know now. He'd lived in North Beach all his life, seventy-two years, and he was a big shot, more or less—at least on this hill of dirt—but he still didn't know what to do. They'd made their share of money, he and his brother. They'd raised their sons. They'd eaten a million meatballs and smoked a million cigars— but in the end he was as ignorant as at the beginning, and now his brother was inside that black box, and his own hands were shaking.

Salvatore had a decision to make regarding his nephew and the circumstance of his brother's death.

And the truth was, he was fearful for himself.

A silly fear, an old man's fear. Passed along to him by his brother on his deathbed. All that hysterical talk.

He was sitting alone in the limo, behind the mortuary, waiting. There was a breeze outside but in the car it was hot and he could smell his own sweat. Three funerals in the last two months, all in this same suit. And he had an envelope in his pocket. The envelope had been given to him by his brother on his deathbed. Inside the envelope were three strips of film— negatives. Salvatore had held them up to the light but the images were difficult to read. But what difference did it make? The doctor had told them death was coming. His brother's hysteria, there at the end, it was because of the tumor, maybe, the deteri- oration of the brain, the trauma of death itself.

I will drop this envelope in the grave, Salvatore thought. *Let it all be buried. Lay my brother to rest.*

Now his nephew appeared. Dante emerged from the funeral parlor with that odd lope of his, headed toward the limo. Salva- tore's wife and his son were in another car, farther up the caravan, riding with the daughter-in-law and the grandkids. Giovanni's old buddies were occupied with their prostates and would be along in a moment.

Alone with his nephew, Salvatore found himself unable to hold his tongue.

"Your aunt, she has a tendency to spit things out," Salvatore said. "You know how she is."

"She says what she thinks."

Salvatore smiled then. He couldn't help himself because it was true.

"Was there an autopsy?"

Dante wasn't going to let it alone, he could see. He had his father's shrewdness, his nephew, the dog-headed persistence— but his mother's looks. His brother's wife had been a beautiful woman in the old-world way, with that high head of hers and the long nose and the eyes that tore you apart with a glance.

"No. There was no need for an autopsy." Salvatore shook his head. "The cancer was painful. The doctor fixed your father up with one of those medication implants. Demerol, morphine. I don't know. Your father overdid it—he overdosed, a heart attack. Maybe it was better though, all things considered."

"He thought someone was trying to kill him?"

"Delirium." Salvatore shrugged. "It happens."

He felt his nephew studying him, peering into him. If they sat here much longer, Salvatore feared, he would change his mind and come forward with the specifics of his brother's rantings— how he'd started going on about Strehli there at the end. Mark Strehli, who'd worked out at the customs yard in Oakland. Who'd been shot in the head and whose murder investigation Dante had challenged—to ill effect. Himself, he didn't quite understand. His brother's rantings were tangled with memories of business deals, arrangements that had seemed reasonable at the time but had a certain stickiness about them now. Much of that stickiness, though, was due to Salvatore's own son, he had to admit. Pushing the boundaries. Looking for the easy dollar.

Now Ernesto Mollini and George Marinetti appeared on the sidewalk, old buddies, his brother's die-hard friends.

Uncle Salvatore greeted them enthusiastically.

"Come in," he said. "Into the big, black car. We are waiting for you."

The two men had hung out with Giovanni almost everyday these last years, down in Paesano's card room, and they would be pallbearers—or titular ones, anyway, walking behind the casket while younger men did the carrying—so it made sense for them all to be together.

Before the limo could pull away from the curb, Joe Rossi hustled up to the car. "Let me ride with you?"

The former mayor was a thickset man with luminous eyes and absolutely no hair. His head was a bald dome that showed off the dents in his skull. Though he was past seventy, the mayor was still the same old glad-hander he'd always been.

"I thought you were going with Di Nido. In his Cadillac."

"That Di Nido, he's blind as a monkey. My heart can't take it."

"Mine neither," said Marinetti. "Jesus himself wouldn't ride in that car."

Uncle Salvatore relented. Ordinarily, he liked the mayor well enough. But Giovanni and his Lordship had had some kind of squabble in the days before his brother died. Rossi had gotten an odd manner about him, bullish in that way he could be, nosey as hell, as if somehow all this had something to do with him. *And maybe it did,* thought Salvatore. The mayor had directed a thing or two their way in difficult times, back when it looked like the warehouse would go under.

The limo headed for the cemetery. Mollini and Marinetti began to banter, the way they often bantered these days, taking sides in an imaginary debate, mocking the rituals they had grown up with.

"The way you tell me, Marinetti, I take the rites, there on my deathbed, the priest waves his cross, then I go straight to heaven?" asked Mollini. "No time in purgatory?"

"That's the truth. Approximately."

"Who told you that?"

"It's an article of faith. Like the virgin birth. You don't believe it, so far as God's concerned, you don't exist."

"I have to believe it my whole life, or just then, at the last minute?"

"If there's no priest around, you can imagine him. You confess your sins, it's an easy ride."

"What's the deadline on this?"

Marinetti hummed around. They could be maddening, these two, a distraction to whatever you had on your mind, and at the moment Salvatore was trying to sort through how much of his brother's agony to pass along to his nephew, who slouched sideways in the seat in the same manner as his father used to do. *Should I give him the film?* he wondered.

"There's a little time—after you stop breathing, after your heart stops beating—when you're alone there inside the dark of your head. That's the deadline," Marinetti said. "Right then, before your soul leaves your body."

"I don't believe it."

"You will, the time comes."

"How long I got before the soul leaves the body?"

"Three seconds. Isn't that right, Lord Mayor? Three—that's the holy number?"

Mayor Rossi did not answer this question. He was not comfortable with the wry tone, Salvatore knew, with the suggestion that there was something ludicrous at the heart of things. Rossi turned to him then.

"Did your brother take the last rites?"

Salvatore nodded, but he did not like the question. As if Rossi wanted to know what his brother—in his deluded state— had told the priest.

The truth was his brother had no doubt overdosed, like the doctor said. Died from a heart failure, technically, head buried in his pillow. If it hadn't been the heart, then it would have been the cancer. He was an old man, going to die anyway, so who would bother to kill him?

It was ludicrous.

Even so, Salvatore had been itching to talk to his nephew alone. Not about this necessarily, he told himself, but about the estate, the family business. There were lots of issues, even the possibility—though his son Gary would not like this—that Dante would want an active stake. They must schedule a time—but he did not want to do so now, with the mayor in the car.

Finally they pulled into Cemetery Drive, and made their way down into the part of the graveyard known as Little Italy because of all the Italians buried in the dirt. Marinetti and Mollini got out of the limo, and looked rather grimly ahead. A Chinese from the funeral parlor stood by its open door, waiting for the pallbearers. Behind the cars lay the open grave and an endless line of stones.

"I want to believe," said Mollini. "But I don't. For this, you tell me, I'm going to burn in hell?"

"Nonbelievers, they get nothing, no heaven, no hell."

"Nothing?"

"Nothing," insisted Marinetti.

"No walking through eternal fires, my body covered with sores?"

"None of that for you."

"No pustules? No buckets of shit?"

"I told you, you miss out on the whole business. You don't believe, it's an empty picture. God forgets all about you."

"I still don't believe."

"You will change your mind, those last three seconds. I can already hearing you crying out."

"Nothing?"

"Absolutely."

"Mama Mia!" shouted Ernesto.

He made a motion as if tearing at his hair, frightened by all that nothing stretching out in front of him. The two men laughed and patted one another on the shoulders. But in a little while the joke was over. They stood by the grave, all of them. Mollini and Marinetti submitted, too, heads bowed. Teary-eyed, sentimental, they watched their old buddy disappear into the abyss. Salvatore touched the envelope in his pocket, walked toward the grave. *Throw it in,* he told himself. He fingered the negatives. Then he hesitated. He didn't know what the hell to do.

Ben years ago at his mother's funeral, Dante had stood in this same spot, more or less, and watched as his father cast in a red rose after his mother. It was a tradition, to throw something into the grave. That day, while he and his father stood by, neighbors and friends had come forward, tossing thimbles and wine glasses, figs and old photographs, holy cards, a plastic statue of the Virgin Everlasting. Today, by his father's grave, Dante stood alone. His father's friends came up and tossed in a little bit of this and that. A red poker chip and the ace of spades. A rosary. A Molinari salami and a Cuban cigar. A snort of grappa. Meanwhile, Uncle Salvatore lingered nearby, his hand in his pocket—hovering in such a way that Dante thought for a minute he might fall in after his brother.

Dante had nothing with him. His gun. His wallet. He kneeled to the ground then and dug his hand into the thick loam the gravediggers had mounded at the edge of the grave. He threw in a handful of dirt, and his uncle sobbed.

There were other traditions as well. One of them had its roots in a sentimental tradition of the fading Italian nobility, who in their waning years would paste photographs and remembrances of themselves into scrapbooks. *Il Libro di Vita Segreta,* these were called, remembrances of a secret life, and at some point this tradition had migrated to the middle class, then to the peasants, and they had brought it with them over the sea. Usually these books were entrusted to a family priest who passed them along to the deceased's children after death.

At the end of the service, Father Campanella walked up to Dante. Like his friends, Dante's father had mocked the religion—with all its smoke and its hand waving and its embroidered vestments—but in the end they all succumbed. Or the people who were left behind succumbed for them, submitting the corpse to Father Campanella.

"Your father had a final gift for you," said the priest. He smiled wanly, and Dante realized his father had put together an *Il Libro.* Dante was surprised. It was not the kind of thing his father would do—but then Dante knew how it went. When the end was coming, the priest would stop by. He would ask to see some old pictures. He would listen to your old stories. And the next thing you knew, there you were with a pen in your hand and a bottle of glue.

"I'll stop by the church, Father," Dante said.

He knew the routine, how the priest used it as a chance to get you on your knees, to pray for the soul of the deceased, and for your own soul, too. He was curious about his father's book, maybe, but he did not know if he could submit himself to the old priest.

The mourners came, pressing close. All of North Beach, it seemed. They embraced him. They kissed his cheeks. The old men in their dry-cleaned suits. The shopkeepers and the hangers-on. People whose names he no longer remembered. Old women with their perfumed smell and their cigarette stink, their teary eyes and rouged-up cheeks. There were some young ones, too, mixed-bloods, children of children, thin kids with freckles and yellow hair. And somewhere among them all was Marilyn Visconti, who brushed against him in her black skirt, her eyes lingering a moment as she took his hands between her own.

Then there was Wiesinski. The only representative from Dante's days at the SFPD.

"We'll get together."

"Sure."

"The Naked Moon." He winked. "We'll tie one down. For old times' sake."

After the funeral was over, while walking back to the limo, Salvatore had a second alone with his nephew. Or he thought they were alone. He didn't realize until later that the mayor had been a few steps behind him, within earshot, though it was also true he did not know exactly when the mayor had appeared, or what he had heard, or whether or not it mattered. This is my brother's paranoia, he told himself, not my own.

"You and I, we need to talk."

"Yes."

"Come to my house. Thursday afternoon—twelve. There's some family business. Your father . . ." he hesitated. "You and I, we'll talk. We'll have a glass of wine."

Dante nodded. "Who's handling the estate?"

"Tony Mora."

"Mora?"

Salvatore explained. Mora was the man who'd been standing with Marilyn, back at the Diamond Mortuary. An attorney. And as Salvatore explained, he watched Dante's eyes go dark.

"Here," said Uncle Salvatore.

He reached into his pocket. In the end, by the grave, he had done nothing—and now he handed Dante the envelope, as his brother had wished him to do. "Take this. Safekeeping. You never know what's going to happen."

The second he gave Dante the pictures, he regretted the action. The mayor was behind them and had seen, maybe, but then he told himself it made no difference.

"Family pictures?"

Salvatore hesitated, nodded. "Sure," he said, speaking loudly, though the truth was he did not know what the photos might be. "Me and you, your dad. From the old days."

"I'll get them developed. Copies for us both."

"Sure. You and me, we'll talk things over on Thursday. Family business," he said. "But today, we grieve."

Then he embraced his nephew. As he did, pulling him close, his hands clutching the boy's side, he felt something beneath the jacket.

A gun.

He looked his nephew in those eyes of his, dark like the shaft of a mine, and he wondered what the hell was going to happen next.

SIX

arilyn Visconti stood at the top of the hill, on her front stoop, still in her funeral clothes. She had just finished kissing Tony Mora good-bye. He was a hungry kisser, always with a hand on her blouse. He wasn't quick to leave—he enjoyed dallying, stretching things out—so she lingered with him for a minute or two, leaning against the red Alfa. Every once in a while, though, she glanced behind her.

A few minutes before, a sedan had driven by. A rental sedan, late model, gray and nondescript. She had noticed it swing around and park on the corner. No one had gotten out. The driver was still behind the wheel, just sitting there. It was too far to tell for sure, but she had a pretty good idea who that driver might be.

Finally Mora cantilevered his Alfa out of her driveway. The house was on the steep, like everything around here, but Mora managed it expertly, jacktailing the car backward up the hill, then pitching nose down toward the view.

At the last minute, he jammed on the brakes.

"Friday," he called to her. "We take that trip to Sonoma."

"Yes," she said.

Inside she poured herself a glass of wine. After awhile, when no one came to the door, she wondered if maybe she had been mistaken about the sedan. She glanced out the bedroom window. The car was still there, but there was no one inside, no one in the street.

I was wrong, she thought.

In her bedroom, she undressed and ran a bath. She stripped off her blouse and skirt and gave herself a cursory glance in the mirror, the kind you might give a stranger on the street. Then she unhooked her bra and lay back on the bed.

It had been a long time since she'd seen Dante. When they'd first gotten together, she'd been dating his cousin Gary. It wasn't a serious thing, her and Gary, no; part of the charm—for both of them—was the fact that the relationship was out of bounds, given the enmity between their families. The affair would have fallen apart on its own accord, no doubt. Then one day, leaving Il Fior d'Italia, the old *ristorante,* she and Gary had run into Dante.

That weekend, Dante had taken her out on his grandfather's felucca—one of those flat-bottomed sailing boats that no one used anymore. With its single sail and a net, it looked like a cocked hat floating on the water. They'd spread their towels on the small hull and lay there under the sun, talking. Above them the white sail ruffled the sky. There'd been a magnetism between them, an electrical charge—and they rolled toward each other on the hull.

But that was a long time ago. She was thirty-three years old now, a different person. Her mother was dead, her father in an institution, and she really wasn't sure why she was still here, in North Beach, other than the fact she worked for Hank Gumina, her father's old partner—lecherous old Mr. Gumina—and that was where she'd met Mora, a little over a year ago, when he'd stopped by to pick up some estate work.

Her bath was ready now. She took off her panties—caught a glimpse of the stranger in the mirror again, the naked woman with the green eyes—and was readying to dip herself in, just then, when the doorbell rang.

Outside, on the steps to Marilyn's apartment, Dante waited. He had retrieved the gray sedan, an airport rental, after the reception, and then driven here not quite sure what he planned to do. He had not expected to see Marilyn and Mora out front, flirting. He could have driven away, he supposed, but he had parked and watched instead—with a surprising detachment. After all, he told himself, he was only here because the company wanted him to be. Because it was a logical part of his cover—to pursue his old girl. After Mora had driven off, he had gotten out of the car and walked to the top of Union, looking down the stone face of Telegraph Hill toward the Golden Gate. The view beneath him was unchanged: the same blue water with the same white sails, and the same golden headlands off in the distance. Then he'd come back and rung the bell.

It took awhile, but now he heard footsteps. The door opened and Marilyn regarded him from the other side of the threshold.

"Dante," she said.

He was still in his dark suit, but Marilyn had changed clothes since the funeral. She wore a sweater now and jeans. She looked a bit mussed, though, quickly put together.

She let him in.

Inside, she had redecorated—bright-colored stuff, in the Milanese fashion, with simple lines. Tucked here and there, however, was the old Italian bric-a-brac: the family heirlooms, the floral vases and absurd lamps. On the wall hung gilt-framed pictures of her family, parents and grandparents, and ancestors before that, going back into the nineteenth century, to the time of the docks and the canneries, when her family had first come—Swiss Italians, Italian Jews, Germans, whatever they were—and helped develop the land along the waterfront. Hers had been a prosperous family once. And though that prosperity was not yet gone, it was wearing thin.

"I wanted to thank you for stopping by the funeral," he said. "Given everything that's happened."

"Your father was kind to me."

This surprised him. The old man, as far as he knew, had never relented in his dislike of Marilyn's father. Partly it had to do with the tangled history of the Italian provinces. Dante's family was from the south, but the Viscontis were wealthy Luccans who'd intermarried with the Germans here in California. They had been labeled as sympathizers during the war, a rumor that had hurt their business—and helped the Mancusos.

As a result unpleasantries were exchanged some fifty years ago, during a meeting at Fugazi Hall. Exactly what those unpleasantries had been Dante did not know, but the effects had lingered.

"I wasn't aware that you and my father ever talked."

"A couple of times, on the street. After my mother died. He spoke to me—and he was very charming."

"He could be like that," Dante said. And it was true; his father had a public face, the ability to embrace, to show that nothing mattered, all was forgiven. What he thought to himself at home, sitting alone in his favorite chair, might be different altogether.

"And things have changed, you know. In the neighborhood—with all the newcomers—the old battles don't matter so much anymore. It's forgotten."

"I don't know if that's possible," said Dante. "I didn't know they forgot anything."

Marilyn laughed. "It's true," she said. "But you're right. Aunt Regina would as soon strangle me as look at me. Your father and your uncle, though—they have been gracious. Maybe on account of Tony, I don't know."

Her voice stumbled a little, mentioning Mora. He was glad to see her awkwardness. Still, Dante had caught a glimpse at the funeral, and he understood how things had changed. Mora worked with Judge Romano's son, and Dante's family had always done business with Romano. They might not like it when they saw Mora with the Visconti girl, but she was just a woman, after all, and you could not help who a man went to bed with, and anyway Marilyn's father was out of the picture, all but dead, and it was easy to be generous.

D ante had changed, Marilyn thought. He was not the same. The last time she had been alone with him, it had been some seven years ago. He'd had a quick smile then, and way of leaning across the table—a confidence. He'd been on his way up, a homicide cop with his eyes on the DA's office, studying the bar, and he'd liked to talk. He'd had a cynical veneer, it was true (what cop didn't?)—but his crust was thin, and underneath it all there was a certain vulnerability.

Anyway, he was different now. He was still lean, and his eyes were the same dark pools, but there was something a little harder, a little meaner. Still, underneath, the same softness. Maybe even softer now.

She could not help it. She wanted to hurt him. She wanted to penetrate to that softness.

"I'm engaged," she said.

"Mora?" Dante nodded his head in the direction in which the Alfa had driven.

"Yes."

Dante nodded again.

If she had gotten to him, Marilyn could not tell, and Dante for his part would not let it show. No. Maybe he glanced at the view and remembered their time out on the bay, she in her white blouse and shorts. It had been one of those days, rare and beautiful, where the wind was down and it was warm and the water was like glass and you could imagine how it had been once upon a time, the men working the nets and the fish swimming in thick schools. But she could not know his thoughts, just as he could not know hers.

H ow's Alberto?" he asked.

She shrugged, giving him the shoulder. It was something Dante had always liked about her. The way she shrugged, the hollow in her cheeks, the quick flash in her eyes.

"St. Vincent's."

Dante knew what this meant. Marilyn's father had gone downhill fast after his retirement. St. Vincent's was a sanatorium for the worst cases. Old folks with jelly-in-the-head. Figs-for-brains. Senile frogs with bladders that wouldn't hold.

"We worried so much about them," Marilyn said suddenly. "Your father, my father. Gary . . ."

She trailed off. At the mention of his cousin's name, he tasted something like bile in his throat.

"I wasn't thinking about Gary."

"We made our choices," said Marilyn. "We could've done things differently."

"You were supposed to meet me that night."

"Don't give me this."

"No?"

"*You* were the one who left town."

There were things about the whole business Dante still didn't understand. All he knew was that everything had been set for him. He'd worked eight years in the department, and he'd studied the bar—and it was all in front of him, the good life—then he'd gone blind, self-destructed. Fallen in love with Marilyn, and pushed his objections to the Strehli case so hard that they'd blown up in his face. Everyone in the neighborhood knew Strehli. He was the only child of Dominic Strehli, one of his father's war buddies. After the elder Strehli died, the son had hung around with the old ones by night, playing poker at the Portofino Café. Then one night Strehli was found with a bullet in his head. The SFPD arrested Vince Caselli, but the evidence was weak—and after a while Dante began to suspect something else was at play. Dante had gone to Mayor Rossi at his house on top of Russian Hill, asking him to intervene, but the mayor had said no. Even his father had asked Dante to beg off. He wouldn't listen. Then all of a sudden he had found himself in the midst of a payoff scandal, a newspaper story claiming he'd been paid to squelch the evidence against Vince Caselli. The story was utter nonsense, but Internal Affairs had come after him anyway.

In the middle of all this, Caselli confessed, and the confession made Dante look like a fool. Ultimately the man died in a jail-house stabbing—but by that time the story had dropped from the news, and Dante was gone.

"How long are you going to be in town?"

He shrugged. "I've got business here. Odds and ends."

"Don't you have to get home to New Orleans?"

"New Orleans is just a base for me. My business, it keeps me traveling," he said. That part was true enough. "Before I leave, I have to meet with my uncle about the estate."

She looked at him again, and maybe, for an instant, they were both thinking the same thing. Maybe what had almost been true once could be true now. If instead of running, he had stayed. But it was foolishness. He was not here for himself. He was here for the company. Because he had a cover to establish.

It was all a routine, another masquerade.

She turned her back on him now, and they regarded one another in the mirror. In that mirror, they looked a lot younger than they were. They could be those other people. In that mirror things could happen, maybe, that could not happen here. In the mirror, he still had the power, the wisdom. *La Saggezza.* He could glance into the looking glass and see all the secret mechanisms. He could see the truth behind the Strehli business, maybe . . . the truth behind his father's death . . . the real reason the company had sent him here. . . .

And Marilyn . . .

He watched himself walk up behind her in the mirror, and she watched, too. He touched her hair, her cheek. There had been something sweet and wild between them once, a ferociousness about to break loose—a wildness they had never really unleashed, or tamed, or whatever it was two people were supposed to do with the emotions that ran between them. He put his arm around her waist, and she watched him in the mirror, and he felt the desire surge in his chest and saw at the same time the vulnerability in her eyes, there in that land of the mirror, not here, and then he pulled her toward him, and they kissed, and it was, for a minute, as if they had somehow walked into that land on the other side.

They had made their plans once upon a time. To take the trip up to Tahoe, to the Nevada side. Where you could be married at the drop of a hat.

"Where were you that night? How come you didn't show up?"

In response she pulled away. Her eyes avoided his.

"Go," Marilyn said. There was anger in her voice. And maybe something else, as well. "Get the hell out of here."

He turned and left. Outside an old woman shunted her way up the sidewalk, struggling up the hill, her back to the view: all that blue water, and those white boats on the bay.

SEVEN

It was twilight in Chinatown, and Homicide Detective Frank Ying found himself hustling down Stockton on a mission of diminishing importance. Ying was on his way to an apartment at the top of the Kearny Street Stairs to interview the mother of a suspected homicide victim who—according to the latest pathology report—had not been a murder victim at all, but a suicide. The interview was a formality, a necessary one—but the kind of thing Ying found himself doing too often since he'd left Special Investigations and returned to Homicide. Gopher work, more or less, and he didn't think it was coincidence.

Ying was forty-two. He had grown up in Chinatown, back when the neighborhood had stricter boundaries than it did now. Grant had been the border then, the line between Little Italy and Chinatown, and you did not walk across without a certain risk. That boundary had long since been overrun. City Hall might paint Italian flags on the telephone poles, and the Italian Preservation Society might hang its banners, but the Italians themselves were not so numerous. Even so, Detective Ying could not cross Grant Street without some sense he was straying into danger.

Ying was a tall man, lanky and not particularly graceful. He had black hair. He had sinuous lips and gray eyes—a glance that was at once both reserved and probing. He was not a dapper man, but he was not slovenly either. His face was weathered and gave him the look of someone who had been out a long time in the wind.

On Grant, he turned up Fresno Street. Despite its name, Fresno was not so much a street as it was an alley—the heart of the Italian neighborhood when Ying was a kid: cats everywhere; laundry over the fire rails; and mean-as-hell Italian boys on the corners, hands in their pockets how they liked to do, knocking the old billiards about, touching their dicks. The laundry was still there, and the cats, too, but the kids nowadays were Chinese, just as mean, maybe, but quieter and less promiscuous with their hands, at least in public.

Still there were some old Italians here, he knew. Ying had been down this alley just a couple weeks back to talk to an old man who lived in one of the houses at the top of the street— and claimed someone was trying to kill him. Ordinarily those kind of calls were left to the regular beat guys, but somehow Ying had gotten the honors.

Giovanni Mancuso was the old man's name: a wide-eyed Italian, weak at the knees—who had denied even calling when Ying came by to check on the story.

"No, not me. You make a mistake."

"Are you sure?"

"Everything's A-okay."

"That's not what you said on the phone."

"It's someone else scared for his life, not me," the old man had said, smiling, laughing, panting for breath as he hung onto the doorknob. Then he had leaned back, appraising him, the way Ying remembered old Italians doing since he was a kid, surprised at his height. He realized that he could talk to this old coot till the end of time but the man would never reveal anything to him, a Chinese cop. Then Giovanni smiled with a kind of toothy pride.

"You know, my son was a cop, too."

The old man had died a few days later, overdosing on his pain medicine. Dementia, the doctor had told Ying. Giovanni Mancuso had gone a little wacky at the end, prone to imagining things—as sometimes happened when the cancer traveled to the brain.

Ying supposed it was true, but there was a part of him that wondered. He recognized the name Mancuso from his time with SI, maybe, but he could not be sure. He rummaged through his notes to see if he could find a connection between the Mancuso family and the Wus—obsessive behavior, his wife had told him, unhealthy, to focus on these criminals—but he found nothing, and the Wu family had so many arms, so many businesses, the legitimate intertwined with the not-so-legitimate, that he wrote it off to coincidence. Then he ran a computer search and found the name of the son, the ex-policeman. Ying had still been working the Sunset District then, seven years ago, when Dante Mancuso had left the force—but it had been big news for a while.

It was funny how a career could shift on you. Ying himself had been transferred off Special Investigations back to Homicide. True, the transfer had been at his own request—and his wife's insistence—after things had gotten ugly. He'd been investigating the Wus at the time, looking into the disappearance of a Shanghai businessman by the name of Ru Shen. That's when the threats had started. Phone calls, his house trashed, his wife's car smeared with pig guts. It had gotten so bad, he'd moved his family over to the East Bay.

Leaving SI had been the right thing to do, he supposed—to put himself and his family out of danger—but the truth was his wife was not satisfied. She wanted him off the force altogether, into private industry, and if not that then at least out of Chinatown.

Now, as he approached the top of Fresno Street, he was surprised to see a light on upstairs in Giovanni Mancuso's house.

Relatives, he guessed. Maybe Giovanni's son had returned home. The cop in disgrace, home to collect the inheritance. To sell the house.

Now Ying noticed a second figure farther up the street, like him, studying the Mancuso house. Ying stepped back in the shadows, and after a while the other person started down the hill. A woman in a black coat, short hair—but she walked by now without giving the Mancuso house another glance. A tourist, maybe, checking out the view, or the row house architecture.

Ying was about to move on when he saw a man in the upstairs window. He was looking in Ying's direction. Not wanting to be seen, Ying instinctively stepped away, slipping a little further back into the shadows. The man disappeared, and the upstairs went dark. Ying waited a beat or two. Then he continued up the hill, embarrassed at himself, at all this cloak-and-dagger. There was no need. The old man had died in his sleep.

The little house on Fresno Street was musty inside. Dante saw immediately his father had done little, if anything, to the place since he'd left town. Everything was the same as always, though a little dingier, as in some fading Polaroid: the double-hung curtains on the windows, yellowing the light; the chairs draped with lace; the ancient carpet, handwoven, lions and jackals in the tapestry border. There was a ceramic pig on the mantle, and a humpback sofa in the living room, and family pictures everywhere. In the den, an RCA. No cable, of course. Just jackrabbit ears and an antenna wire that hung out the window to catch the signal from Mount Davidson.

His father had a woman come in once a week to wipe the dust, but it seemed everything was in the same place as the day Dante's mother had been buried.

Downstairs, in the basement, Dante found a casement window with a broken hasp—as if someone had forced it open. Most likely it had been his father, he guessed, after locking himself out. Dante pushed the casement into place and went back up. There was a mirror on the second-floor landing, so Dante could see himself growing larger with each step. Dante's grandmother had used to cross herself whenever she climbed the stairs, mumbling some cautionary phrase her own grandmother had mumbled before her: a protection against the world behind the looking glass.

Nanna Pellicano had heard voices sometimes as well. People

from beyond the grave. The devil. His mother had used to joke about it—*runs in the family*—but sometime in midlife the voices had started to speak to her as well. Conspiracies revealed by the laundry detergent. By the noodles as they boiled. By the pipes moaning in the wall. Nanna Pellicano had known how to deal with such things. Counting to seven on her fingers, then seven again. Invoking the saints. His mother on the other hand had no belief in such things. She died in the asylum.

Tomorrow Dante had work to do. He would get rid of the rental car. He would pick up a bag out at Federal Express, then taxi down to the Fillmore District and meet with Williams. He would give him the cash from the bag and set the sting in motion. Then a few days later he would walk into the Wu Benevolent Society and make contact with Mason Wu. Dante's role in all this seemed simple. The details had been worked out by an advance contact, someone the principals trusted. But somehow he doubted things would turn out simple.

Inside the company there were layers within layers. Headquarters had its primary network of agents, all accountable in some way, under the government wing. There was another network a step removed, people contacted via proxy, paid by secondary funding. People such as himself, who worked on projects from which the government wanted a certain distance. Sometimes lines were crossed, though, and it was hard to know on which side you stood, and whether the intentions of those who spoke to you were exactly as they seemed.

There was a mirror in his father's room, too. Mirrors everywhere. He lit up one of the old man's cigars and studied himself. His parents' wedding pictures were tucked into the edges along the frame, and a picture of Dante, too, when he'd first joined the force. In the mirror, he could see the open bedroom closet: the old man's clothes and his mother's dresses still hanging alongside. His father had never thrown her wardrobe out.

Dante ambled down to the hall window. He used to stand here when he was a kid. You could see the neon down on Grant, and Coit Tower up on the hill, and old lady Musso with her big tits washing dishes in the window across the way.

He heard the floorboards creak behind him. There were times when he wondered if he, too, were prone to the family disease.

Ghosts were real, Nanna Pellicano had liked to say.

You could hear them in the creaking of the floors, and you could feel them pass through you, and you could see them in the faces of your children, all those ancestors peering back.

Just as he was about to step away, Dante glimpsed a figure in the alley below—a shadow retreating into the alcove—and at the same moment, up at the corner, a woman in a dark coat, head bowed, crossed the street. Instinctively Dante moved away from the window: The hall light illuminated him from behind, making him visible from the street. He killed the light and edged back to the window.

After a beat or two a man emerged from the alley and headed up the hill. The woman had already disappeared. Dante could not be sure if the appearance of either figure was a matter of concern, but he felt the hackles rise on his neck. He went back into his father's bedroom. Dante let the cigar burn in the ashtray and lay back all the way on the bed. He unbuttoned his shirt, removed the gun from its holster, and lay there with the gun resting on his belly as he listened to the sounds of the floorboards, the creaking he remembered from childhood.

He fell asleep with the gun on his chest.

EIGHT

The Fillmore District had its ghosts, too. It had been a neighborhood of old Victorians. Ornate as hell, ramshackle, decaying grandly along the avenues. Filled with transplants from Louisiana and the Deep South: dirt farmers turned dockhands, shipbuilders, porters on the railroad; women in flowered blouses and tight skirts, hair slicked with straightener; little girls in pinafores. A neighborhood of barbecue joints and jazz clubs and tenements and corner churches. Streets where the street cleaners never came. Men doing the New Orleans mambo, the Atlanta chicken fry, the Detroit Staggerlee. A mosaic, full of this, full of that, spreading from Hayes Valley all the way out to Geary. Then came the change. Instituted from on high with the best of intentions, or the worst of intentions, depending upon whom you talked to, but either way the change came. The best of the old houses—the ones with sound timbers—were sold at auction, loosened from their foundations and dragged on wide-bed trailers up to Pacific Heights. Everything else was torn down. Bulldozers pushed it over and the government built public housing. Out Laguna. Up Hayes. At the Heights on Webster, in the shadow of the U.S. Mint.

The meeting place was up a dead-end street that overlooked the projects. There were old gangbangers hanging out nearby. Men in their thirties, burned out, dressed in baggies that had been hip a decade before, cutting edge—but the men were clichés now, hanging around in their corny clothes, caps twisted bill backward.

Nonetheless, they might be watching him, Dante knew. They might be the eyes, as the expression went. When you made a drop like this, there were always eyes.

Williams's place was at the top, up a narrow staircase. At length a man opened the door. Maybe thirty-five years old, a little bit heavy, he had a real ordinary quality about him and dressed in a regular kind of way: jeans, a plaid shirt, loafers. He did not look like a drug dealer so much as the owner of a hardware store. But Williams had served time, Dante knew, and he was affiliated with another ex-con by the name of Yusef Fakir. Fakir was the man the company really wanted. He had been associated with left-wing politics in his youth, out to break the chains, tear down the wall, but how it ended up was in armed robbery. He was suspected of killing a county judge, though no one had been able to prove it. Either way, Fakir had done his time and was now a preacher for a local offshoot of the Nation of Islam down in Cole Valley: preaching the gospel, telling the congregation the CIA was behind the drugs in the black community. Meanwhile, he was pushing glory himself, building a bank account.

Or this was the story Anita Blonde had told him, back in New Orleans, under the statue of Andrew Jackson, in the square where they used to auction off the slaves. Who knew how much of it was true.

To Dante's surprise, there was no one in the apartment with Williams, or at least there didn't appear to be. But perhaps this was not so surprising. There was no transfer of drugs going on, nothing for Williams to protect. The risk was all on Dante's side.

"What's in the case?" Williams asked.

"I think you have a pretty good idea."

Williams unzipped the bag and peered at the money.

"How much?"

"Half."

"When do we get the rest?"

"On delivery."

He and Williams sat down at a kitchen table in a bay window. It was a modest apartment, with furniture that was old but well kept. There were some pictures of kids up on the mantle, and a lot of little homey touches. There was something incongruous here. He doubted the apartment belonged to Williams. To some parishioner down in Cole Valley, maybe. A woman, from the look of things—someone with a vanished husband and a couple of kids—who more than likely didn't quite know what Williams was up to.

The bag rested on the table between them.

"So what's your story?"

"Story? I don't know what you mean," said Dante.

"You're an ex-cop, aren't you?"

"Ex. That's the important part."

"Can't you find other work?"

Dante said nothing.

"I mean you're a white man, local boy. Seems like you could find yourself some respectable work."

Williams was pulling Dante's chain, goading him. But there was a point underneath, maybe. Williams was letting him know he had his suspicions.

"I had to leave my old profession," Dante smiled. "But I've been compensated. Traveling around, bringing things in and out of the country. Now I'm home. And I want to make my own mark."

Williams smiled in return. It was a wry smile, and the look of the hardware clerk was gone. He had instead the look of a man who knew there was something else beneath the surface, and who knew that you knew, too, and who didn't want to be taken for a fool.

"All right," Williams said. "We've got a mule coming."

"When?"

"One week. Maybe two."

"What's the source?"

"Colombia. The Medellin fields."

Dante nodded. He knew the trade route. There was a certain irony in it. In Bangkok, he'd been working to infiltrate the operation in northern Thailand—or so they told him—but even then the South American cartels had been moving their fields out of cocoa into opium, undercutting the Asians in the U.S. market.

He had sampled the wares himself more than once. In Bangkok, yes, of course, but in New Orleans, too. Down Esplanade, through the iron gates. Behind the mausoleum walls. You found dealers, people on their knees. *Chasing the dragon,* as the saying went. Unfurling the aluminum foil, lighting the powder, and breathing in the smoke. Trying to get every bit of that smoke before it vanished. Pursuing it with your whole being.

"We don't want you selling it here," Williams pointed out the window.

"I understand."

"No, you don't understand. We don't want it here in these projects—or anywhere in the Fillmore, or Valencia Gardens."

"We don't have any intention to sell it here."

"Sell it to the Chinese. Sell it to the goddamn Italians. Sell it to the goddamn Haight, but stay out of nigger country, you understand."

"You protecting the good folks in the 'hood? Or keeping that market for yourself?"

"Take it out to the suburbs."

Something was wrong. On an assignment like this, it took time to penetrate to the point where he was now. You did not waltz into the inner circle so easily, no matter the advance work. The Nation recruited out of the black prisons, and there was no reason for them to trust him. So Dante wondered about Williams. What kind of role was this man playing? You never knew on these kinds of things, because oftentimes the company had its people in roles you didn't expect, playing every side against the middle, operating on hidden logic. Or on no logic at all.

Williams grabbed the gym bag and zippered it shut. He hadn't bothered to count.

"I'll call you when the shipment comes in."

"You bring the boss when you come."

"What are you talking about?"

"When we make the trade, you bring Fakir. To the family

warehouse—that's where we'll do the deal. My partners will be there to check the purity."

"That's not usual. He doesn't associate himself."

"We're laying the groundwork for the future. If Fakir doesn't come, then nothing happens. No deal."

Williams shrugged. "I'll see what I can do."

"If Fakir can't be there, we might as well end this now. My partners want to meet him."

Williams swelled a little. "He'll be there."

Dante left. This was the most dangerous moment. He had dropped off his money. If Williams had no intention of working a deal—if there was no dope, no connection—then there was a chance that he might have already made arrangements, given one of his buddies on the street here a few dollars to take care of Dante, to end the business while Williams himself slipped out with the money. Dante studied the gangbangers, and he scanned the windows up above. He decided to double back through the service alley, into the projects. Around the corner, a boy stepped out of a stairwell in front of him.

"You want something?" the boy asked.

"No."

"I can get you anything you want. Horse, rock, Liquid X—hell, you want that yuppie shit, I can get that for you, too."

"No."

"Acid, dope?"

"No thanks. Not today."

"Fuck you, then." The boy planted his feet wide. He was a small-time dealer, street level, high himself and ready to explode. "What the hell you doing here?"

"Fuck you, too," said Dante.

Then he showed the boy his gun and kept on walking. He knew better than to look back.

In The Beach, Dante stopped at Cassinelli's corner drug for a pack of cigarettes. By the counter, same as the old days, he saw a drop box for sending your photos over to Monaco's Lab. He remembered the envelope in his jacket pocket, the one his uncle had given him with the family pictures, and he dropped the negatives in the box. Then he walked up the hill past Marilyn's house and stood looking at the bay. The sky was darkening and the wind was picking up. There was a light on inside Marilyn's house. He lingered for a moment. He wanted to see her, but there were a lot of things he wanted. To walk down Esplanade. To kneel among the statuary, the tombs littered with aluminum foil. He decided to get a drink instead and headed down the hill to the Naked Moon.

NINE

All things are interconnected, even if by happenstance. Maybe once, when things were simpler, it was possible to divine the deeper intention, but now the connections . . . they are too many, too random. There is for example the black gangster on the street, the little fuck whose uncle had worked years ago in the Mancuso warehouse—and whom Dante's mother had admired once as an infant in a carriage— but there is no way to know these connections. Just as there is no way for Dante to know, as he takes a seat at the Naked Moon, that Marilyn is at that moment packing her organza blouse and her silk skirt, getting ready for her trip to Sonoma with Mora the next day—but in the middle of packing she goes to the bottom shelf of the bookcase, looking for a picture from seven years ago. Just as there is no way to know that Uncle Salvatore is in heated conversation with his son Gary, telling him how he will meet with Dante tomorrow afternoon to discuss the family estate. And at the mention of Dante's name Gary feels a sickness in his stomach. Meantime the Chinese detective drags out an old file, and Love Wu sits in his wheelchair on a balcony over-looking Chinatown, and Dante watches the girls at the Naked Moon, trying to fight off a craving rising in his chest, drinking, then drinking some more, eventually returning home, lying in his father's bed, sweating as he used to sweat in the Ninth Ward, waking up to an image of the Bangkok girl with her body slashed, his mind skittering to the Strehli case, to Marilyn, to his uncle's odd behavior, the convergence of past and present, a deeper meaning, connections he is able to fathom just for an instant, or so he believes, at the edge of sleep, but then he awakes and the understanding all vanishes. He counts on his fingers, mutters, and in a fugitive moment even crosses himself in the dark. Then at midnight, he goes out to the family warehouse. To make sure that the layout is as he remembered, and nothing has changed.

TEN

Uncle Salvatore lived up the steep side of Telegraph Hill, in a double-story Edwardian that looked back over Vallejo Gulch. It was the same house his uncle had lived in for the past thirty years. To reach it, Dante climbed the Filbert Steps, where more than a few old-timers had had heart attacks, the blood rushing to their heads as they plodded up the hill, stubborn as donkeys, one foot in front of the other, carrying in paper sacks their groceries and their bottles of wine.

Better to drop dead, your heart beating like a cement mixer inside your head, than give a goddamn taxi driver four bucks to take you two and a half blocks.

The Widow Bolinni lived at the crest of the hill, across from his uncle. She'd been a peeper, always at the window. Judging from the curtains, the yellowing lace, she still lived there now. Dante climbed up his uncle's stairs. The front door was ajar, but that wasn't unusual. Aunt Regina often opened the door to let in the air, despite her husband's objection that it might let in other things as well.

Dante knocked. When no one answered, he rang the bell.

"Uncle Salvatore," he called.

There was no answer, but this did not surprise him. The stairs were around back, off the kitchen, and his uncle's office was at the top of those stairs, toward the rear of the house. And Aunt Regina, he knew, was on her weekly visit across the bay, to her sister in Alameda.

The house was bigger than his father's house—light and full of air. There were none of Grandmother Pellicano's talismans here, and not much in the way of old world Italiana. Aunt Regina was a modern woman who did not like her place to look like a museum.

In the kitchen, Dante found the back door open, as well. He stood on the rear landing and noticed that the gate leading into the alley was thrown wide. Dante had an ill feeling in his gut that he told himself was foolishness, paranoia, based on nothing, too many years in the company.

Upstairs, he found his uncle.

The old man lay on the floor, with his feet straddled wide on the imported carpet. The air smelled of cordite. The room around him was in disarray, papers and books scattered everywhere.

Uncle Salvatore had been shot in the head, and there was a large amount of blood, as yet uncongealed. The skin had lost its pink, but the extremities did not yet have the mottled look that came when the blood settles into the lowest parts of the body.

After his years in Homicide, Dante was familiar with crime scenes. Maybe it was because the professional part of him took over. He knew better than to touch anything. He did not want to jeopardize the evidence, or somehow implicate himself. From the looks of things, the wound was fresh, the killing very recent. And something else: there was a great deal of splatter, but no smearing. It suggested that the visitor had searched the room before the shooting. Otherwise the blood droplets would lay on top of the scattered papers.

Dante took out his gun. He searched all the rooms, but found no one.

The killer had left through the back door, Dante surmised, through the alley.

If Dante called the police, he would be in for a lot of questions. He did not want the attention. The company had him here on assignment, and it would be best to keep his distance.

He holstered his gun. He had disturbed nothing, touched nothing. The problem was to leave without being seen. In the alley, just beyond the back gate, a tree crew had just pulled up, going after an old Bay Laurel in a nearby yard. So Dante went out the front.

He left the front door ajar, just as it had been. He guessed that the killer, whoever it was, had stuck the gun in Uncle Salvatore's face as soon as he opened the door. Bossed him into the house. Sat him down while he searched the room.

The street was deserted, and Dante was glad for that. As he hit the sidewalk he glanced up at the Widow Bolinni's. One of the lace panels parted, then fell closed.

And he knew he had been seen.

PART TWO

ELEVEN

Ying should have been at home hours ago, in his little house in El Cerrito with the Queen Palm out front. He should have taken the five o'clock tube under the bay. Then he would have been home when the call came, home with his wife, Lei, and their two kids, and somebody else would have been assigned to the case. Instead he'd worked late, then dallied in Chinatown, stopping in Portsmouth Square to watch some old bachelors from Guangdong haggle over a game of go. Afterward he'd doubled back to his grandmother's house in Winter Alley.

His grandmother's place was tiny, and the rooms were small, closet-sized. A fire escape jagged to the rooftop. On more than one occasion Ying had folded the escape ladder back up because the gangbangers in the neighborhood were always yanking it down, using it as a way onto the roof. There was a small desk in one of the rooms, and a bed where Ying slept when his work kept him in the city.

About a year ago, he had walked in to find the upstairs room trashed, his files scattered and the bed overturned. Whether it had been the doing of the neighborhood gangbangers or some- one else, he didn't know. It had happened when he was still with SI, investigating the disappearance of Ru Shen.

Today, his grandmother was not in the front room, but no doubt she had already sensed his presence. Grandmother Ying could see very little and hear even less, or so the doctor said; but it rarely happened that Ying took her by surprise. She was attuned to the subtle vibrations of the house and sensed in advance, it seemed, his key turning in the front lock. By the time he reached the little kitchen, she had already turned in her chair. As he stepped toward her, she offered him her cheek. Since he was a boy, it had been their greeting; he pressed his cheek against hers and whispered her name.

Ying did not know the old woman's exact age. Grandmother Ying had been smuggled into the country decades ago, back when the exclusion laws still prohibited Chinese women. Ying's grandfather had been a successful tradesman, so he'd made ar- rangements through a Shanghai broker who specialized in young women. She had outlived her husband and a number of her chil- dren and several of her grandchildren as well. At some point along the way, Ying was not sure exactly when, she had passed into this blind silence.

Now the old woman got up to make tea. She negotiated the little kitchen without hesitation. This was all part of their ritual, the boiling of the water and the steeping of the tea. Then they would go sit together in the front room, which was really nothing more than a parlor. Grandmother Ying had raised five children in these tiny rooms, though that seemed hardly possible now.

The front room was spare. She was quiet and he was quiet

and the only thing in the room was the smell of the orchid in the vase on the rattan table in front of them.

It was beautiful, that orchid. Ying lingered in the silence of the old woman's house and found it hard to pull himself away. He often came here. They sipped their tea together, and he closed his eyes, dwelling in the old woman's quietude. He thought about his wife, Lei. Even though she was only just across the bay—and he could be on his way home to her any minute— he closed his eyes and for a moment yearned for her in the way the Chinese bachelors must have yearned for wives of their own, dreaming of the day when they would have enough money to smuggle a woman into the country. Most of them never did.

Then his cell rang. It was Maxine Hong, the desk sergeant at the Night Division.

"Are you in the city?" asked Hong.

Ying said nothing. He could guess what was coming. The Night Division was perpetually shorthanded.

"Where are you?"

The tunnel, Ying wanted to say. I am in the tunnel, in the train, deep under the bay. On my way home. And in another moment the tunnel will emerge into the light and I will step onto the platform and . . .

"I'm here," he said. "In The Beach."

"There's been a homicide up on Union. Toliveri's on the scene—but Angelo says it's yours to head up. If you want it."

Ying got the implication. Ever since he'd left SI the implication was the same. He'd gone soft.

By the time Ying got to the scene, the patrol car had cordoned off the house and the gawkers were starting to gather. The ME was on the steps with the photographer, but Toliveri was holding Forensics out of the house until Ying had a chance to walk the scene.

"We've got the wife and the son sequestered in the den." Toliveri jabbed a thumb over his shoulders. "Do you want to talk to them?"

"Let me take a look around first."

There were blood smears on the carpet, and Ying followed the tracks though the kitchen and up the stairs. The stains got darker as he went up, and darker still on the hall carpet—until he turned the corner and saw the old man lying on the hardwood, then the prints got muddled with the blood on the floor. Ying glanced at the corpse and could see at once that lividity had set in. Dead maybe six, seven hours. The ME could be more precise. The room itself was a mess, paper scattered all around—as if someone had been searching for something.

"Who reported the murder?" Ying asked

"The victim's wife."

Toliveri was in his early fifties. He had grown up in the neighborhood, but he was a second stringer in the department. He was a good detective when he wanted to be, but he had some gripes—the main one being he wanted a promotion before he quit so he could boost his pension status. He was genial enough. Witnesses tended to trust him, at least in the early going. But he had a way of undermining the investigation. Holding back too long, then bulling forward for no apparent reason. There were times, too, when he just didn't do what you asked.

"These footprints," said Ying. "They look like a woman's shoe."

"The wife, like I said. She's got blood on her dress as well."

"You had a chance to talk to her?"

"She says she came home at three o'clock. But she didn't come up here right away. Took a nap on the couch first. Then she found the body. She's the one who tracked things up."

"How about the son?"

"Gary Mancuso. He lives up the street. His mother called him after she found the body."

Ying felt a spear of panic. Maybe it showed on his face.

"What's the name again?"

"Mancuso."

And he had the feeling it was all connected, it was all the same case, just a million different manifestations. A hydra. Cut off the head, and it grew a dozen more.

"Big name in The Beach. Or used to be," Toliveri said. He gestured toward the corpse. "That was Salvatore. Owns the warehouse down China Basin. His brother Giovanni died a few days back."

"I'm aware of that."

"The son, Salvatore's nephew—he used to be with Homicide. He's back in town for the old man's funeral."

"I know."

"How do you know? You keeping tabs on the Italians these days?"

Toliveri meant it as funny, but it didn't come out right. Like there were things Ying couldn't possibly know. Ying had gotten this kind of treatment before, just as he was sure Toliveri had gotten it when he worked Chinatown. There were things you couldn't know if you were not of the blood. Things you shouldn't know. Ying understood the attitude, even shared it to a degree, but the comment still played on his nerves.

"I'm going to go talk to the wife," he said.

When he went downstairs, though, he found a man in the den with Regina Mancuso and her son. He was the family doctor, and he had Mrs. Mancuso stretched out on the daybed. It was a brightly colored piece of furniture, and there was something incongruous about the woman lying there. She wore expensive clothes but she had a peasant face, and there was that blood on her dress.

"She's in no condition to talk with you," said the doctor.

"How did you get in here?" Ying turned to Toliveri. "This place is supposed to be secure."

Toliveri shrugged. The answer lay in the shrug. Loose discipline. The crew didn't pay attention to Toliveri, because everyone knew how he was. But Ying knew if there was a breach in evidence, he would get the grief.

"Her heart—she appears to be fibrillating," the doctor said. "From the shock, possibly. I need to get her to the hospital."

"I want to talk to her first."

The doctor shook his head. "You can talk to her later. This is a medical emergency."

"I've already taken her statement," said Toliveri.

Just then Ying heard the ambulance in the distance, wailing down Columbus. The mother grasped for her son.

"I want the son with her," the doctor said, "riding in the ambulance. It's a matter of keeping her calm."

"I got the broad strokes in the preliminary," Toliveri said. "We can catch the details later."

The ambulance was closer now, and the mother moaned again. Given her condition, Ying wondered how much information, if any, Toliveri had gotten. Ying didn't want to push the old woman over the edge, but the police work so far had not been as tight as it should be, and in cases like this family members were always suspect. He forced himself past the doctor and took Gary Mancuso by the arm.

"I just need a minute."

"What, what?" said the old woman. She was disoriented and her color was bad. Ying edged the son away.

"Where were you this afternoon?

The son gave him a vague look, and Ying repeated the question. "Where were you?"

"At the warehouse."

"Anybody around who can verify that?"

"Huh?"

The paramedics were coming in the door now. There was a rush of activity and Ying used the confusion to push himself into Gary Mancuso's face. The man was nervous. Ying did not like the curl to his lip, or the way he averted his eyes.

"I said can anybody verify where you were this afternoon?"

"The men on the dock, I guess. I was in and out."

"You guess?"

"Listen—"

"You work on the dock."

The guy looked offended. "It's the family business. I had paperwork this morning, in the office, then I went out to lunch."

"But you spent some time on the dock, this afternoon."

"That isn't what I said."

"You have a secretary there, in the office?"

"Of course, but . . . I can't do this now."

The doctor cut in. "Listen, can't this wait?"

Ying glanced back. The paramedics had strapped the women into the gurney, but she was looking toward her son, her eyes very wide and full of fear. Ying could see he wasn't going to get anything else out of Mancuso, not now. He turned to Toliveri. "All right," he said. "Let's seal this scene. But do it right this time. And get Forensics in here."

Outside, Ying watched the old woman and her son and the doctor make their way to the ambulance. He was tempted to send Toliveri along to push things, to get a formal statement from Gary, and maybe something from his mother, if possible, but he needed Toliveri here. So he called Central and told them to get a detective out to the hospital, a woman preferably, maybe Louise Roma. After the ambulance was gone, he lingered on the front porch. He studied the neighboring residences, looking for windows and doors that had a direct sight line into Salvatore Mancuso's house. There was a place across the street, with the blinds half open, and those curtains fell closed as he watched.

Ying strolled down into the crowd that had gathered on the street. The street crackled with the odd energy it had at times like this, and they gawked at the gangly Chinese detective in his white shirt and thin tie.

"Who lives across the street?"

"The Widow Bolinni," said one of the old-timers.

The crowd had questions of their own, but Ying paid no attention. He went inside and got Toliveri, then sent him over to talk to the woman while he supervised the scene. It took him a while, but eventually Toliveri came back with the news.

"I got something," said Toliveri. He looked excited. "The Widow Bollini—she says she saw the deceased's nephew outside the house around two o'clock."

"What's the nephew's name?"

"Dante. Dante Mancuso. She saw him leaving the house."

"The ex-cop?"

"Used to work Homicide. He was Angelo's partner. That was before the Strehli business, if you remember all that."

"Two o'clock, she said?"

"Yeah. Two o'clock."

"That puts him here at the time of death."

"Pretty close."

"Let's go talk to him."

"He lives down on Fresno."

"I know."

"Of course," said Toliveri. "You know everything."

The man who opened the door on Fresno Street was not soft or pretty. He had hard, angular features. His nose was prominent, his skin dark, his lips thin—with a downward turn, almost sensuous—and altogether he had about him the looks of the old world, Moorish and cruel, but handsome, too. He wore pajamas, expensive pajamas, but he did not seem entirely comfortable in them. If there was one thing that struck Ying about the man it was the nose. An admirable nose—ancient in its profile, big as a peninsula. It made you unlikely to forget his face in the future.

The man's hair was short-cropped, unlike his father's, and this accentuated his features. Ying saw the family resemblance. He had stood in this same doorway a couple weeks back talking with the father Giovanni. But Ying was with Toliveri now, and the man in the doorway was Dante Mancuso.

"Hi, Toli," Mancuso said. His voice carried a note of irony. It was a natural irony directed at the order of things, of which Toliveri was only the most recent manifestation. "You still with Homicide?"

"Sorry to get you up at this hour." Toliveri shied backward, straightening himself. On the way over, Ying had suggested Toliveri lead the questioning, at least at first. It seemed to make sense. Toliveri and Dante were acquainted; they knew each other from the neighborhood as well as from their time on the force. Already, though, Ying was beginning to think this was a mistake.

"If we could come in for a moment?" Toliveri asked.

"Is this a social call?"

"I wish so. I haven't seen you for so long." Toliveri paused, trying to be gracious in his way. "This is Detective Ying. He used to be with Special Investigations."

"Who's he with now?"

"Do you mind if we come in?"

Mancuso nodded, but he kept himself wedged in the doorway.

"There was an incident," Toliveri said. "And we were wondering if you could help us out."

Instead of revealing the uncle's death up front, Toliveri was holding back to see how much Dante would reveal on his own. To see if the man would contradict himself or come out with some detail that gave his involvement away. But Dante had been a detective, Ying thought, and would not be so easily taken in.

This was obviously a Homicide detail, and there was no way the two of them would be here at this time of night if it didn't have to do with a murder. Still, Dante seemed to warm to Toliveri, though perhaps this was pretense as well; it was hard to tell who was working who. In the meantime, the two men turned their shoulders in such a way as to exclude him from the conversation. The old neighborhood thing.

"What kind of incident?"

"We'll give you the details in a minute. It would be better, more helpful, if you could tell us where you were this afternoon."

"I'm in town for my father's funeral."

"I know. I'm sorry. I liked your dad."

"I appreciate your sympathy. Especially in the small hours of the morning like this."

Toliveri laughed at Dante's remark. It was an uncomfortable laugh and made the detective look foolish.

"So tell me, what's this about?" Dante asked. He was not smiling.

"Where were you this afternoon?"

"What time? Just tell me exactly the time you want to know about, and I'll tell you where I was."

"About two."

"Two," Dante hesitated. "About that time, I walked up the hill to see my Uncle Salvatore. Up Union. You know where that is, don't you?"

"Your uncle's? Yes, I know where it is."

"We were supposed to get together. Discuss some family business. But he wasn't there."

"What do you mean?"

"I mean I knocked on the door—but he didn't answer."

"And then?"

"I came back here."

The two cops looked at one another. The game had gone about as far as it could go.

"What's going on?" Dante asked. "What's this about?"

Ying took over now. "I'm sorry to tell you this. You're uncle's dead."

"No." Dante looked genuinely confused. A little too genuine, maybe. "No," he said again. "It's my father who died. We buried him Tuesday."

"I'm sorry. But your uncle was shot to death earlier today. He was found on the floor of his office, upstairs in his house."

"Jesus," said Dante. And in the instant he uttered the word, his eyes met Ying's. It was the kind of naked moment you looked for while cross-examining a suspect, when the two of you looked into one another's eyes, and you tried to see if the grief, the surprise, was a lie, and what was hidden underneath. It was the tiniest of instants, but sometimes it was all you had to go on, and you had to make up your mind whether there was something to pursue.

In this case, Ying didn't know. His gut pulled him two ways. Given the circumstance, though, he had little doubt about what to do next.

"We're going to need to take you downtown. We need a statement."

"It's routine," said Toliveri. "As you know."

But it wasn't routine, of course. Just as it wasn't routine to have a couple of cops knock on your door in the middle of the night to tell you your uncle had just been murdered.

"You want to change your clothes?" asked Ying. "Toliveri here, he will accompany you back into the house."

Toliveri bristled. Ying realized he didn't like being told what to do in front of Mancuso. Sensitive about his rank. Didn't want Dante to see that it was Ying leading the investigation, a Chinese dragging an Italian around by the nose.

"No," said Dante. "Just let me grab my jacket, and I'll come the way I am."

A smile crossed Dante's lips, a smirk, as if there were part of him that thought it was a joke, going down to Columbus Station in his imported pajamas. *Before this is over,* Ying thought, *we'll be back with a warrant.* But if Dante was as smart as he suspected, they wouldn't find a damned thing.

TWELVE

Columbus Station was an anonymous building composed of steel and glass. Despite its name, the station was not on Columbus Avenue at all but squatted on the edge of Chinatown a couple blocks up Vallejo, between the old Italia Café and the Wung Family Vegetable Emporium. The police station was remarkable only in its anonymity, resembling from the outside nothing so much as the back office processing center for an insurance company.

Dante had worked at Columbus Station for close to a decade, and he knew it well enough. The overcrowded garage underneath. The elevator up. The interrogation room at the end of the hall. One floor above was the Homicide pen, and above that was the chief's office.

Inside the interrogation room, Toliveri gave him a cordite test—to see if there was gunpowder residue on his hand.

Toliveri was not near as chatty as he had been earlier.

"Where's our buddy Mr. Ying?" said Dante.

"He'll be back shortly."

"Used to be with SI?"

"Yes."

"Why did he leave?"

"I don't know. Lost his nerve."

"He doesn't seem like the type to lose his nerve."

"People say what people say. You know how things are around here. It isn't always fair."

"No, it isn't," said Dante, but he remembered how it was to work with Toli. He had his insights, but he spent a lot of time grousing. He worked in fits and starts. In the beginning he was affable, but when the case got hard, he resisted—and sometimes bulled off in the wrong direction.

Now Toliveri went away. It had been almost three A.M. when Ying and Toliveri woke him from his slumber, and it was getting close to dawn now. Likely he would still be sitting here after the sun went up. Dante knew the routine. Let you sit. Then let you sit some more. It was a hackneyed technique but it had its uses.

When Ying came back, he came back alone.

"Coffee?" Ying asked. His manner was matter-of-fact, neither cordial nor otherwise.

Dante shook his head. "I'm fine."

"Are you sure? I'm going to get myself a refill. We've got a new brewing system. You know how it is these days—people and their coffee. Everybody's a connoisseur."

Dante knew what was going on—and he knew Ying knew he knew—but he decided to play along.

"All right," said Dante. "Get me some coffee."

Ying went away again. He was a long time away. Much longer than it took to get to the coffee trough and back. It was part of the old routine, and Dante remembered doing the same. Offering fresh coffee, then coming back a year later with cold mud.

And that was the way Ying played it. Handing him the coffee as if it were some kind of gift, when it was the same awful stuff. Sitting there in the pot since Dante had left seven years ago. Coffee that had been burnt to begin with, then allowed to go cold, then reheated again a couple million times. Packets of powdered milk on the side and enough artificial sugar to kill a rat.

"Sorry it took me so long," said Ying. "I got caught up in something."

"Sure."

"How's the coffee?"

"Delicious."

"Always is."

Ying stared into his cup, disguising a smile, perhaps, or maybe just weariness. Or maybe he really thought the coffee was good. Ying had the hangdog look of a man who had been up all night. His eyes were way back there in a tunnel someplace. He was about Dante's age—but taller, lanky, and loose-jointed. He had a strong jaw and wore his tie loose around his neck. His hair was black and disheveled.

"So you used to work in Homicide, here in Columbus Station?"

"Yes," Dante said.

Dante guessed the man already knew the whole business: how Dante had gotten tangled up on the wrong side of the Strehli case and left the department under a cloud. Dante wondered if those allegations had grown over the years, reiterated in rumors, repeated and fleshed out with invented details, augmented and then augmented again. The truth was, Internal Affairs had nothing on him—and he'd quit in disgust.

"I appreciate your cooperation," Ying said.

The cop settled in across the table, and his composure changed in some indefinable way. Dante recognized the small talk was all but over, and he was grateful. He wanted to get on with it.

"I spoke with your father before he died," said Ying.

Dante was taken aback. His aunt had mentioned something at the funeral home: how a Chinese cop had been by to talk with his father. Dante was surprised at the coincidence, but this was the way things went in The Beach. Like a small town, you were always stumbling into someone.

"He thought someone was out to kill him, apparently. But when I spoke with him, he backed off."

"The doctor said he was delusional."

"Was there anyone with a reason to kill him?"

"I don't think so."

Dante could guess the question on Ying's mind. It had occurred to him as well. He wondered if his father's death was what it seemed. Or if there was some connection between his father's passing and his uncle's murder.

Ying sat with his hands flat on the table—and Dante saw an earnestness there. Ying had been in SI, then transferred off, and now here he was back in Homicide. It was an unusual move—not a step forward for a guy thinking about career—and Dante wondered what lay behind it.

"Why are you in town?" asked Ying.

"I was attending my father's funeral."

"Did you visit your uncle yesterday?"

"We went over this."

"I know, but there are a few details that I need clarity on. I think you understand."

"I did visit him, yes. But as I told you, he wasn't in."

"Did you go inside?"

Dante had given this some thought. If he were Ying, and this was his investigation, and a relative had been sighted outside the house at the time of the murder, he would pursue the obvious. He would try to tie the suspect to the scene—to the crime inside.

"No. I didn't."

"Why not?"

"I knocked. I rang the bell—but no one answered. So I left."

"It didn't occur to you to go inside and look around?"

"Yes, but the door was locked." He was lying now, of course, but there was no way for Ying to know this.

"What was the reason for that visit?"

"My uncle asked me over. He had some things he wanted to talk about. Family business. He didn't elaborate—and I didn't ask."

"Did your father leave behind a will?"

"Yes."

"Have you seen it?"

"A few months back, yes. I saw him in Houston, and he showed me a copy."

"Were there any provisions you—or somebody else—might have found troublesome?"

"I was an only child. He left everything to me."

Dante knew what was going on here. The cop was trying to establish motive, though the truth was his father's will had been pretty straightforward. The only catch was that part of his father's money was tied up in the warehouse. After his father quit the business, he'd stayed on as a silent partner. The way things were set up, Dante had a chance to reactivate the partnership if he wanted, or sell out. Either way, he gained nothing from his uncle's death. He explained this to Ying, but the cop wouldn't let go.

"Given what you describe about the estate, and the arrangement of the business, could there be a conflict down the line between you and your cousin?"

"I suppose it's possible."

"Sometimes, things get emotional, things happen quickly." Ying's voice softened, and there was a note of invitation. "Did you and your uncle have an argument?"

Ying paused, waiting. Dante let the pause linger.

"I lost my father a few days ago," he said at last. "And now my uncle. As a cop, I understand what you're doing here." Dante's voice was calm. When he spoke again he himself could hear the venom underneath. "But maybe you'd be better off out there, looking for the murderer."

Ying didn't flinch. As an interrogator, Dante knew, you expected a reaction when you pushed someone; it was almost instinctive—odd if they did not push back. If they responded too vociferously, though, or not at all, that's when you wondered. Still, even then, you didn't know for sure. There were innocent people who trembled and fell apart, looking guilty as hell, and then there were the actors, the sociopaths who shrugged off their crime like an ill-fitting suit.

"All right," Ying said. "I'll be back in a moment."

Dante put his head in his hands and all of sudden his anger

gave way and his grief washed over him, here in this peculiar little room with the smudged walls, the plastic chairs, the table
anchored to the floor. There was an emptiness the size of the
moon inside his heart. His father and his uncle had vanished,
taking with them a part of himself, as well. Because who else
was there to remember the boy he had been, hobbling his first
steps down the wharf while the brothers Mancuso joked and
laughed? Who else to remember the crabs crawling from their
silver buckets, and the fish flopping in their purse seines, and his
mother before she went nuts? He held his head in his hands, and
as he did he imagined the Homicide cops watching from the
other side of the one-way mirror as he himself had once done,
studying the suspect, trying to figure out how to entrap him.
Ying would be there, of course, and Toliveri. And probably
Angelo, too, his ex-partner. But at the moment Dante didn't
give a shit. They could watch till kingdom come.

After a while Ying and Toliveri returned to the interrogation
room together. Ying took the plastic chair and slid it
around; he sat with his hands hanging between his legs. They
were long hands, with finely sculpted fingers. Meanwhile Toliveri made a show of turning on the tape then he leaned against
the wall, regarding him with that same empty countenance
Dante remembered from years ago. When you got down to it,
he had little fondness for Toliveri.

"Earlier tonight, we did house-to-house interviews," said
Ying. "And Toliveri here talked to a woman who lives across the
street from your uncle."

"The Widow Bolinni," said Toliveri. Dante could see that

Toliveri wanted him to know that the Widow Bolinni had been *his* interview: that *he* was the one who'd wriggled his ass up the stairs and sweet-talked the old witch. "She saw you on the walkway outside your uncle's house yesterday. About the time of the murder."

"That's not surprising," said Dante. "I was there. I told you that before."

"Did you go inside the house?"

"I already told Mr. Ying what happened."

"Did you kill your uncle?" Toliveri staggered forward a little as he spoke, like a boxer, but punch-drunk, a little too eager. Dante recognized the behavior.

"You got the cordite tests?" asked Dante.

"Yes."

"Then you know I didn't fire a gun."

"You could have been wearing gloves."

"Then where are they?"

"You could have thrown them away. Or they could be up at your house."

"They're not."

Ying cut in now. "The Widow Bolinni, she told Toliveri you were wearing a red shirt and white slacks. Is that correct?"

"Yes. It is."

"You still have those clothes?"

"Not on, obviously."

"At home?"

"Dry cleaners. I took a load last night."

Ying's eyes narrowed, and Dante knew how that made things look. Like he'd run the clothes down to remove any fiber evidence that might be there. And he'd considered doing that, it was true. There was always the off chance he'd brushed against a sofa or a wall. That something had clung to him that might tie him to the inside of the house. But dry cleaning didn't remove everything. And Ying would know that, too.

"What cleaners?"

"Red Wing. Down off Grant."

"And the shoes?"

"I'm wearing them."

Ying's eyes went bright for a second then dead again, realizing perhaps that he had no way of knowing if these were indeed the shoes. If Dante had not dumped them—with blood smears on the bottom, carpet fibers—into a debris box somewhere. Which, of course, was exactly what he had done. Along with the clothes.

Then he'd gone down and bought a new red polo, new white slacks, identical to the ones he'd thrown away. These were the clothes he'd dropped at the dry cleaners, crumpled up, mixed with old laundry. So even if he'd brushed against something during his brief time in his uncle's house, there was nothing for them to find.

"Unless things have changed since I left the force, you've got forty-eight hours to bring formal charges against me. If you've got the evidence, then bring the charges. Otherwise—let me go."

Ying shut off the tape. Toliveri went lax. He could only play the bull for so long, then reverted to his usual demeanor.

"I can't let you go," said Ying.

"You don't have any evidence."

"We'll search your apartment, you know. We'll get a warrant."

"You won't find anything."

"It's our job to check, you know that."

"I understand." Dante was irritated now. His father was dead, and his uncle, and he had to put up with this treatment. And the day after tomorrow he was supposed to meet with the Wus.

"I'm going to have put you in a cell," said Ying.

Dante didn't argue. He was pretty sure how this would work out. They would check his apartment. They would find his gun, but it hadn't been fired recently, and they would find never get a match on ballistics. They would examine his clothes for blood stains—but again, they would find nothing. They could hold him for a little while, but eventually they would have to let him loose.

THIRTEEN

Later that same morning, Marilyn Visconti and Tony Mora crossed the Golden Gate in the red Alfa. Mora drove in the center lane with the top down. It was cold. They were on the way to wine country, and Marilyn's heart fluttered with misgivings, whether at the onrushing traffic—just inches away, across an unprotected divider—or for some other reason, she didn't know. Or if she did know the reason, she was not about to admit it. Rather she shivered and adjusted her scarf. It was a silk scarf, bright and flimsy, very beautiful, but it did little against the wind. Though it was miserable on the bridge, the tourists were out, regular as seabirds, clinging to the chain link. Overhead, the giant suspension towers caught the sun, then disappeared in a confusion of fog. The traffic slowed, and Mora jammed the brakes. Just as suddenly the traffic let loose. They crossed into Marin and the fog was gone. The hills were flooded with a hard light.

"There's a place on the way I want to show you," Mora said. "Just up here." Mora's voice was difficult to hear in the wind, but he took the next exit and rumbled the Alfa down the hill-side. "Mia Rancadore's father died. And the estate wants to sell."

The Rancadores were an old North Beach family who had left the city some twenty years before. Mia was a few years older than herself, and Marilyn remembered watching the moving van, wishing she could go, too. Everyone had been leaving then.

Tony pulled into the drive, and now she could see what had drawn the Rancadores away. It was the kind of place you didn't find much anymore. Off on its own. Or it had that illusion. In truth it lay in a skelter of houses screened from each other by a jagged terrace of madrone and wild eucalyptus. The bay was below. On the hill above, at the precipice, a bank of fog hung as in a photograph, ready to run down a slope covered with gnarled oaks and yellow grass.

"It's hard to find the perfect place," Tony said. "But I think this might be it."

And maybe it was, here on this sheltered hillside. An older house with a bit of grace. A backyard with a grape arbor and a view of the city.

"If we want this, I can probably do something, but we should move fast. Otherwise, they're going to put it on the market."

Marilyn toyed with the ring on her finger. Tony had given it to her. She had wandered the North Bay towns with him more than once, walking over pink flagstones with the sun in her face, intoxicated by the light. She had yearned for a place that was warmer, less confined, away from the alleys, the mildew and dry rot, the stench of the past, the familiar faces. But now, imagining herself in this house, sitting on the couch, under these redwood timbers, she felt overcome by nostalgia.

"No."

"Why not? It's the kind of place we've been looking for. Lots of upgrades."

"It's not right."

"Well," Tony looked around somewhat wistfully, "I admit, it is a bit on the small side."

They drove north, taking the turn at Black Point, winding through what remained of the old marshes, up through Carneros, into the Valley of the Moon. Her family had owned a place up here once, a summer retreat, but they'd had to sell when they put their father in St. Vincent's. It didn't matter. Stepping out of the Alfa into the parking lot—in her traveling clothes— her slacks, her turtleneck, her shades, and the bright scarf around her neck—she felt as if the whole valley were hers. It was a transitory feeling: a sense of ownership that fleeted away with the birdsong and left her hollow.

The hotel spa was fed by hot springs, and Marilyn soaked for a long while in one of the stone tubs under the terrace. Then she went inside for a massage. At times the young man's fingertips lingered overly long, but she said nothing. What could you say? Sometimes it was better to give in. To let your body relax and your mind drift.

She had been supposed to meet Dante that day, seven years ago. They'd made plans. They were going to go off, to hell with everyone—but a few days before she'd been overcome by bouts of nausea, and the tests confirmed her suspicions. She knew the truth, but there was no way to tell him. Because there was something hideous about the truth, and ugly, and she did not know how to explain. So she'd gotten the procedure, then gone to Italy. With her parents. To lay in the splendid light and forget the vacuum inside.

Now the masseuse helped her from the table.

"Enjoy," he said. There was an invitation in his eyes. Once upon a time she might have accepted, but she strolled away from him, down the stone path to her room.

The hotel room was rustic and posh at the same time, done in the current ideation of Tuscany. She dressed for dinner. A gold blouse and pale skirt. Stockings just a shade darker than her normal skin. A blouse that required buttoning from behind.

"Tony?" she asked. "My buttons?"

Tony was thirty-five. When it came to his business, he was very sharp. When it came to women, he was part boy, part man. He had curly hair and bedroom eyes, and he wore a cologne that smelled of one of her father's friends. In some way she couldn't explain, it made sense she would be with Tony.

He took her to bed. In another moment, her skirt was up, her hose down. This was the way things always unfolded between them: Just as they were on the verge of going someplace, in the midst of departing, his hand found its way into her panties. She felt a trigger inside her, a door about to slip off its hinges, gaping into another world. He unbuttoned his shirt and pushed her blouse up so they could feel their chests one against the other. Except she wasn't here, no. She was somewhere else. In an alley, maybe. Leaning against the seawall. Behind her was the squall of the seagulls over the old fishing grounds, and off on the horizon, somewhere, beyond all those sailboats floating like cocked hats on the blue water, was another land, a place they were all straining toward, trying to create in their heads. But when she opened her eyes it was Tony Mora, only Mora, looming over her with his tight curls and his good looks and his clothes that smelled like an old man with money.

"Over," he said.

She turned on her stomach, and he got rougher now, grabbing her ass, all but penetrating, then backing off, starting over.

"Oh," he said, "oh."

He petted her, running his fingers over her body—but the truth was he could not keep his hands off her clothes, fiddling with the buttons, the collar of her blouse, and she knew that for him desire was not so much about the flesh but about the clothing. He exhausted himself on her skirt. He rolled over.

"Let's set a date," he said.

She felt the anxiety again, same as she had felt earlier crossing the bridge. She put a hand between her legs. He put his hand on top of hers, "Let me do that," but instead his hand drifted to her collar, to the fabric.

"Let's set a date," he said again. "We've been engaged awhile."

Then the phone rang.

"I thought you turned the ringer off."

"I thought I did, too."

He stood naked, talking on the phone. The conversation went on awhile. She saw his eyes go wide, and she knew something had happened.

"Salvatore Mancuso," he said. "He's been murdered."

"What?"

"He was shot to death. And they have his nephew in jail."

"Dante?"

"Yes."

"Oh," she said. Her heart was racing.

"I was supposed to meet with him and his uncle later this week, you know, regarding his father's will." He put on his slacks as he spoke, zipping them up. He glanced at his watch. "We're late for our dinner reservations. We'll lose them."

"Dante's in jail?"

"It happened last night. It's been on the news. And the viewing's scheduled for Monday—down on Green Street." He turned to her then. He looked a little like a gigolo, with his silk shirt and the way his hair fell into his eyes. "Will you go with me?"

It was part of his job, the funerals. A way of showing his respect—and recruiting new clients. Like a mortician, or a rabbi.

"Either way I have to go to the city tomorrow." Tony's voice grew anxious, and she could see the boy in his face. "I'm sorry to cut our trip short. But I don't have a choice."

"We were lovers."

"Who?"

"Dante and I."

His face registered no surprise. He knew, she guessed, the way people in The Beach knew everything.

"I've had lovers before, too," he said.

"I'm sure you have."

"But not one that's murdered his uncle, I admit." His voice was both bitter and wistful. He looked at her hungrily.

"He's been charged?" she asked.

"They're holding him for questioning. That's all I know."

"He used to be with the police, you know. A Homicide detective."

"Well, isn't the way it goes? People who investigate a thing—they're drawn to it. You know how chefs—they're so fat, most of them. The same thing, psychiatrists and crazy people. Detectives and criminals. We're drawn to the things we despise."

"I suppose."

For some reason, she found it hard to meet his eyes. She went to the closet to get a clean skirt. The lamé, she decided.

"Let's go to dinner," he said, eyeing the lamé. "We'll drive back in the morning."

"Button me up."

"All right. But we have to hurry if we're going to make our reservation."

When he was behind her, though, he put his lips against her neck, crushing against her. His dick was hard. He wanted to fuck her again. Or to fuck her lamé skirt, it was hard to tell.

FOURTEEN

So far the warrant had turned up nothing. It was as Ying suspected. The crew had pulled some fibers, confiscated a firearm, and otherwise torn the house on Fresno Street upside down, but found nothing of consequence. Ying wasn't hopeful. In addition, Louisa Roma had talked to Regina Mancuso in the hospital, and the old woman's story had checked out pretty well. There was no evidence of powder burns, no weapon at the scene. Gary Mancuso was another matter. He was evasive, hard to pin down. Ying needed talked to him again soon, even if it meant following him to his father's funeral. Meanwhile, he had sent Toliveri to chase down the man's alibi, starting with his colleagues at the warehouse.

At the same time, in regard to Dante, the forty-eight hours were just about up. Ying needed to make a decision—though he already had a pretty good idea what the decision might be. Dante Mancuso's personal information was clean; he wasn't wanted for anything, no criminal record. The only thing unusual had been the accusations around the Strehli murder, that

Dante was somehow suppressing evidence—but nothing had come of it. Still, the name triggered something and Ying went back to his notes from SI. As it turned out, he had jotted Strehli's name down during his investigation into the disappearance of Ru Shen. Strehli worked at Customs, and apparently he'd been on duty the day a Chinese family was found suffocated in a shipping container. Later, there were rumors that the dead were Ru Shen and his family, but it was only a rumor, and Ying had not had time to investigate before he left SI. Anyway, it seemed tangential at the moment. What Ying needed was to wrap up his check into Dante's background, and he still hadn't heard from the New Orleans police. He had a friend in the department down there, running an off-hours check. Ying decided to call and give things a push.

"I was just getting back to you," his friend said, but something about his voice told him it wasn't true.

"What did you find?"

"Well, the address checks out. He's lived there for the last five years. In and out of town a lot. Mostly out. And the firm he works for . . ."

"Yes."

The man hesitated. "This is confidential."

"All right."

"Run it through a system, you get a vinyl sheet."

Ying hadn't heard the term in a long time, but he knew what it meant. It was from the old days before the computer, when you ran a make on somebody and stumbled into an undercover investigation. You'd be investigating something—drug activity, maybe, a house with ammunition, odd comings and goings—

and then suddenly you'd get a desist order. Such orders, the paper used to come inside a clear sheet of plastic. A vinyl sheet.

"That's official?" said Ying.

"Officially, you and I, we never spoke."

FIFTEEN

The Mancuso brothers were dead now, both of them, and everyone knew. The news of the brothers' deaths lay strewn on coffee tables and front porches. It was in the air at Cavelli's. In the cigar smoke that clouded the back booth of Il Fior d'Italia, under the gold record of Tony Bennett. The cops had let Dante loose, and as he walked down Vallejo, still in his father's pajamas, he could see the evidence of those deaths all about him. In the way the awning kiltered over Rossi's Grocery, and in the bent heads of the old women inside Mara's Pastries. In the eyes of the passersby. In the drooping clothes of the old Chinese man and in the fat ass of the tourist clutching to her chest a purse as big as Texas.

There were ghosts everywhere, Nanna Pellicano had said. The land of the living and the land of the dead, they overlapped.

Later that day Dante had an appointment with the Wus, and he needed to change. The cops meantime had made a mess of his father's house. They'd pulled things out of drawers and left the drawers hanging out of the bureaus, extending like tongues in some kind of cartoon show. They'd piled his mother's and father's clothes onto the furniture, and they'd opened the refrigerator, and rolled back the carpets, and torn down the drapes. They'd taken his Glock into evidence, his .40 caliber, and most of his clothes, hauling them down to the lab, looking for fibers, for samples. They'd left him little to wear. They'd left his father's clothes, though, so Dante began looking through them.

His father had been a flashy dresser. Chintz Polo shirts. Baggy pants. Double-breasted jackets of raw silk. Shoes of calves' leather with toes that came to a point.

He dressed himself and left. Off to his appointment.

When Dante was growing up it seemed Chinatown had a million doors, all forbidden, and those doors opened into a labyrinth of the unknown, visible only in glimpses. Chinese women on balconies. Girls who turned away when you looked. Men gathered in circles in the dark end of the alley.

Child eaters. Kidnappers. Traders in severed testicles and loose eyeballs.

Now he made his way to the Wu Benevolent Society. It was an old building faced with stucco and balustraded in the Chinese style. It had been allowed to decay, but the art deco lamps still hung over the outdoor balconies. On the windows above street level you could see the gold-lacquered names of Wus numerous associates, but on the street level the building was a Chinatown bazaar: stores full of statuettes and paper fans and cheap jade.

Dante headed to the back of the bazaar, as he had been instructed, to a small office where a young Chinese woman in a polka-dot dress sat behind a travel desk stacked with invoices. Though she was younger than himself, when she looked at him it was the same look he remembered from when he was a boy—as if he had crossed some line into a place he didn't belong.

"I'm looking for Mason Wu."

She shook her head. "He doesn't have an office in this building."

"I was told I could make arrangements here."

She regarded him blankly from the other side of the desk. Her features were cold and beautiful, and she wore a white flower in her hair.

"My name's Dante Mancuso," he said, and handed her his card. "I'm looking for Mason Wu."

The woman pushed through the door behind her and left Dante alone. Behind him the bazaar was in full swing. He could hear the cacophony of the market.

Buy a fish from a Chinaman and your dick will fall off.

People bought the fish anyway. They slept with Chinese whores. They used the laborers in their truck farms and in their restaurants. And when the Chinese money came from Hong Kong, they sold them their houses and moved down to Burlingame.

The woman in the polka-dot dress returned, head up; she carried herself with a marvelous disdain, avoiding eye contact. At the same time it was clear there was very little she missed. She hand him back his card, flip side up; there was an address handwritten on the back.

Step through a door in Chinatown, enter the labyrinth, and you could end up anywhere.

Dante took a taxi to the address on the card. It was across town in Presidio Heights, but he was in the labyrinth all the same. He paid the driver and walked up the manicured walk and the man who opened the door was Mason Wu himself. He wore wire-rimmed glasses, Dockers, and a denim shirt rolled up at the sleeves. He was maybe thirty-five years old and had the healthy, recently scrubbed look of a software engineer, but around his neck hung a gold chain that did not quite fit the look.

"It is good to meet with you, Mr. Mancuso."

"The pleasure is mine."

"Given recent events, this must be a hard time for you to be discussing business."

"Very hard."

"Yet you seek us out."

"Sometimes, you must seize the opportunity."

It was true. By all rights he should have been in mourning, adhering to the formalities of grief. Still, such callousness played to his advantage. It would make Wu wonder—like others wondered, no doubt—if he had in truth killed his uncle, or at least arranged to have it done. The fact that he had been released by the police suggested either he was clever enough to have had done it right, leaving no trace, or else he had connections inside the force.

"How is it that the Wu family can help you?"

"I believe I'm the one who can help you."

The man smiled and you could see the arrogance. It was something you didn't see in the old-timers so much, but it was there in the new generation—the dawning suspicion that they were superior to the so-called natives and would soon own it all.

"I understand your source from Thailand, it's not quite what it was."

"Source?" asked Mason Wu.

"My expertise is bringing in things from around the world.

Finding the best, the highest qualities. All types of merchandise. I believe you understand what I mean. And my family, and your family, there is an existing relationship."

The exact nature of that relationship, Dante didn't know. He did know the warehouse had started handling shipments from China about ten years ago—clothing exports, toys, soccer balls— all sent on the older barges that didn't require the crane equipment they used over in Oakland: a deal that had been arranged back when Mayor Rossi was scraping to keep the waterfront alive. How closely this was tied to the Wus, and how nefarious those ties might be beneath the surface, Dante had no idea. Either way, Mason Wu himself said nothing, and Dante read this for what it was: a businessman's precaution. Because if Dante was wearing a wire—if he was not what he pretended to be— then Wu was better off saying as little as possible.

"Let me be blunt. I know currently you're getting under-priced by quality product out of Colombia and Mexico. And we both know there are poppy fields here in California now, in the Sierra Nevadas. The Latin cartels are moving their product closer to the market—and you can't compete. Not in quality. Not in price."

Dante saw the quiver in the man's cheek, and he knew he had touched something. According to what Anita Blonde had told him, Love Wu's old-line family lieutenants were getting pushed out of the drug market, and young Mason Wu was ambitious. In the Wu hierarchy, he was a midlevel guy who worked a step or two above the street with a character named Charles Yi. Mason provided the capital and Yi the muscle.

Rumor had it that Love Wu wanted to be rid of his ambitious young nephew. Meanwhile, the company's plan was to rake in Yi and Mason and Fakir all at once, then offer immunity if they'd roll over on the higher-ups, on Love Wu himself. Maybe it would work, Dante didn't know. Part of him still thought this whole thing was going too easily, too smoothly.

"I must consult with my great-uncle."

Dante handed him a piece of paper. On it was a layout of the Mancuso warehouse. They went over the details.

"You come by boat," said Dante. "And you leave the same way. This first transfer, if it goes smoothly, will be just the beginning."

"When?"

"In three days, a week," said Dante. "Give me your cell number, and I'll let you know when it's time."

Then the deal was set. And Dante stepped outside again, back into the labyrinth.

SIXTEEN

Gary Mancuso was nervous as hell, jittery by nature, and it didn't help things when he pulled up and saw Detective Ying on the sidewalk in front of his house. He had just gotten home from his father's service, and there was the detective waiting on the curb. It gave him a start, seeing the man; it made him angry and fearful at the same time. People were on their way, friends and relatives and well-wishers, to give their condolences to himself and his mother—who had just been released from the hospital yesterday. He didn't like the cop hovering out on the sidewalk.

Gary had his oldest son with him in the car. "Go inside," he told the boy. "Tell your mother I'll be along in a minute."

Then he walked over to Ying.

"I'm sorry," Ying said. "Just a few questions . . ."

"You picked a swell time."

"I understand. But it's important we get all the information as soon as we can after the incident. Time is of the essence in a case like this."

"I have people arriving."

"You told Detective Roma you would come down yesterday," said Ying. "And when I called . . ."

"Yesterday I was talking to morticians all day."

"Just a few questions . . ."

Gary wanted to tell the cop to fuck off, to get the hell away from his house, but he held his tongue. There were people pulling up now, fresh from the funeral. Gary did not want to cause a scene or make the cop think he had something to hide.

"Let's step over here," said Ying. "It will give us more privacy."

It was thoughtful for the cop to suggest, but for some reason it just made Gary resent Ying all the more. Even so, he obliged. He followed the cop around the corner, and they stood in the driveway that serviced the apartments behind his house.

"Before your father died, how were things at the warehouse?"

"What do you mean?"

"Businesswise?

"Not so good, not so bad."

"No money problems?"

"What are you getting at?"

"Any financial problems? Your dad owe anyone money?"

"No."

"How about the other way around?"

"You know, I can't help but resent this."

"I understand. But I'm sure you want to catch your father's murderer. I'm sure you want to help."

"Like I said, he didn't owe anyone any money. And no one owed him."

"What did your father keep in the room where he was killed?"

"Some old files, but family stuff mostly. Pictures. Mementos. Nothing anybody would want."

"It was ransacked. Somebody tore it apart."

"I know," said Gary. "But I don't know what they could have been looking for."

"You were at the warehouse the afternoon he was killed."

"I was working, yes."

"All day?"

"I went out for lunch."

"What time did you get back?"

Gary could see where the cop was going, and he didn't like it.

"About one thirty."

"Did anyone see you come back?"

"I don't know."

"You don't know?"

"I didn't make a fuss, if that's what you mean. I had some account files to work on."

"At the hospital, you told Detective Roma you didn't get home till seven. You were here the whole time?"

Gary swallowed uncomfortably. He didn't like this. "Yes," he said. "That's right."

Ying paused. Gary feared he was going to make him go through it all again, but all the sudden the cop left off this line of pursuit.

"Your father wasn't feuding with anyone?"

"No."

"No arguments? No reason for anyone you know to do something like this?"

Gary shook his head. His insides were shaking, too, but he did his best to hold himself together.

"Is there anything else you want to tell me?"

The cop looked him in the eye. Gary looked back.

"No."

"All right," said Ying. Then he shook Gary's hand and told him to give him a call if he thought of anything.

"I will."

The sudden change made Gary more nervous, and he knew in his gut this wasn't going to hold. But he didn't know what else he could do. He walked back up to the house. Inside, he saw his secretary, Anna Jones. Anna knew more than he would like. She had worked with the business for a half dozen years, an ample woman who always dressed in black and wore loose clothes to hide her weight. Anna was by a nature a friendly person and had done him a favor or two in the past, but she was not the kind who would lie to the police. He greeted her, and she gave him a big-breasted hug but her eyes flitted from his and she didn't stay long. She gave her condolences to his mother, then she left. He felt the fear in his throat. He'd made a mistake. The cops would talk to her eventually, they would be all over the warehouse, and his story wouldn't hold.

G ary Mancuso was an only son, adopted out of an orphanage in Rome by Salvatore and Regina. Gary knew the story: how his parents had made the trip to Italy because they'd wanted an Italian child. It was a story he'd heard over and over. How they'd bundled him up and taken him on the plane, across that gray ocean, then showed him off the next Sunday to the shopkeepers along Columbus Avenue. Himself, he remembered nothing of Italy. He had spent his whole life in North Beach, played in the streets, gone to the church, hung close by his father and mother. When he was a young man and just about everyone his age had left The Beach—down the peninsula, across the bay, any place to get away from the windy streets and cramped apartments—Gary had stayed. He had gone into the family business. Despite all this he was still an outsider, the adopted kid whose claim to the neighborhood was secondhand. He had one of the nicest spots in The Beach now, on top of Telegraph, with a view all around and Italian furniture, everything you could want. But people still talked. He hadn't worked for it, they said. He was pampered. And who knew what else.

His parents had doted on Gary, it was true. His mother always with her fingers in his hair. When he was young he had spent endless hours around tables with his mother's friends—the same women who were here in Gary's house now, gathered around his mother in her grief.

Beautiful women. With their black eyes and their black hair and their darted sweaters. Their tight skirts and high-heeled pumps. Or they had been beautiful once. At some point, they had begun to resemble the crones of his youth. Painted moles and bagging eyes. Drooping hose. Hairnets to hold their wigs in place.

The women formed a kind of circle around Regina on the couch. One at a time the arriving visitors would penetrate that circle to offer their condolences.

Even so, there was an air of suspicion, an undercurrent of whispering and speculation. *There is something behind this death, some other business.* It didn't help that Detective Ying had been out front, lurking on the walk. Mayor Rossi made him nervous, too. Penetrating the circle now, come to press his cheek against Gary's mother's.

"Your husband, he was one of the most respected men in this town." The mayor dabbed at his eyes and smiled at the same time. He was clownish in his grief, with his bald head and shining eyes. "I remember when I was on the town council, he went door to door with me. Helping get out the vote."

All the while the crones regarded the mayor, and everyone else around them as well. Slitting their eyes. Peering. Lips pushed out. Chins nodding. Heads tilted like crows on the wire. They might humor the mayor, but later they would talk. *Rossi ruined this goddamn town, him and his big plans.* As a kid, their opinions, their gossip, were all Gary had known. He had wanted their approval, and he internalized their thoughts so often that after a while their imagined voices were like a running commentary in his head.

"Bring me a cookie," said Aunt Regina, "a chocolate leaf"— though in fact she had a small plate of these cookies at her elbow.

It didn't matter. Gary got more from the table. Her heart fibrillations had been induced by the trauma the doctor said. Though they had subsided, she was still pale and winded easily.

"I'm afraid I can't hear a word the mayor is saying," said Michele Salini. Mrs. Salini had been gorgeous beyond belief at one time. Now she had an inoperable tumor in her brain; it dulled her senses intermittently—and without warning—but for some reason did not give her any pain.

"What did you say?" asked Eva Besozzi.

"She's says she can't hear anything," said Gary.

"Say again?"

"Hearing!" said Mrs. Mollini. "Who cares about hearing when you can't stand up? This diabetes gets any worse, doctor's going to amputate my feet."

"That happened with my brother," said Eva.

"They start with your feet, then it's the knees," said Mrs. Mollini. "Piece by piece. I tell you. There won't be anything left of me to put in the grave."

No one was paying any attention to the mayor any more. Rossi glanced up at Gary. He elbowed his way over, and Gary felt the dread all over again, the sense that everyone was watching him.

"How's the investigation going?"

"I'm not sure."

"I saw the police outside."

"Just doing their jobs," said Gary. "They have to get their information."

"Do they have any leads?"

"Nothing solid," he said. "Excuse me. My wife needs my assistance in the kitchen."

Rossi was too damn curious. Old fool. Probably he just wanted to be consoled, patted on the head. He was that way, the mayor, as if everything had to do with him, but even so, Gary didn't have a good feeling about it. His father and his uncle and the mayor had had their dealings in the past, and the mayor had always had a proprietary attitude, as if somehow the business of the warehouse were his business too.

Gary went into the kitchen, but things were no better there. His wife, Alice, was in a foul mood. She was a second wife, an Irish blonde full of freckles, whose big ass had driven him wild once upon a time. It was even bigger now, but the effect diminished after a certain point. He had grown weary of looking at her. His ex, Gina, was here as well, and that was part of the reason for Alice's mood. Gina had kept her looks; in fact, she looked better than ever. They didn't like each other, Alice and Gina, but he'd had two children by Gina, and she had brought them to their grandfather's funeral.

"She's driving me nuts," said Alice.

"Who?"

"Who do you think? One little crack after another."

"That's why I divorced her."

"She goes on she's not got enough alimony. In front of everyone. She smells the inheritance, and she wants to rob us blind."

He looked back at the couch and saw the crones regarding him, studying. No doubt they'd gossiped him up over the years, him and his two wives. Now Eva Besozzi and Michele Salini whispered something to one another, shaking their heads. *There's a secret here, something. Something this ugly happens, a man shot in the head, the brother delirious, there's something going on. How do you think Gary affords a place like this?* There had been grief in the air at the funeral, the welling of tears, but also suspicion. As if the answer to the puzzle of his father's death might rest in the crowd hovering by the casket.

Now Tony Mora arrived with Marilyn Visconti, and together they made the pilgrimage to the sofa. Then came Dante, his cousin, unabashed, though he'd spent the last two days in jail. There was a sudden hush in the room, everyone watching as Aunt Regina embraced him, letting the crowd know it meant nothing to her, this was her nephew whom she had cradled at his birth, who had played with her son in the street. Gary's cheeks went red. He was looking at Dante and Marilyn, and he saw the glance they shared when Mora wasn't looking. It wasn't right. *I was with her first,* Gary thought. *Dante took her away, and everyone here knows the story.* And if Dante hadn't interfered, then none of this would have happened either. He wouldn't have bounced into that marriage with Gina, then bounced again to Alice; he wouldn't be standing here quivering over just how far the cops would poke into his life. For a moment this line of reasoning seemed to make sense. If only Dante had kept his hands to himself. If only . . .

The crones looked at him, and Gary knew they knew everything, those goddamn women. There was no way to keep a secret in this town.

Now Mora was here. Right in front of him. Taking a slice of melon off the tray, wrapping it in prosciutto. Holding a glass of wine. Mora the well-dressed, Raybans cocked on his head.

"I'm sorry for your loss."

"Thank you."

"A real devastation."

"Yes."

"Your mother seems, well, she is a strong woman. . . ."

"They've got on her on antidepressants."

And then there was some foot shuffling, some more muttering, and he saw the old ladies staring at him.

There's something rotten here. This adopted child, his real parents, who knows who they were, what criminal blood . . .

"Anything I could do to help you," said Mora.

Suddenly Gary wondered where Dante had gone. Off with Marilyn. Out the kitchen door, onto the terrace. He felt the old jealousy, absurd as it might be—as if he could stop now what he couldn't stop then.

"Excuse me," he said.

He nudged away from Mora, determined to find them.

SEVENTEEN

Ying was at home when his cell rang. It was late afternoon, and the blinds were at a slant, so the light had the half-cast look of twilight. Lei lay on the bed beside him, faceup, her lace shirt unbuttoned and her feet hanging over the bed. They were talking about the kids, and Ying had his hand on her stomach, studying her face, her lips. Meanwhile, she stared at the ceiling, occasionally casting a glance at him; aware of his desire or not, he had no idea. She had a marvelous self-possession, his wife. He moved to kiss her. And it was in that instant the phone rang.

"No," she said. "Don't answer."

Her manner had changed. Her voice was still soft—it was always soft, trained to delicate pitch by her proper mother, Hong Kongese with a touch of English blood—but there was a steeliness there as well, the same urgency he recognized from months back when they'd still lived in the city and he'd been investigating the Wus. Back when the threats had come.

"It's my work phone," he said.

He glanced at the incoming number. The exchange was familiar. Chinatown. But the particular number was not one he recognized.

"Don't answer," she said.

He shrugged. "Honey . . . ," he said, and let it falter. There was nothing else to say. She knew his response.

"Whoever it is, whatever—it will keep. This is your day off. And you already spent this morning interviewing that man's son."

She was right. He had gone this morning out to Telegraph Hill, to pigeonhole Gary Mancuso. Toliveri was supposed to pick up where he left off, looking into the details of the man's alibi, talking to employees at the warehouse, but it wasn't Toliveri's number on the line. Even so, it was hard to ignore the phone. There were times, in the middle of a case, when somebody might step forward, when they might have something to say. And if you missed the opportunity, you might never get it back.

"Lei," he said. "It's my job."

The look she shot him reminded him of the arguments they'd had a year ago: her insistence that he transfer out of SI, if not leave the force altogether, and in the end they had settled for this, a compromise. It had not been easy for him to let it go, but he'd done it. He transferred back into Homicide and they'd moved the family across the bay. It seemed to have worked. There were no more scrawled messages, no more threats on the phone.

He turned his back to her, clicked on the cell.

"Detective Ying," he said.

There was a pause on the other side. Then a woman's voice.

"We haven't spoken for a long time."

He recognize the voice, low and sultry, and felt a twinge of excitement. The voice belong to Miss Lin. Or that was the name she gave herself.

Miss Lin was an informer—an insider at the Wus'. He had not heard from her for some time, since back when he was still active in SI, and the truth was she had never given him anything of value. He had met with her only once—a good-looking woman with a haughty air who worked in the Wu Benevolent Society. The one time he'd met with her, she had a flower in her hair. A chrysanthemum, maybe. He'd asked her then about Ru Shen—the Shanghai businessman who'd disappeared—and she'd gone cold on him. He did not know her motives, or her reliability as an informant, but he was not about to send her off. He glanced at his wife, still on the bed, and felt vaguely disloyal. Not because anything had gone on between himself and Miss Lin, but because he felt himself drawn to the whole miasma once again, where he had promised he wouldn't go. To the Wu family, the benevolent associations, the intertwined businesses of racketeering and everyday commerce that stretched across the sea, to Hong Kong, to Guangdong, to the markets where chickens sat in cages next to frogs and jungle monkeys and snakes, delicacies waiting to be skinned and gutted. Illegal contraband that traveled like the flu, making its way along subterranean routes, unseen yet in full view, as impossible to suppress as a handshake on a busy street.

"I have some information. I know you are investigating the murder of this man in the paper, Salvatore Mancuso."

"Yes."

"A man came here yesterday to make a connection with Mason Wu."

Ying knew about Mason Wu, of course. He was the youngest of Love Wu's grand-nephews—anxious to make his mark in the drug trade. From what Ying had heard at SI, there was friction between Mason Wu and his great-uncle, but maybe it was just talk.

"What kind of connection?"

"Am I going to get something for my trouble?"

"It depends on what you have."

"It has to do with drugs. I don't know when or where. But I know the name of the man who's making the arrangements."

"Okay."

"Dante Mancuso."

Ying was surprised but then he was not surprised. You worked a case, and worked it, seeking out the logical connections, unearthing little bits of this, of that, none of it adding up—and when you found something it was in a place you didn't expect, something you tripped over on your way to somewhere else. Except he was not sure what this meant, either, or why it had been offered up to him like this, all of a sudden. He remembered the vinyl sheet and wondered which side of the law Dante was working.

"I can't talk much longer," Miss Lin said. "Is it worth anything to you?"

"Perhaps."

"Perhaps? I don't know if I can put that in my pocket."

"Remember before, we talked about Ru Shen."

"I remember."

"I am curious about his disappearance."

"That is more dangerous. For me. For you."

"I understand."

"But if you have money, if you are generous . . ."

Ying heard something in the background. The woman was in a market, it sounded like, there were the sounds of cash registers and someone speaking Cantonese dialect.

"I have to go," said Miss Lin. "You know how to contact me."

Ying knew he shouldn't be messing with this informant; his days with SI were over. His job now was to close the book on the murder of Salvatore Mancuso, though he was beginning to realize this might not be so easy to do. Especially if his nephew was involved in some kind of covert operation.

He did not know Miss Lin's motive. She could be in it for the money, and if that was the case she might be playing both sides against the middle—hawking information to the Wus as well.

"So how important was it?" Lei asked.

"Not very."

And he felt it there between them again, the secrecy, the way he'd kept an empty face during the Wu investigation.

Ying walked over to the open window and looked out at the street. Every once in a while, he'd see someone out here, someone lingering under a sycamore, a man in a parked car, a solicitor, and wonder if they were who they seemed. Or if instead it was someone else, watching, biding time. If it was really all behind them.

"Are you going to have to run off to a murder scene?"

"No."

"I'm sorry," she said. "It's just . . ."

"I know. You don't have to explain."

"The kids will be gone for another hour. We still have time."

He turned and smiled at her. Then he glanced back out the window. It was a quiet street. A man walking his dog. A woman trimming her wisteria on the corner. You could hear the soft woosh of traffic up on Hearn, and some starlings going after one another down in the grass. It was all green and peaceful, the twilight filtering beautifully through the slatted blinds.

Everything was calm. There was nothing to worry about. Nothing at all.

An hour later the kids came home. In the intervening time, Ying and Lei had been intimate, and now the air inside the house had a little bit of a glow. The kids were chattering and full of themselves, and there was a certain magic in the mere sound of their voices.

"Did you work today?" his girl asked.

"For a little while."

"Did you kill anyone?" asked his son.

It was the family joke. His son, who had just turned seven, asked it every time Ying came home from work lately, and they all laughed, even though it was not so funny as it had been.

"No," said Ying. "Not today."

He went back to the window. It was dark outside now, but the street was serene and beautiful. *I'll stay away from Miss Lin,* Ying decided. *There is no reason to stir things up. No reason to ruin our beautiful life.*

EIGHTEEN

Earlier that same evening, before leaving his uncle's wake, Dante had lingered a moment on his cousin's balcony. Inside, he had embraced the old ones and smelled the wine on their breaths, and there was something comforting in all this, he had to admit, in the pressing of the flesh, in the raising of the glass, in the long liquid glances and sudden laughter—but there was also a question left unasked in those eyes, a suspicion. He had seen it in Aunt Regina, up close, even as she embraced him, and in the others as well. It was natural enough given the circumstances, but Dante could not help wanting to put it to rest. Meanwhile, the sun was down and he could see the hard glitter of North Beach below, and for an instant he felt the craving that would overcome him in New Orleans.

Now he heard a footstep on the balcony, a woman's step, and then Marilyn Visconti leaned over the railing beside him.

"So this is not the best homecoming for you."

"It could be better."

The wind was blowing hard, and an offshore fog had begun to form, billowing against the black sky.

"Gary has a nice place here," she said.

"Yes."

It was idle talk, but he wondered about the opulence. A three-story house, balconies on every side. Slate on the outside and imported marble in the foyer, The warehouse was a decent business, but neither his father nor Uncle Salvatore had lived like this.

"Your uncle," she said. "Do the police have any idea what happened, I mean—who was responsible?"

"I don't know what the police are thinking."

"I'm sorry. I thought, someone you know in the department, maybe, you know, cop talk—that you might have some kind of knowledge."

"They don't confide in me."

"No, I guess not."

She was being polite, he supposed, acting as if his time with the police had been some sort of cooperative venture, a meeting of the minds, friendly detectives filtering through the clues.

"I'm sorry," he said.

"About what?"

"The other day, up at your place—I should have kept my hands to myself."

"You had just buried your father," she said, as if this some-how explained things. Maybe it did. Off to the east, the sky had gotten yet blacker, and from offshore the fog was moving quickly. The wind was cold. Marilyn was dressed in her funeral blacks, but her clothes were thin, and she shivered. "Those years—it wasn't like I stopped thinking of you. There are things I didn't get to explain."

"Have you set a date?"

"For what?"

"The wedding."

She didn't answer. Dante turned and leaned with his back to the railing. He was surprised to see that the fog was up around Coit Tower now, and in a little while it would be here, and the view would disappear. "You remember," she said. "That day we spent out on the water."

Her smile was self-deprecatory, embarrassed. She shivered again, and he took a step closer.

"I remember," he said. "I'll take you out there again. If you want to go."

Then Gary blundered onto the balcony, just like the old days, standing there with that lost-kid look on his face, lips in a twist, eyes watering.

"What are you two doing?" he said. "It's cold out here."

Neither of them moved. Then Mora appeared on the balcony, a piece of melon in one hand, a glass of wine in the other.

"Excuse me," said Dante.

He left. On the street, Coit Tower had all but vanished. The fog had descended and North Beach was covered in a black mist.

Later that evening, Dante headed down to the Naked Moon. Wiesinski had phoned again, wanting to meet him there: for old time's sake, he said, some commiseration and troublemaking. And Dante had agreed to come.

In its own kind of way, the Naked Moon was a family place. The owner, Jojo LoCoco, worked behind the bar. Jojo's father had worked it before him, and his father's father before that, back when the navy still let its boys loose in The Beach, and Broadway Avenue was all about big tits and Mama Mia's spaghetti and finding someone to suck your cock. But things were different now—what with home video and pay-for-view—and it wasn't quite as easy to make your money off an old-fashioned grind show. Jojo sat behind the counter smoking a cigar, and he greeted Dante in the same way he had seven years ago, as if he hadn't been gone a day.

"If it isn't the Pelican," he said. "Sit down, my friend, water your beak."

Dante ordered a beer with a chaser and put some money on the counter. Jojo's eyes grew rheumy and sad.

"Sorry about your dad."

"Thanks."

"Sorry about your uncle, too."

"I appreciate it, Jojo."

"It just don't make any sense."

"No."

"You need something, let me know. One of the girls. Between shows. A blow job."

"I'm waiting on somebody. But I need anything, I'll let you know."

Dante took his beer and sat in the back to wait for Wiesinski. In a little while the show started. First it was a blonde girl that came out, then a black, and then a Vietnamese.

This was a midweek show, and the routines had a certain clumsiness, but then that was always the case. The blonde girl did "Yankee Doodle Dandy," and the black one danced to "Dixie," and the Vietnamese girl did some kind of sayonara-sounding good-bye song, with a voice-over à la Tokyo Rose. Her movements were jerky and odd. She was very young, but Dante felt compelled to watch her as she took off her kimono then jutted about the stage, with black pasties covering her tiny breasts and a bird of paradise perched in her hair. She tried to make her moves graceful—rising to her tiptoes, then a series of half-rendered pliés—but the effort only made her seem more ungainly, her arms and feet hurly-burly over the floor. Her eyes were doll-like, glassy and black.

She was about halfway through this routine when Wiesinski tapped him on the shoulder. "Ah, my old friend," he said. "So we meet again."

"It appears so."

"Why are you sitting so far back?"

Dante shrugged. "I like the dark."

"I can understand that, seeing without being seen. Certainly," he said, "not my way, of course, but hell . . ."

Wiesinski had grown up in the Excelsior district, out near the Alemany projects, but he didn't carry that with him. When he was with the SFPD, he'd been known for his suits. Well tailored, very sharp. At times Wiesinski looked more like a well-heeled mark than a cop, but apparently it served him well, even after most everyone on the beat knew his game. He'd worked vice all over the city—Polk Gulch, Lower Market, the Barbary Coast—and you couldn't walk too many places without people kissing his shoes.

As a vice cop, he'd played out in the open like he said, not undercover. But he'd had his pigeons like anyone else. Eyes in the dark.

"Long time," said Dante. "Who'd you say you were working for these days?"

Wiesinski hummed a minute. "Security work. Downtown. That kind of thing."

"So you're a night watchman."

It was a calculated remark. Wiesinski laughed. "That's me, watching the night," but then he bit, like Dante guessed he would bite, not wanting to be played low. "There's some intrigue. Corporate espionage, call it what you will, it's all about money. I go abroad sometimes. Three, four months at a time. But hell. You tell me, my friend, how are *you* doing? First your dad, and now . . ."

Wiesinski shook his head. There was something like tears welling up in his eyes. Crocodile tears, maybe, it was hard to judge. Even the people he put away, Dante remembered, they would joke with Wiesinski on the way to the tombs. He was a dapper guy, the kind of guy you liked right away—even if you did not quite trust him. The truth was he'd been one of the few people on the force to hang with him back when the Strehli business was coming down.

"They got any suspects?"

"Aside from me?"

Wiesinski laughed. "Yeah, well, you can't blame 'em. You dagos. One killing the next."

"You're a dago."

"Only half, my friend. Only fucking half."

On the stage, the Vietnamese girl had finished the solo part of her act. The other two returned—the blonde and the black girl—and it was the three of them up there all at once now. Nothing sophisticated, just straight-up grind.

"You going to stick around town?"

"I'm thinking about it," Dante said, "exploring possibilities."

"You know I never liked how the SFPD treated you. You had a career here."

"Well, I made a mistake."

"Butted the wrong heads. That Strehli business." Wiesinski shook his head, but his face had gone flush. Then he leaned in. "So what's it you're into now?"

"Export business," said Dante.

"Get to use any of your old skills?"

"Not much."

The man was peering at him. Dante wasn't sure what to think. There were a hundred ways you could read Wiesinski. It could be he suspected that the export business was some kind of cover, that there was something to tap into there, and he wanted a piece. But it could be something else, too. Wiesinski, with his job, his connections . . .

"Tell me something. This cop investigating your uncle's murder . . ."

"Ying."

"He used to be with SI. Now he's back with Homicide. Brass doesn't like that kind of thing—downward movement."

Dante wondered how Wiesinski knew so much. Apparently he was still keeping tabs on things, staying in touch. A finger in the pie.

"Guess he didn't have the taste for it."

"Homicide dicks—most of what they deal with is arbitrary. Impulse, greed—jacked-up hormones, skewed biochemistry.

"But SI—it's a different thing. You look for the calculated stuff. The mind behind the mind. Some people—they look at that, they see a consciousness behind it all. The kind of mind that works in SI thinks the world's got an explanation, just study the book long enough and you'll understand. You get this bug in you, it's hard to go back to Homicide.

"But the truth is, evil, it's both things. It's the calculated *and* it's the arbitrary—the careful plan juiced up with sudden improvisation. That's the genius of evil. Why you can never bring it under control."

He was a bit drunk, and Dante remembered this side of him, the philosopher gone askew. It was how he'd gotten his nickname, rants like this. Wiesinski got around. He hung in the gutter, but he hung with the elites, too, the mayor and the businessmen. Dante thought again how he'd run into him once down in New Orleans, at Mardi Gras, not long after he'd left the SFPD. A few days later, he'd been approached by the company— and he'd always wondered if that was happenstance. Ultimately, he dismissed it. You could drive yourself mad floundering over coincidence. Especially in New Orleans.

The Big Why raised his glass. "To genius. The inscrutable text, the unknowable secret. May it keep us long employed."

Wiesinski was on his feet now. On stage, the grind act was over. Wiesinski raised a finger—every bit the gentleman. "Hey, sweetie, a word, please, a word." His voice was the perfect pitch, loud but not too loud, friendly, like that of some uncle who'd recognized you on the street. The girl turned.

Wiesinski went over and spoke to the girl. Then he came back.

"The three of them are coming off shift here. I invited them for a drink. Soon as they get some clothes on."

"They're never off shift. Those drinks are going to cost."

"Of course. We'll have a couple. Let Jojo make his money."

"I was getting ready to go."

"We'll take them to the Romolo Hotel. Get twin beds. You screw one, I screw the other. Treat the girls to a night of luxury. Hell, I'll pay. I'll pay for it all."

"There's three girls."

"The third can watch."

Dante hesitated. "Who you working for downtown?"

"Come on, which girl you want?"

Dante leaned in now. "Caselli didn't kill Strehli, you know that?"

"This is out of the blue, my friend. Who cares about Caselli? He signed a confession, the way I remember."

"But he didn't do it. It was someone else—and everyone knew. But they didn't want to investigate. Why?"

Wiesinski shrugged. "Why do you think, my friend? Because the world is a web of sin, and the truth wasn't in their interest. Once you're in the web, you're in, and there's no getting out. Survive anyway you can. But you know this, my friend. Come spend some time with the girls."

"I've got someplace to be."

"No, you don't. We'll go to the Romolo. We can get some treats on the way?"

"Treats?"

"Something recreational, you know. Whatever you want."

There was a glimmer in Wiesinski's eyes, and Dante realized what he was saying. Wiesinski would know every street vendor between here and South City. The Vietnamese girl was headed their way now, dressed in jeans and a denim shirt. She couldn't have been more than sixteen.

"You spent too much time in vice."

"Old habits—they die hard. If they die at all. Anyway, ours is not to reason why. Like the poet says. Ours is to pleasure ourselves. And pleasure ourselves some more." The crocodile tears were back now. Wiesinski reached out and touched his arm. "Come on," he said. "Old time's sake."

"Sure," said Dante. "Just let me take a leak."

Dante went to the bathroom. As he stood there with his cock in his hand, he wondered what the hell Wiesinski was up to. If all this was anything more than the usual shenanigans, a late-night plunge into darkness. Dante washed his hands and thought of Marilyn, and the possibility he had seen in her eyes, there on his cousin's balcony. He could pursue that possibility, but what was the point of that? The sting would be set soon, and he would be gone, out of her life.

He stepped out of the restroom and stood a minute looking through the blue light and the smoke back at Wiesinski—all the girls were at the table now. Jojo was bringing a fresh round.

The hunger was as fierce as it had been, as fierce as he could remember.

No, he told himself.

Dante ducked out the rear exit and headed once more toward the little house on Fresno Street.

NINETEEN

Dante's first impulse always was to head toward the kitchen, to where his mother and father had spent their time in the old days, his father leaning backward in his chair, holding forth, a glass of wine in his hand, while his mother stood tending the stove, his dark-eyed mother with her auburn hair, her delirious laugh. Through the windows behind them you could see the flattop roof, where Mrs. Fiora hung her laundry, and beyond that the rusted spires of the Coppola Building. It was an old instinct, heading toward that room, one that persisted even now with his parents gone and the house empty. Tonight, though, he did not take three steps before he pulled up short. He had caught the movement too late. There was nothing he could do—even if his gun had not been confiscated during the warrant search.

A woman faced him from the shadows, and she held a revolver pointed at his chest. He did not recognize her at first, but when he heard that voice, cool and implacable, he remembered it from their encounter in New Orleans.

"You're sloppy," said Anita Blonde. "And unarmed. You should be more careful."

She had changed her looks since the last time he'd seen her. The blonde hair was gone, with its delicate flip, and so was the straw hat. Her hair was cut close now, coal black. She wore a waist jacket and pants that flared at the bottom. Jazz pants, like dancers wore, black and close-fitting. For agility, he guessed. So she would blend easier into the shadows.

"You could announce your arrival in advance," he said.

"What happened here?" She pointed to the disarray—the clothing scattered by the police in their search.

"My uncle was murdered, and the cops came here with a warrant."

She holstered her gun in an ankle strap under the flare of her pants. The gun was tucked away nicely, but at a long reach. He could see how it might be difficult to retrieve in certain circumstances.

"Are you a suspect?"

"I'm on their list."

"That's not the kind of attention we need."

"You could replace me."

She shook her head. "I don't think that's possible, at this point. I assume you've made the arrangements. With the Wus. And Williams."

"Yes."

She strolled over and looked at the family pictures then, contemplating Dante as a young man, maybe nineteen years old, the summer he'd worked at the warehouse.

"Aren't you going to offer me a place to sit?"

"Sure. Take a seat."

"Can I move these clothes?"

"I'll do it for you."

Some of his mother's clothes had been taken out of the downstairs closet by the cops and laid over the chair. Dante picked them up and noticed a scent he had all but forgotten. He remembered himself as a kid watching his mother getting ready for church, back when she was still beautiful and both he and his father had taken a special pleasure in strolling with her down to the cathedral. The clothes smelled liked perfume. Like dry-cleaning fluid. Like his mother walking down the street.

"Give me the details," said Blonde. "Tell me what you've been doing."

He told her then, more or less, about his contacts with Williams and Mason Wu. And about his interactions with Ying down at Columbus Station. Then he drew for her a diagram of the Mancuso warehouse and showed her the positions from which the tactical squads might emerge. The deal would go down in his father's office, recorded on video by hidden cameras. His notion was to have the Wus come in by boat, then grab them when they left, as they headed out to the dock. Williams and Fakir could be apprehended in the parking lot.

"I suppose I should bring my cousin into the loop."

"Do you know when the mule arrives?"

"I'm waiting to hear."

"When you get the date, you call our local contact at the DEA. But not before. In the meantime, he'll get the squad together. They'll plant the cameras and make sure everything's ready."

"How are they going to get access?"

"That's not your concern."

"You have someone else on the inside?"

"Like I said, that's not you're concern. And as far as your cousin goes, wait. We don't want any leaks."

Blonde picked up a hat that had been his mother's—a stylish bit of felt with netting that hung over the brim and a feather on the side. His mother used to wear it when she was young, when she and Giovanni still went out in the evenings.

"You grew up in this house?"

He heard the flat midwestern forever in her voice, the prairie reaching across Nebraska, all that corn waving around under the blue sky.

"Sure."

"Your room was upstairs, and in the morning you came down the stairs—in pajamas with little feet—and ate at that yellow table."

"That's right."

It was the same kind of banter they had done back at the Du Monde, fooling with identity. She got a certain pleasure out of it, he supposed. And so did Dante, up to a point.

"You watched your dad go off to work, and you smelled the clean smell of his aftershave, and though your heart ached when he left, you were glad, too—because then you could just look at Mama. You and her together, both of you, with your big brown eyes."

"You've got it dialed," he said. The hat looked good on her, he had to admit. Even so, it bothered him. "And you? What are you doing here in our living room?"

"I'm a schoolteacher. From out of town. Someone the little boy used to think about in a certain way."

"What town?"

She shrugged.

"Chicago?" he asked.

"Sure," she said. "Chicago."

"A girl from the Midwest who grew up in the town of slaughterhouses—and moved out here because she couldn't stand anymore the smell of meat in the air."

"You're very perceptive," she said. "I always wanted to live next to the ocean."

They were standing close now. "Take the hat off," he said.

"And the little boy, when his mother turned her back, and he was alone on the couch, he thought of his schoolteacher, imagining her here in his living room, in his mother's hat. You know how boys are about their teachers."

"Our teachers were nuns."

He'd had enough. He reached up now, intending to pull the hat from her head, but instead touched her cheek with the back of his hand.

"The teacher, alone at night, she's not thinking of the little boy, but of a man she knows. A man in slacks and a white shirt."

"Is he unshaven?"

She reached out and felt his cheek.

"No. But his father has died, he has an inheritance, and he has promised her a trip to Tahiti."

They kissed. It was the kind of kiss that people like themselves exchanged. Strangers acting at roles. Lingering between the pulse of this moment and the next. Your mind free to create and fill in the blanks, racing as it did so, as one illusion slipped into another. He had done the same thing, more or less, in other places, with other women—not knowing the degree to which they, too, were acting, though he suspected in a way it was what all people did. There was always a notion out there, an idea unformed, a child racing in the void. And that was what you chased. Because the instant that notion was solidified you were dealing with an object in the world—flesh, bone, a hank of hair—and then everything changed.

It was a paradox, maybe, he didn't know. All he knew was that his dick was hard, and he was pressed up tight against this woman in the hallway of his parent's house, in a way that he had dreamed of when he was a kid: like he had dreamed of his mother's friends and his Italian cousins. Anita Blonde pulled his shirt from his pants, and he found her crotch, reached under the waistband, then jerked her toward him, his other hand over her breast, her tongue inside his mouth, and they slid to the floor, his mother's and father's clothes scattered around, and he was thinking of Anthony Mora and his Alfa, and of his dead uncle, and of the smell of blood, and all the time Anita Blonde's eyes were half shut—as if she too were off in some other world, pursuing some other vision, there on the Persian carpet with all those animals in the fabric. She began to make noises down in her throat, sounds that were guttural and deep. And for a moment it seemed they might consume one another, there on the floor.

During the night Dante woke up twice. The first time Anita Blonde still lay on her back next to him, asleep. Her skin was almost pearlescent in the dark room. She seemed a bit beautiful to him, and a bit ugly, her black hair too ragged and short, her skin too white, her features too sharp for a person at rest, too harsh. The second time he awoke it was just after dawn—and she was no longer in bed.

He heard the creak and sigh of the house, and he realized she was downstairs, rummaging.

For what?

She had been searching the place when he walked in the door last night, he was pretty sure. She had seduced him, maybe for the fun of it, but maybe to buy herself a little more time, another look around. He thought about the broken window hasp in this father's basement, and the two figures he had seen out on the street on his first night he returned: the man ducking into the shadows and the woman strolling by in the close-fitting clothes and the dark jacket, and it occurred to him that woman had been Anita Blonde. Now he heard her coming up the stairs. She tried to be quiet about it, but the old redwood had a considerable amount of give and he could hear her footfalls. Then she came into the room. He lay on his side, eyes partly closed. She went to the dresser and opened the drawer.

"What are you looking for?"

She regarded him in the mirror. "I wondered if you were awake."

"You didn't answer my question."

"Just seeing if there's any perfume around."

"You expect me to believe that?"

"My, my. Aren't we the suspicious one?"

He moved toward her. Outside the dawn was breaking and the room filled with its half light.

"What were you doing?" he asked again.

"We all have our jobs to do."

She tried to brush past him, but he grabbed her by the forearm and saw something cold in her eyes. The ankle holster was out of reach. He held her an instant longer, wanting to frighten her—and maybe he saw the fear for a second, naked inside of her.

"I'll see you in Tahiti," he said, then let her go.

TWENTY

Later, Dante had a hunch, one of those hunches people who have worked Homicide are supposed to have, though perhaps he should have had it a week earlier at his father's funeral, when his uncle had nervously handed him some film. Family pictures, he'd assumed. A roll of sentiment that had been stashed away and forgotten. Dante had dropped the film off at the local pharmacy, then he'd forgotten it, too.

Now he wondered.

His uncle's office had been pretty well torn apart. And Anita Blonde's visit had not been without ulterior motive.

Dante returned to Cassinelli's Drugs and picked up the pictures. As it turned out, they were not family photos. They had been taken out at the Oakland waterfront. The subject was a large freight container, the kind sent over on container ships preloaded with merchandise, then picked up with a crane and placed on a tractor trailer. The next photo showed the interior of the container—a makeshift living quarters of the type inhabited by stowaways, illegals looking for a way into the country.

Then came the ghostly images, taken with the flash: the family intertwined on a pile of rags—a man and a woman and two children—girls, most likely, if you were to judge from the hair and clothing. The corpses had decomposed considerably, enough to suggest they had died early in the voyage. Other photos showed what looked like scratch marks on the interior of the trailer, and a broken tube on the outside—both of which, when combined with the posture of the corpses, suggested death by asphyxiation. It was not uncommon. Sometimes, when the containers were being loaded one on top of the other, the tubes providing air would snap or become otherwise obstructed.

His father had given this film to his uncle; he'd wanted Dante to see it. It didn't seem his uncle had known what the pictures were, but Dante couldn't know for sure. He did know that Strehli—his father's friend—had been a customs inspector down at the shipyard. An amateur photographer.

Strehli.

Dead of a gunshot wound to the head.

Strehli had gone over to the dark side, or that's what the cops had said. Murdered by Caselli over a drug deal gone bad. Dante hadn't believed it then—and he wasn't any more inclined to believe it now.

TWENTY-ONE

All his life, the ex-convict Yusef Fakir had been the target of investigations, and in his dark moments he feared the Cole Valley Mosque had been infiltrated, too. The white man was a parasite. Bite into the sweetest fruit and you would find him there, multiplying himself, wriggly and wormy. There was no garden that was safe, no sanctuary. At least not for Yusef Fakir. The blunt truth of it was that the government was after him; Fakir had no doubt of this. There were people who wouldn't be satisfied until they had seen him laid into the ground. Until they had squatted down and shat upon his grave.

Fakir was in his late fifties. He had spent about half his life in jail, where he had read Marcuse and Camus and Marx and Malcolm X, of course, and also the writings of Muhammad. He had always been a good speaker, and when he was young he had worked the soapbox along Telegraph Avenue, then started a community center down in West Oakland under the shadow of the Nimitz Freeway, but the place had been raided a dozen times, no fucking reason. Then a county judge had been murdered and the powers that be came for him. Fakir was on the road for almost a decade before they got their fingers in his collar, and when they dragged him to trial it was not just for the murder of the judge, but for every unsolved murder and robbery in the state.

Fakir had participated in some of those robberies, it was true, and a brother had wounded a cop during a bank heist. As for the murder of the judge, Fakir had been innocent, and in the end the prosecution had been unable to prove otherwise.

For the rest they gave him twenty-five years, and he'd served them all, no time for good behavior, and when he got out he'd started preaching the word of Muhammad, speaking the truth about the society that had badgered him and put him away, and defining, too, his own vision of the struggle, the need for a Third Force, a new union of the oppressed. But the more success he had, the more people who came to hear him speak, the more trouble that lay ahead. Because he knew that behind the scenes the state prosecutors were still at work. The grubs penetrated unseen until the sweet heart was gone and there was only rot. He could all but smell their presence. They had agents everywhere.

This afternoon, Fakir met with some brothers and sisters at the Cole Valley Mosque. Brother Williams, his right-hand man, sat next to him. Brother Williams was soft spoken and clean-shaven, with eyes that seemed to have a natural tenderness—but Fakir knew there was hardness inside Williams, because he had seen that hardness in prison and he had the same hardness within himself. It was what you needed to survive in the prison yard, and maybe on the outside, too: a shell around the heart and a ruthless eye for that which wanted to destroy you.

The subject of conversation was the church's bakery, which had lost its lease down on Haight Street.

"What about if we move the bakery into one of our houses?"

"Impossible," said Sister Lakeesha. She was swinging her foot as she spoke. She may have been a sister of Muhammad, but she still had her brashness. (Meantime, Sister Hannah cut a sideways look at Williams—a half-smile that revealed what was up between them. But it was no secret to Fakir. He knew how much time Williams spent in her apartment.)

"Why?"

"The city," she said. "I've explained this already. We can't operate a commercial bakery inside a residence. It's against code."

"Code. Is that the real reason?" Fakir asked.

The others did not answer, but everyone knew his opinion on such things because he'd spoken it clear enough, often enough. The master will cite many reasons, Fakir knew, but in the end the real reason is only one. What the master cannot control, he must destroy. If we make our own bread, then we cease to be his slaves. And our freedom is the one thing the master cannot tolerate.

Sister Lakeesha was still swinging her foot. "All I know," she said. "We don't get the bakery started up, this place gonna close down big time."

"Amen," said Sister Hannah.

The Nation of Islam might follow in the law of Muhammad, in which the woman follows in the footsteps of man, but in Cole Valley all the economic livelihood was from the bakery, and the bakery was run by Sister Lakeesha.

"How much longer can we go as we are?" asked Imam

Harold. He was the old man who had founded the Cole Valley Mosque. It did not follow in the exact precepts of the Nation— and was considered by some to be renegade—but it was nonetheless a member of the tribe. Harold had been a fiery one in his day, and was glad to see the new life brought here by Fakir.

"We are a month behind on our lease here at the mosque," said Lakeesha. "If we don't have a find a place for the bakery soon, it isn't just the business we will lose. Everyone we hire, our bakers, our drivers, they will be in the street. And we will lose this building, too."

Fakir felt their eyes. Before he had come to the pulpit, this place had been thriving. The ministry paid its way; they had an outreach to the poor and handed out food and clothes. Lately they had been in the papers, and the crowds were larger, but who was in those crowds you could not be sure. Suddenly there were demands from this quarter and that, questions about building safety, permits, lease arrangements. And now the regulars of the church had started to fade away, and it was gawkers in the crowd, and agents, and who knew which was which.

"We will find a new place for the bakery."

Fakir wanted to say more, but the prayer siren went off. In these matters, they followed the old practices, as adapted by Imam Harold. The women separated themselves and the men gathered in line on the pillows and bowed toward Mecca. To the place where the ancestors had come out of Africa and gone into the desert and rebelled against the slave traders, where the True Prophet had spoken his words about the redemption of the black tribes and the corruption of the white, and as you knelt there and felt the outside crushing in on you, you knew it was universal, this corruption. How else the owner of the bakery building suddenly enact the renegotiation clause? How else the city forbid them to operate the retail booth on the church property? How else the tax audit and the parking tickets? How else the projects and the drugs on every corner and the scattering of the tribe while the gentiles of every foreign land and color were given succor here and his own people tormented? How else himself put into jail for a crime he had not committed—and now these rumors spreading through the congregation that he himself was an agent, a dealer, spreading the poison even as he spoke against it?

How else?

When the afternoon prayers were over, Fakir walked down Fillmore with Williams at his side. He felt again the bond between them. It was the bond of all brothers who had spent time in the yard: time doing push-ups and watching your ass and keeping the Hispanics and the whites away from you with their sharpened spoons, their drugs, their stubby little cocks.

Williams's face was set and quiet and at such moments there was something relaxed and ordinary-looking about him, but Fakir knew about the underneath. There were times in prison where you glanced into a man's eyes and you saw the veil, and you realized there were things beneath the surface you could not know, and you knew better than to ask. He saw that look on Williams's face now, but then Williams gave him a sudden grin.

"We will find a bakery, God willing," said Williams.

"That's right," said Fakir, "God willing," and he was glad to have his prison buddy by his side.

TWENTY-TWO

When Dante had been working on the Strehli case, collecting evidence for the prosecution, there'd been a PI on the other side, doing the same thing for the defense. That investigator's name was Jake Cicero. After seeing Strehli's photos, Dante had made arrangements to meet with Cicero Wednesday afternoon down at the bocce courts in Columbus Gardens.

Once upon a time the old men used to hang around Columbus Gardens all day, rolling the bocce and sitting on the benches, eating their hard-crusted bread, and drinking their wine. There was hardly any hour, day or night, when you couldn't find the old-timers there, passing the time. Eventually the city had put a fence around the court and planted ivy, and now the ivy had grown up along the fence, but the bocce courts were still there, on the other side of the cyclone gate, with weeds growing through the unraked gravel. Dante found Jake Cicero alone in the middle of those weeds, rolling the bocce.

Cicero was in his midsixties. He'd been in the business some thirty years, and he knew most of the undercurrent, the truth that swam below the surface. A good deal of Cicero's work when Dante knew him had been contract work for the city— digging up alibis and mitigating circumstances for the public defender's office. Seven years ago he'd been doing grub work on behalf of Caselli, the man accused of murdering Strehli. Though Dante and Cicero had worked the opposite sides of the line, things were friendly enough between them. At one point, Cicero had even offered him a job.

"So you like bocce."

"I've played a couple times."

"No one around here gives a shit about this game anymore." Cicero took out the pallino and handed it to him. "Here, you start."

The pallino was a small round ball, smaller than the bocce balls themselves. Dante tossed the pallino down the court, past the midline. The pallino acted as the stake, the center point, more or less, and the goal was to roll your bocce as close to it as possible.

Dante's first put was no good. His second was better, a foot or so off the pallino.

Cicero cradled the bocce in his palm, judging the distance.

"Why you coming to me?"

"I was just hoping to pick your brain."

"What about?"

"The Strehli case."

"Strehli's dead and Caselli's dead. And I think even the PD who handled the case is dead, too."

"How?"

"Heart attack. Nothing sinister, if that's what you mean."

Cicero tossed his ball. It was an easy toss, smooth and fluid, and it rolled in front of Dante's into the lead position.

"I was wondering if you might know where Angie Caselli is these days?"

"The wife?"

Dante nodded.

"My part in the case ended when Caselli decided to cop a plea."

"The wife disappeared before that, didn't she?"

"A couple days," Cicero said. "At first she was her husband's primary alibi. Then I found a couple of other witnesses to back her up. Given all that, it looked like we were in good position to undermine the prosecution case. But all of a sudden Caselli rolled over."

"You have any idea why she left town?"

"There were rumors."

"What kind of rumors?"

"A million kinds. Let me ask you a question."

"Okay."

"After Caselli confessed, why didn't you let it go?"

"My father knew Mark Strehli. The idea he'd been killed in a drug deal, it didn't make sense to me."

"So even now, you can't give it up?"

"I guess not."

Dante took his turn. His form was bad but his aim was good and he knocked the old man's ball out of the lead position. His own ball rolled after the kiss, within inches of the pallino. It would be hard to beat.

"My advice: Unless you're getting paid, let it go."

Dante didn't say anything.

"I know what they did to you years ago. Rossi gave you the old pat on the back and fed you to the wolves. So you come back after these many years, it's still in your craw. You want to vindicate yourself."

"Maybe."

"Well, drop it. I just lost a detective. You want to stay in town, I'll give you a job. Same job I promised seven years ago. Long hours. Lousy pay."

Cicero held the bocce in his hand. The detective had two puts remaining. Dante remembered how he'd used to come here when he was a boy and watch the old men play. They'd be grilling the Italian sausages, and talking in Italian, mocking the man with the bocce, trying to laugh him off his throw. And they'd drag out the family pictures here, too, and the letters from Italy, and one time, after Marinetti's twin boys had died in a car crash, he remembered seeing the father out here weeping and wailing, hurling the bocce into the fence.

Cicero took his pitch then. The form was perfect but there was no force behind it. The ball rolled short.

Dante reached in his pocket and took out the pictures of the dead family in the container ship.

"What are these?" asked Cicero.

"Not long before Strehli was murdered, there was an incident at the port. Some Chinese immigrants. Illegals, trying to get into the country. They were found dead in a container ship. Suffocated."

"And so?"

"Strehli took these pictures, or I think he did."

"Okay, so he took the pictures. What if he did?"

"He sent the pictures to my father. Before he was killed. My father hung on to them all these years. Then at the end, my father got the idea someone was after him. He thought someone was trying to kill him."

"I heard he died in his sleep."

"Before he died he gave the pictures to my uncle—and now my uncle's dead, too."

"So you think somebody's after those pictures?"

"Maybe."

"Well, then, maybe you better get rid of them."

If Cicero meant this as a joke, he couldn't tell. The man had his eyes on the pallino and was judging the distance. Then he backed off. "There are a lot of mysteries in this life," said Cicero suddenly, "and you can't solve them all. You chase and chase. You spend your time looking for the little nugget, the secret at the heart of things. But the truth is, that nugget, sometimes, it's better not to find it. Sometimes, it's better not to know."

"You sound like my father."

"Your father was a wise man."

"Do you know how I can find the Caselli woman?"

"You can't."

"Why not?"

"She's dead. Caselli was killed in jail. The wife died in a car accident. Nevada, maybe a year later."

"Another coincidence?"

Cicero shrugged. "You want to know the rumor, I'll tell you. Caselli was paid to confess. To take the fall for Strehli's murder. He made a deal. He would serve some time—but then he would get out. Assume a new identity, meet up with his wife. Except Caselli decided to renege. So, he was stabbed to death in the county jail. And his wife—it just took them a little longer to catch up with her, that's all. But it's all rumor, like I said. A theory."

"But who's behind it all?"

"It's all a goose chase on that one. You'll end up chasing your own tail."

"You don't have any ideas?"

"None worth repeating. I can tell you this, though. You want to know more about those bodies in those containers, you might start with your buddy down there in Homicide."

"I don't follow."

"Ying. He used to be in SI. I heard he was looking into the container deaths a while back. But like I said: You'd be better off forgetting that business."

Then Cicero rolled the bocce. It was a beautiful roll. It hit Dante's front bocce on the bounce and sent it caroming to the side. Meanwhile, Cicero's ball rolled forward and kissed the pallino.

Cicero smiled, and you could see all the creases in his leathered face. "I've still got the touch," he said. "I still got the goddamn touch."

TWENTY-THREE

It was coming on four o'clock, and for once Ying intended to get across the bay at a reasonable time, so he could sit with Lei and his kids around the dinner table. He had an errand to run on the way—up Grant Street to buy a certain rejuvenating tea for his grandmother: a foul mixture prepared especially for her by the herbalist Mr. Chan. Grandmother Ying took the potion every day at dinner time. Ying knew it was important for him to pick it up. She was almost out of the tea, and if he did not bring it home for her, then she would head out herself, with her white cane, tapping her way through the crowded streets.

There was another reason, too, that Ying wanted to visit the herbalist. In the adjoining trinket shop, run by Chan's daughter, there was a bank of mailboxes. One of those mailboxes was his contact point with Miss Lin, his informant.

On the way out of Columbus Station, Ying ran into Angelo, the Homicide chief. There had been no morning briefing, and

Angelo wanted to know how things were going on the Mancuso murder.

"So, Dante Mancuso—he's still your prime?"

"I haven't crossed him off."

Angelo was in his late forties, a half-bald Italian with wire-rimmed glasses and a studious expression. He and Dante Mancuso had been partners once, Ying knew—but after Dante fell from grace, Angelo had risen. Ying had never worked with the man in the field, but he had noticed in his superior officer the ability to ask seemingly innocuous questions in such a way that you sensed an underlying implication, even when his manner was friendly.

"How about the rest of the family? The mother and the son?"

"Toliveri talked to them both at the scene. And I sent Detective Roma over to interview the old woman in the hospital."

"Louise?"

"It seemed better to send a woman. The old woman was frail. And Detective Roma, she has a good touch for these kind of situations."

"Have *you* talked to the old woman yet?"

"I was out to the house yesterday, and I talked to the son."

"Does his story hold?"

"He told me the same thing he told the first time around. Added a few details. Toliveri's hunting down the alibi—but apparently the son put the warehouse on a skeleton crew. With the funeral and everything. So it's taking some footwork."

"Nothing from Forensics? Nothing on Dante Mancuso?"

"No. No breakthroughs."

There are other things I could bring up, Ying thought. *The dubi-*

ous nature of Dante's employment. The fact he'd been seen outside the Wus. Or his own growing suspicion that this was leading somewhere else altogether. But there was that little voice inside him. *You still have your head in SI*, it said. *You have to let that go. You're reading patterns in the tea leaves when all you've got is wet grass. You're not focused on the task at hand.*

"I assume you're going to catch up with Toliveri."

"Of course."

"All right," said Angelo. "You do that. Then we'll all crack our heads on this one at the Friday briefing. Me, you, and the rest of the troop."

The herbalist's shop up was off Grant, down a nameless alley—a narrow bit of asphalt strung with fire escapes. There were residences overhead, and the fire escapes were hung with laundry. The shop's window was smudged, but inside the place was clean, and there were hundreds of tiny vials filled with liquids and powders.

"I have something to pick up," he said, "for Elenore Ying."

The young woman at the counter gave him a dour look. She was one of Chan's daughters. Ying wasn't as welcome as he used to be. There was another trade that went on here, he knew—in the ground-up remains of endangered animals: elephant tusks and rhinoceros ears and the beaks of eagles—and the trade in such substances was against the law. Part of his job with SI had been to crack down on that trade.

"Ah, Frank Ying," said the old herbalist, a wizened man with a black toupee. "Here is for your grandmother."

"Thank you."

"You are a good son."

Ying took out his wallet. It was part of the reason he came. This little concoction was not cheap; the old woman was on a fixed income, and it was the least he could do. As to the efficacy of the remedy he had no idea. He knew that the exact nature of the ingredients had changed over time as she grew older, the proportion of sweet to sour, of hot to cold, but no matter the proportions the content maintained its rank odor.

"Maybe you let me make up something for you," said Chan.

"Not now."

"Something for you—your wife. Make life nicer at home." The man smiled in a way too kindly to resent. "Some people say I shouldn't sell to you. But I say no problem."

"No, not to worry," said Ying.

Ying understood. Despite his overtures, the herbalist feared he would take the little bag down to be analyzed. And it was true, more than once he'd wondered what he might find if he did. Tiger balls. Panda intestines. Tip of a kangaroo's tongue.

"I tell people you understand how it is. It is for your grand-mother. You are Chinese, like us, after all."

"Yes," said Ying.

He put up with little lectures such as this often enough in Chinatown. People who did not like him going after the Wus. People who regarded it as a betrayal of his people. He had been taken aside and chided by old women. Spit on. Laughed at and hooted on down the street.

Or that's the way it felt, anyway.

He was a hypocrite, who bought the medicine for himself, his own family, but persecuted others. And now that he had backed off the Wu investigation, rumor was, no doubt, he was on the take.

He turned out of the store and down Grant, glancing for a minute back at the building of the Wu Benevolent Society, with its balustrades trimmed like pagodas, its deco lights over gilded balconies, cracked now and sagging. Love Wu was up there somewhere. Or so rumor went. In his wheelchair these days. Blue oxygen bottles by his side. A lovely nurse. Too lovely for words.

Ying went on down the street. His informant's mailbox was in the back of a trinket store adjacent to the herbalist. There was a bank of such boxes there, frequented by immigrants and other passers-through, legal or otherwise.

He kept walking.

He couldn't worry anymore about the larger picture, he told himself. He had his wife to worry about, his grandmother. The world was full of contradictions, of paradox. He couldn't worry about Angelo and the look in his eyes and the fact that the Wus were bringing in not just the ground-up intestines of endangered animals but assault rifles and heroin in its most purified form.

Fuck it, he thought.

But he couldn't help himself. He pulled out his pad. Wrote out a message there in the middle of the avenue. *Meet me. At the New Asia Lounge.* He scrawled out a time and a date. Then went to the back of the trinket store and dropped it in the informant's box.

TWENTY-FOUR

Dante caught Ying as he was entering Columbus Station. Dante had just finished talking to the desk sergeant—who'd told him that Ying had left, gone for the day—but as he turned to leave there was Ying, coming in the door. They stood for a moment in the over-lit lobby, with the fluorescents too bright overhead, while the desk sergeant turned his attention to a Chinese woman who had parked herself in one of the vinyl chairs. The woman had come to complain about some boys in the neighborhood who made a practice of throwing rocks at her cat. Dante could not know this, but Ying did, because the woman came in every day.

The two men regarded each other without surprise. They were both intense men. Dante with his close-cut hair and his dark eyes. Ying with his strong jaw and his skewed, angular looks. Ying still held the paper bag containing his grandmother's tea. His intention had been to drop it off and go home, but then he'd decided at the last minute to swing by the station and check on a report he was expecting from the lab.

"What can I do for you?" asked Ying.

"I'd like to talk."

"Okay, let's go to my office."

"Not here. Off the record."

"Nothing's off the record with a cop, you know that."

"Not here," said Dante. "And off the record."

"Where?"

"Your choice," said Dante. "Someplace where they don't speak much English. And where they won't pay much attention to us."

Ying led him down Stockton and up the heights to a small place at the edge of Chinatown. Ying had been here a few times before. The service was slow and the help surly but they left you alone.

"My treat," said Ying.

"How come the place is so empty?"

"Food's horrible."

Dante nodded. They ordered a couple of Tsingtaos and passed on the dim sum.

"I thought maybe we could help each other."

Dante tossed the photos onto the table.

"What are these?"

"I was hoping you could tell me."

Ying dwelled a moment on the corpses inside the shipping container. It was a hardened glance, professional and a little sad. Saddened not at the deaths themselves but because the part of him that had once been shocked by such sights wasn't shocked anymore.

"My uncle gave me the negatives before he died. Negatives," Dante repeated. "Not undeveloped film. So that means other prints were made, some time or other. Though I don't know if my uncle ever saw those prints. My father, maybe. I don't know."

"Your father?"

"Apparently he's the one who gave the negatives to my uncle. To give to me."

"Why didn't you tell me before?"

"I just picked them up."

The men drank. Dante was a more vigorous drinker and ordered another. Ying held back.

"You've checked my background, haven't you?" asked Dante.

"Yes."

"And what did you find?"

"New Orleans Export . . ." Ying looked at Dante—at the half-smile, the square shoulders, the eyes with their dark sheen. He was not sure really what to think of this man. "It's a vinyl sheet," he said. "Or it appears to be."

Dante didn't argue with this or acknowledge it, either. The thin smile played across his lips.

"Seven years ago, a man named Strehli was murdered. He was a customs inspector. I think he took those pictures—and was killed on account of them. And I think whoever killed my father, my uncle, both of them, I think it has to do with those pictures."

Dante pushed a pair of photos at Ying. One was a tight shot of a man's face, partially decayed.

"Do you know who this man might be?"

Ying studied the face. It was pretty well decomposed, but

when he looked at the other photos—a woman, two children—
the circumstances brought back the old rumors.

Ru Shen.

Ying kept his opinion to himself. Partly because it was only
a guess, but also because he was not sure of Dante's intentions.
He didn't know if what he told Dante might be used in some
other way than he expected. And at the same time he saw Dante
was reading him, realizing that he was holding back, or wondering at least, and wondering, too, if Ying was working more than
one angle, more than one game. The two men sipped at their
beers and regarded one another and in this mutual mistrust there
was a kind of bond.

"Why are you showing me this?"

"I want to find my uncle's murderer. The killer, I think he
was harassing my father at the end."

"You think these pictures are connected to their deaths?"

"I'm going to find out."

"That's my job." Ying was about to launch into the bit about
how Dante should leave the investigation to the police, but he
knew the man wouldn't listen "What branch are you with?" he
asked. "What's with the vinyl sheet?"

"You were with SI?"

"Yes."

"But you left."

"Family reasons."

"They wouldn't protect you, would they?"

Ying didn't respond, but it was true. When he had started
pressing the investigation, the threats had come—and there
hadn't been much anybody could do.

Dante leaned in. "The Wus," he said. "You were after the Wus. And we are, too."

"You think they're behind the murders."

"I don't know. But if you can tell me who's in that picture, maybe we can work together. Maybe we can help one another."

"Give me the pictures, I can run some facial comparisons. See what we find."

Dante hesitated. "Who will run them?"

"I'll run them myself. I won't tell a soul."

Dante picked up the envelope. He reached inside and took out the negatives. He slid those into his own pocket and handed the photos to Ying.

The two men parted at the top of Winter Alley. It was just past twilight. Ying went down the road toward his grandmother's house, and Dante went on up the hill. He hadn't gone more than a half block before he turned around and headed back.

La Saggezza, his grandmother might say. The wisdom. Because there was a part of him that had sensed something in the shadows, back there in Winter Alley. Or maybe it was just because he'd been overcome by a craving and didn't know what to do with it and decided to fill it, however shoddily, with a pack of Luckies and a pint of Jack from Coit Liquors.

Either way, when he returned to the corner of Winter Alley, he stopped for a moment. He saw Ying at the front door of his grandmother's cottage—or rather he saw Ying disappear inside, closing the door behind him. An instant later he saw a figure emerge on the fire balcony above Ying's door. A woman, he thought. All in black, thin and lithe, working the ladder, attempting to work her way down.

Dante broke into a run.

The figure disappeared back into the house. *A mistake,* Dante realized. *I should have waited.* But it was too late. Dante grabbed the fire escape ladder, dislodging it, and headed up.

The instant Ying walked into his grandmother's place, he knew something was wrong. The old woman sat motionless on the rattan couch. She was not meditating, though; her position was too rigid—and she did not offer him her cheek in greeting, but instead held her head in such a way as to suggest she was listening to something from up above. Then Ying heard the noise, too.

An intruder, he thought, and headed up the stairs. Goddamn kids—though another part of him feared it was not kids at all. He was remembering how the room had been trashed.

Then he heard the noise on the street, the sound of the fire escape being pulled down.

He pushed through the door, gun drawn.

Dante had scampered up the ladder and onto the balcony. Inside, the room was dark. Ying would be coming up the other way, he guessed, drawn by the noise, and he realized the situation here could get out of control, and he himself was illuminated, out on the balcony, unarmed, a complete and utter target. Just as he realized this, the woman said "Dante," and he saw her form emerge from the darkness inside, stepping toward him—then the door on the other side pushed open, and there was a flash of gunfire.

An instant later the lights were on. Ying was standing with his gun drawn, and on the ground lay the prone figure of Anita Blonde.

PART THREE

TWENTY-FIVE

Anita Blonde was bleeding badly. The blood was seeping through her shirt, and Dante started to unbutton her front, thinking to somehow staunch the flow. She gasped. His fingers fumbled. Then she gasped again, and the sound of the gasp made him stop.

Ying hovered a few feet back, his gun slack in his hand.

Blonde sputtered, lifting her head. Her eyes were swimming but she recognized him, and for a moment Dante thought she might try to say something. Her lips moved and there was a bubble of pink froth. Her eyes closed. She looked like a kid, with her short hair and a face that was boyish, full of freckles, and Dante thought again of hayfields and pitchforks and her voice that was flat as Kansas someplace. She looked a little like Dorothy laying there, the Oz girl with her innocent pigtails sheered away.

"It's all right," he told her.

But it wasn't all right. Her eyes opened and she gasped again, clenching herself. And then she was dead. The room smelled of blood but also of urine and shit because she had voided herself at the end.

Dante got to his feet.

"I saw someone on the balcony," he told Ying. "And I charged up the fire escape."

Her gun lay on the floor nearby. It had all happened so quickly. Ying had pushed open the inside door, and Blonde had turned, swooping low, pulling the gun from the ankle holster. But she was too slow. Ying had fired not once but twice, and her own shot had gone wide, blistering the doorjamb. Standing on the balcony, under the arc lamp, Dante had feared Ying might shoot him as well.

Now Ying pulled a cell phone from his pocket. Dante grabbed his arm.

"What are you doing?"

"Exactly what you think I'm doing. Calling for a car."

"No."

Ying was a by-the-book type, but Dante could not afford for him to go by the book. There was an unwritten rule: When an agent falls, you distance yourself. Another Homicide investigation now would put Dante in a quagmire. It would blow his assignment—or worse—because in the end he did not know what Blonde had been up to. More importantly, he didn't know where the company's involvement ended and where other interests took over, or how those worlds might be intertwined.

He had already taken a chance with Ying, risking his cover to help find his uncle's murderer. A mistake, maybe—but there was no going back now.

"She was my contact."

"What do you mean?"

"My job here was to set up a sting. On the Wus. And she's an agent, working with me."

"What was she doing here at my grandmother's?"

"I don't know. Looking for something. The photos, maybe. Or something else. I ran across her in my place the other day—rummaging." Dante shrugged. "It's not always clear, my business. There are things I am not told. Things I don't know."

Ying gestured at Blonde's gun.

"It's a nine millimeter."

"I see that." It was a Glock, similar to the model Dante carried, only a little smaller and more lightweight, with a shorter handle.

"Same millimeter killed your uncle."

"Either way," said Dante, "we have to get rid of the body."

"I can't do that."

"We report what happened here, no good will come out of it."

"I am not culpable." Ying's voice was weak; he did not sound convinced. "She was in my house. She pulled a gun."

"That's not going to matter," said Dante. "She's an agent. She could've come here to ransack your room, or to kill you, but it doesn't matter. Even if it's true, they're not going to let that story come out—this thing will get twisted some other way."

"I'll just tell the truth."

"Our chance to get the Wus will disappear, and you will be destroyed."

Ying said nothing.

"Your career," said Dante. "Your reputation."

"It doesn't matter," said Ying.

"And whoever was after your family before—"

Ying hesitated. He hesitated long enough to make Dante think he was considering it, and he could guess what was in his head. The bullet had gone through Blonde's body, probably, and there would be a slug somewhere in the wall. There was also the blood. If for some reason there were a search of Ying's room, the cops would drop Luminol on the floor and find the blood traces.

"Won't someone come looking for her?"

"They'll figure she dropped out," said Dante. "Flew the coop for another life. Or else someone caught up with her somewhere, a past assignment. A violent end. But they won't come looking. They won't want the trouble."

Ying twisted the ring on his finger. His wedding ring. For his part, he'd seen a hundred murders bungled: cases where people killed someone by accident or in rage and thought they could get away with it, but in the end they were caught. At the same time there were plenty of other cases where someone went missing and you never found the body. There were times when you had motive and maybe some circumstantial evidence and a gut feeling—but nothing else. He twisted the ring and looked at it and thought about his wife and his little kids and how if he did the thing he'd been trained to do—if he was the honest cop—he would disgrace himself and endanger his family. But if he did the other thing . . .

Which path weakness, which path strength.

"I have a boat," Dante said. "It belonged to my grandfather. We can take her out on the bay."

Together they wrapped Anita Blonde in a plastic tarp and carried her downstairs. The old woman, Ying's grandmother, sat in the tiny parlor below. She sat with her legs crossed, eyes open, dead eyes, seeing nothing, and at the same time she moaned a low moan—some Buddhist chant, Dante guessed, but it was not particularly sonorous, and he could not escape the sense that the woman, though she saw nothing, heard nothing, knew what was in their bundle. Dante glanced at Ying. The detective lowered his head as he walked past the old woman, not looking in her direction. His lips trembled.

Outside there was no one in the alley, and they struggled to get the corpse into the trunk of Ying's government-issue Ford.

"Where's the boat?"

"On the old pier. Behind Alioto's Restaurant."

"We can't carry her through that way."

Ying was right. The old Wharf was a tourist haunt. Even after hours, when the hotels and the restaurants were closed, people lingered along the gangways.

"You drop me off," said Dante. "Then meet me on the other side of the harbor building, at the public pier."

Dante hit the dock. Out where the old fishing fleet had been—the trawlers and the deep water boats and the crabbers—it was all pleasure craft now. Around the corner, though, along a plank walk that ran between the Alioto's pier and Scoma's Grill, there were still a couple of dozen professional rigs. His grandfather's boat was a refashioned felucca with some deep casting lines and a net for trawling—though the net was of the sort that had gone out of style decades ago, too small for commercial purposes, these days. The boat was really nothing more than a dinghy with a motor in the back and a compartment below that you stuffed with ice and maybe fish if you caught them. The old boat still had its sailing mast—Dante had rigged the mast seven years ago, when he went out with Marilyn Visconti—but it was dark now and he relied on the motor, working his way along the shore, past Fort Mason toward the harbor building and the public landing on the other side.

Ying was waiting there when Dante arrived.

There was not much going on at the public pier this time of night. No doubt there was a person or two sleeping in their boats, and there were drifters under the cypress trees in the park. The patrol cars that worked this beat swung by every few hours, sweeping the park with a flood. When the next sweep might be, Dante had no way of knowing.

"Let's grab her," said Dante.

Though it was only a couple of dozen steps from the car to the boat, it seemed much longer. There were cars on Marina Drive nearby, any one of which might suddenly pull into the lot. There were cars in the lot even now, and inside the parked cars there were people necking, or smoking dope, or maybe just looking out at the view, at the two shadows with the sagging burden between them. As they carried her down the gangway, Dante caught the glow of a cigarette near the sea wall, then a pair of cigarettes, and the sound of laughter echoed over the water. Finally they were on the boat, and they rolled Anita Blonde below deck, into the compartment which his grandfather had once filled with ice and fish.

Anita Blonde with her blue eyes, and her pearlescent skin. Who had sat outdoors at the Café Du Monde in the sweltering heat, and who had followed him here to San Francisco. Anita Blonde. Who'd had another life once upon a time. Another name.

Dante worked the skiff out into the bay. The water was calm, the night clear and dark. Ying's eyes glistened in the blackness. Dante could sense the change in him. He was complicit now, too. It happened to everyone sooner or later, that was the truth of it. In fighting evil, you succumbed to evil—and you tried to hide what you had done. It was an awful thing, maybe. But there were things that were worse.

"Your people were fishermen?"

Dante nodded.

"Mine, too. Generations ago."

It was likely. The red-hulled junks had been here first. When the Luccans came, they forced the Chinese out. North to San Rafael, to China Camp, and Point Richmond. South to Monterey. Then the Sicilians came and forced out the northern Italians, too.

"Where we taking her?"

"Out past Treasure Island."

Ying nodded.

Treasure Island was the name for the naval facility built on slag out in the middle of the bay. Ying knew, like Dante knew, the places where professionals dumped a corpse if they wanted it to stay under. In the deeper water, away from the shipping channels. It was one of those things you learned if you work Homicide in SF. The amateurs, the sociopaths, the wife murderers, and rage freaks, the first thing they did was head for the bay with the body, as if the idea were somehow original and simply dumping the corpse would destroy the crime. But corpses floated; they washed ashore. If you wanted to get rid of the body, you had to place it right. It wasn't an exact science, no, but the currents were seasonal and predictable. You wanted to weigh the body down, submerge it in deep water, but away from the shipping channels, where it might get stirred to the surface by the heavy freighters passing through.

Even with every precaution, though, a body sometimes turned up when the seasons changed, and the cold water started to rise to the surface. But by that time, the corpse was pretty well rotted, the skin separated from the bone, the circumstances of death more difficult to determine.

In this case, Anita Blonde did not have to stay down forever. A couple of weeks, a month. Because even if they did discover her body, the chances of anyone tying her to Dante and Ying would be remote.

They pulled her from the fish compartment. They weighted her down and wrapped her and scooted her abaft.

In the middle of it, Ying's cell phone started to ring. Ying glanced at the number on the screen.

"Don't answer."

"It's my wife."

"We don't want anyone to know we're out here."

"She's going to think I am having an affair."

"Let her think it."

The phone stopped ringing and they finished their work. They lifted Anita to the railing, then dropped her over the stern into the black water. In an instant she was gone.

Dante put his hand to his forehead, as if to cross himself, but the action gave him no comfort. He stared at the water.

Ying bowed his head. "Hey-yung," he said, ever so softly, an expression his grandmother had taught him years ago. An ancient mantra, the origins of which he did not know. Simply something to be whispered upon departure, to the spirit who is passing. Perhaps it was something the old woman had made up herself.

They headed back to the shore.

In the city, a patrol car pulled up behind them, wailing suddenly, then racing by. Then there were more sirens, and engines racing up the hill—toward a calamity of some sort, a fire maybe, people trapped in a building. The sound of the sirens seemed to echo in Dante's head all the way back to North Beach. Ying left him off at the corner of Bay and Columbus, and as Dante walked home he paused a moment out in front of the cathedral. It was not quite dawn, but there were birds chattering up along the belfry, and already some old crones had begun to gather for morning mass. It was Thursday he remembered, and Father Campanella would hold confession this afternoon, and for an instant he wished he believed the way his grandmother had believed: that he could drop on his knees in the confessional and list his sins and then walk away clean and pure. Father Campanella had wanted to see him, to show him his father's *Il Libro Segreto*. Had Campanella been there this moment, standing in the darkness of the cathedral steps, he might have gone up to him, but Campanella was not there and confession was no longer in his realm, so there was nothing he could do but walk up the hill, home to Fresno Street. Nothing to do but go home and lie in his father's bed and wish for sleep as the day got slowly brighter and it became more apparent that sleep was not going to come, and all the while he could not fight the feeling that there was something worse ahead.

Meanwhile, Ying had finished his drive across the bay. He had parked his car and keyed the door, sneaking through the just-graying hallway to lie beside his wife, crossing his arms and staring upward, before realizing he had taken the position of the woman they had slid into the water.

"Hey-yung," he whispered again, thinking of the dead woman. One of his grandmother's mantras, idiosyncratic, no meaning in the world. Give it whatever meaning you wanted.

Go with the spirits.

And as he closed his eyes, floating on the gray void of the morning, Ying wished someone would say the same for him.

TWENTY-SIX

Dante slept for an hour or maybe two, a sleep that despite its brevity was both dark and deep, a plunge into the subterranean. But then he was on the surface again, unrefreshed. The sun was white, and he was both wide awake and dead tired, weighted down with a remorse that felt like a blanket over his head.

Dante thought of Campanella and remembered there had been something teasing at him early this morning as he'd walked by the cathedral.

Guilt, maybe.

He couldn't help but think his own presence here had somehow triggered his uncle's murder—and Blonde's death, as well. Some move he had made without realizing its consequence. A step this way or that. A failure to see what lay ahead.

His grandmother had had rituals to prevent such stumbles. She'd had a picture of St. Alfonso in her kitchen and said a little prayer to him each morning, and sometimes—for no reason at all, it seemed—she would invoke his protection out in the street.

The prayers to Alfonso were prayers to protect yourself against happenstance, from stepping right when you should have stepped left, from walking up Grant when you should have walked down Vallejo because on Grant someone was going to drop a hammer from the scaffold, or a bicyclist was going to run over your foot, or you would talk too long with old Mr. Gizzi, who would therefore forget himself later that afternoon and step in front of an oncoming Cadillac.

These little rituals, they had taken over his grandmother's life as she had gotten older. Protecting herself against the devil. The shadow in the mirror. The creaking at the bottom of the stairs.

Himself, he didn't know. If he'd driven one more time around the block with Angela, his high-school sweetheart . . . If he hadn't run into Marilyn with his cousin that day seven years ago . . . If he had picked up the telephone in New Orleans on the third ring . . . If he hadn't headed back toward Winter Alley last night . . .

The old ones had had their remedies for such folly. The thirteen Stations of the Cross and the three faces of God and the twelve apostles and the forty days of Lent. The ten decades on the rosary, a prayer for each bead and act of confession at the end. When he was a child his grandmother had taught him to run his thumbs over the beads, counting as he prayed, and though he no longer prayed or carried the beads, he still tapped his fingers against his legs as he walked, worked his thumb against the other fingers—and he counted. It didn't seem to help. He had made a wrong turn. He was a company man now and did not know how to get out.

Dante went down the stairs. He left his father's house on Fresno Street and once again paused in front of the cathedral.

What was in his father's *Il Libro Segreto*?

He knocked on the rectory door and after a while a small woman came to the door. She was the housekeeper for the priests, the same woman from years ago; she wore the same gray skirt, it seemed, the same pin-striped blouse, the same crucifix around her neck.

"Father Campanella's gone on retreat."

"Retreat?"

"To pray. He'll be back in a few days."

He was tempted to go around to the rear of the rectory, to open the door and rummage through the priest's desk and find the book for himself. He knew where the priest's room was, and how Father Campanella kept things lying about, but the housekeeper had her eye on him from the window, and he decided it wasn't a good idea, at least not now. Instead he walked up Union to Montgomery Street, toward Marilyn's house. He stood at the top of the hill looking out at the bay, at the sailboats and the blue water, just as he had done that first day after his father's funeral.

Finally he could not hold himself back anymore. He walked across the street and knocked on Marilyn's door.

Hers was not a face that demonstrated surprise easily. Rather she smiled wryly—as if perhaps she had seen him lingering outside. Even so, her demeanor was not without a certain self-doubt, a certain agony. She was dressed in autumnal colors, both bright and subdued at the same time, like a leaf dying on a tree.

"Dante," she said. "You look like hell."

"I need to be with you."

She was wearing too much makeup, or maybe it was the morning light. He saw the age in her face.

"Let's go for a walk," he said.

She hesitated. "I was on my way to work. I could meet you later," she said. "Or I could call in late, I suppose."

She did neither. She closed the door behind her and they headed down the hill together. Out of the wind for the moment. The sun in their faces. Walking. Dante had no idea what he meant to say, or if he even meant to say anything at all. It was her physical presence he wanted, next to him on the street.

"Do you remember Lido's?"

Lido's had been a hangout, a place to go when they were kids. Red booths and polished leather. Somewhere in this block, maybe. Next to the Ligurian Bakery. Or Lucca's Delicatessen. Somewhere in here. Or maybe it had been the next block over. Somewhere.

"Yes," she said.

"How about the Columbo Hotel? With the old men out front?"

"Yes," she said again, looking at him curiously, and just as she spoke, he saw the old place up ahead. It was called the Sam Wong now; no more Italians, only Chinese pensioners lingering out front these days, except for Pesci, the old Black Shirt—but he looked again and Pesci was gone, too. They were on Columbus now, walking a little faster, the way you tended to walk on Columbus, jostling through the crowd—the tourists, the Chinese, the slew-footed old women—all the while looking for a familiar face and feeling the passersby looking back, looking without seeing. The glances penetrated through as if you were not there.

Ghosts.

"And how about Rivini's Restaurant?" Marilyn said. "And the woman with the vegetable cart?"

"And the fishmonger?"

"Yes."

They turned off Columbus, past the old coffee shops, the old vagabond hotels, a street corner where, as a young cop, he'd watched a man die one night, his skull caved in with a tire iron. A kid with a boom box stood there now, alongside his girlfriend, blue hair and tattoos, the heroin fire in their eyes—and Dante felt a longing pierce his heart.

"Where are we going?"

"I just want to walk," he said. "I just want you next to me."

They headed up Russian Hill away from the crowd. He sensed her hesitation, but she kept pace.

At the top, they were winded. They could see down to the bay, and to the city, all that pastel light, all that stucco and brick and steel, little sprouts of green, trumpet vines sprouting from the concrete, palm trees, and meantime the wind up here blew hard and cold, and there was the racket of the cable wires, and you could see all the way to Oakland.

It had always been like this. Walking up the hill made you feel as if you owned the city. She was beautiful beside him.

"Things have changed," Marilyn said. "I don't know . . ."

He looked at her face and saw it was going to be ravaged. How the folds were going to go deep and the worry lines would set in, and at the same time he saw her as she had been just a few years before.

"It doesn't matter," he said.

Then he kissed her. He expected her to pull away. She did, at least at first, but then she kissed him back. It was a long kiss, and it was pure, almost—except for everything that lay beneath the surface—and then he pulled away from her. His body went stiff and he sobbed. Because he was thinking of Anita Blonde. And the dead girl in Bangkok. And a man in Paris. And some son of a bitch in Des Moines. Because while maybe he could say that it had been a wrong step that had killed Blonde, a miscalculation, and maybe it had been the same with the Thai girl, he had killed the Frenchman with his own hands, a knife in the gullet. And there'd been others. And would be more. He had not joined the company altogether by accident, one stumbling foot after another. There had been an act of will at some point.

He began to sob more fiercely, and Marilyn put her arm around him, thinking perhaps it was his father he cried for, thinking these were paroxysms of grief that shook him to the bone, and though that might have been true in part, there were all those other ones, too, all the dead, but more than that he was weeping because of a premonition of how all this was going to end, and how complete would be his loss.

"Take me out on the boat," she said. "Let's go sailing together."

They were necking in the doorway of an abandoned grocery. He pushed his leg between her thighs, unzipped her skirt, pulled at her panties, and she didn't stop him. In the window reflection Dante saw an old woman working her way up the hill.

"Take me sailing," Marilyn whispered. "Take me out on the waves."

He clutched her close. When he looked again the old woman's reflection was gone.

TWENTY-SEVEN

Detective Ying was out of harmony. His wife, Lei, was serene, however, composed and fresh-scrubbed, and they worked together side by side at the counter, as they often did, making breakfast and packing lunches for the kids.

On the surface it was a tranquil scene, but inside his chest was full of dread, and his head felt hollow from lack of sleep.

"Are you driving us, Dad?" his daughter asked. She was the older of the two, a smaller, fiercer version of her mother. His son was another matter. Scatter-headed. Driven by impulse.

"Yes."

"Don't you have to go to work?"

"Not until later. I was out late last night. On assignment." He gave his wife a glance which she did not return.

"Did you kill anyone?" asked his son.

"Daniel—"

"Just joking."

He watched his family at the breakfast table and felt oddly estranged from them. He had made a mistake last night, in more ways than one. He had no idea of Dante's real motives, or if he could believe anything the man had told him about the dead woman or anything else.

One thing, though: Ying had held on to the dead woman's gun. He wanted to run ballistics, to see if the same weapon had killed Salvatore Mancuso. Ying couldn't go to the police lab under the circumstances, but he could go to a friend of his, Max Grudgeon, who these days ran the criminology lab at UC. He got up from the breakfast table to phone Grudgeon and leave a message, saying he would come by to see him later.

When he returned to the table, his children were gathering their things for school.

"You're taking them?" she asked.

"Yes."

"You'll be late."

"No. We'll make it."

He had a hard time meeting her eyes. Lei noticed and reached out to touch his cheek.

"Who were you talking to?"

"It was just the lab."

"Are you investigating the Wus?"

"No."

Her inclination was uncanny. They knew each other well.

"Are you stepping out on me?"

Her tone was lilting, almost flirtatious. She fixed him with her eyes. They were gray eyes, very clear. Even so, there was something hidden there. Her chin tilted, she smiled ever so slightly, and suddenly he feared, despite her question, that she was the one drifting from him.

"Don't worry," he said, kissing her forehead. "It's just another murder."

After he dropped off the kids, Ying drove across the bay. He stopped at Figone's Hardware on Grant to pick up some plaster and some bleach and a small chisel, then he returned to Winter Alley.

His grandmother was not in the kitchen, nor was she in the tiny bedroom at the foot of the stairs. She was upstairs, on her knees, with a brush and a bucket, scrubbing at the blood.

Blind as she was, she had beaten him to it.

Grandmother Ying raised her head as he entered. He bent down and put his cheek against hers.

He put the Clorox on the floor next to her. With the chisel, he dug out the bullets he'd fired the night before. He counted the shots in his memory. Two from himself, one from Anita Blonde. Now he dug her shot from the doorjamb, and one of his own from the plaster opposite. The bullet had gone through her body and into the wall. The third bullet, he guessed, was still inside her. While his grandmother scrubbed, he stirred the plaster. Slowly, methodically, he patched the two holes, then brushed them over with paint.

Then he went to Columbus Station. Technically speaking, the evidence room was under lock and key, but the truth of the matter was that the detectives had unfettered access. He went to the metal drawer and lifted one of the bullets from the Mancuso murder. Then he took the bullet and drove back across the bay to Berkeley.

Ying had studied criminology at UC some fifteen years before. It was where he had met Lei. She'd been a nursing student, and they'd met in a class about emergency trauma. Here on the quad, underneath Sproul Tower, they'd staged a mock triage with student volunteers sprawled on the ground. Lei had been one of the wounded, and he'd helped carry her off on a canvas gurney.

Now he walked down the long halls of the criminology building, seemingly unchanged: the same worn tile, the same yellowing paint made dingier by the overhead fluorescents. Grudgeon was in his office.

"Ah, Frank," said Max. "How's things in the real world?"

"A little too real."

"You back home in Homicide?"

"Yes."

"Feel good?"

"Well, it's home, like you say."

"Well, you know me, pure theory."

There was an awkward moment. Max Grudgeon had been among the brightest of the young criminologists, but instead of going into law enforcement he'd stayed at the university. There was an undercurrent of tension between the two men, as there often was between academics and the people who worked the field. Over the years, Grudgeon had done some consulting work for defense clients, undermining the physical evidence on a couple of murder cases where helping the accused, in Ying's opinion, was of questionable ethics. On one of those cases Ying himself had been the arresting officer—but this was all old news.

"What can I help you with?"

"It's a simple thing, really. A ballistics check. I know you have a lab here for the students."

"Can't the police lab do that for you?"

"In this case, no."

Max smiled. It interested him. Ying could see. It appealed to his anarchist heart.

"You going to tell me what this is about?"

"I can't."

Max nodded his head. The man was obviously pleased to know that Ying, too, had occasion to work outside the boundaries. Exposing himself bothered Ying, but he had no choice.

"Show me what you have."

Ying opened his case and put Anita Blonde's gun on the desk with one of the bullets from Salvatore Mancuso's corpse.

"I need to know if we have a match."

"All right," said Max. "I have to teach a class this morning. And another this afternoon. But talk to me Friday. I should know by then."

"Thanks."

Max Grudgeon looked at the gun on his desk.

"I'm not going to have the SFPD down my throat for this?"

"No. It's confidential. You and me."

Ying walked back across campus to his car. As he opened the door, he glanced around, and he felt again the uneasiness that had plagued him when he was with SI: the suspicion that someone was following him, that everything was about to break loose—but there was no one in the lot.

He went home then. Early, for once. Lei wasn't there. She returned a few hours later, nonchalant in her sleeveless blouse.

"Where have you been?"

"Errands," she said.

She gave him a kiss on the lips. He closed his eyes at her touch. He didn't want to open them. There was a lie at the heart of things, he knew that now. You couldn't hide it forever. No matter how you sanded, no matter how you scrubbed. Go into a dark room—with the ultraviolet, the Luminol—and you would see it glowing, a puddle of luminescence where the blood had been.

TWENTY-EIGHT

Across the bay, in Duboce Park, the Cole Valley Mosque was holding a benefit for their bakery. The community was out in their dashikis and cornrows, listening to a man named Pharaoh play his saxophone. It wasn't the real Pharaoh—not the Pharaoh from the old days of jazz, who'd played the clubs along Fillmore—but one of his children, so to speak, a disciple: a man in purple raiment with a quartet behind him, filling the breeze with the sound of electricity and light.

It was a sweet moment and Joe Williams felt its sweetness flutter through him, but at the same time the coldness at the core of his being was untouched. While the music played, Williams worked the edge of the crowd, handing out leaflets to the passersby. He wore gray slacks and a white shirt and was clean-cut-looking and earnest.

He was the kind of man who could smile warmly as he shook your hand while inside he felt nothing at all, or almost nothing; the machinery clicked and spun. His own time in San

Francisco was all but over, he figured. He would do the thing he had come to do and get gone.

All around him the people were grooving: the hipsters and gangsters, together with the crack freaks and kids from the Haight, playing homeboy for the day, and also some gay boys from the Castro.

Sister Hannah flashed him a little wave from the booth where she was selling cookies and all-natural bread. Fakir was working the booth, too, standing next to Hannah. She and Fakir exchanged a laugh, and Williams felt the jealousy sear through him, then vanish in the coldness at his center. The women liked Fakir, with his beard and his righteous demeanor and his talk of the Third Force. Fakir had his share of opportunities. Still, he wasn't the kind of man to lay down with a brother's woman.

A feeling like guilt pricked at his chest, but it did not pierce very deep. Fakir had brought all this on himself, Williams thought. This business about the Third Force, it was delusion. Just like this bakery benefit was delusion. Raise fifteen cents by the end of the day. No, there wasn't any Third Force rising, no Black Kingdom. And if it did rise, it would be crushed soon enough, and the people who'd do the crushing would be your Howard graduates, your up-and-coming niggers. Men from West Point. Women from the Stanford School of Minority Business. People who spent all day scrubbing their faces with pumice and at night fingered themselves dreaming about the white man and his money.

Everyone was a traitor.

After the benefit, Williams walked with Sister Hannah and her two kids up to the apartment. They ate a dinner of grits and ribs and afterward watched the television daughter of Bill

Cosby, whatever her name was; fat and sassy, she had her own show now.

The sweetness fluttered against him once more and he smiled at Hannah, but the smile was just muscles moving, a trick he had learned. Even if he wanted to stay here, he couldn't. He had made a deal.

Fifteen years left on his sentence, now to forever, and another case pending—double homicide—and they'd told him he could walk. A protection program and a new life.

Just a small favor in return.

The first night he had met Hannah, he had made love to her on the couch here in this apartment. He had reached up under the muslin dress and felt her taut brown breasts. It was the kind of behavior the daughters of Islam were supposed to avoid, and the sons, too, but she had that wiggle in her and he wasn't a fool. You didn't get two kids locked up in a chastity belt.

It was a sweet little apartment, with two kids and the dinner smell, and she had the job at the bakery, and he himself was respected on the street, being the right-hand man of Brother Fakir. Maybe he wished for a moment that this could be his life—but that was like wishing he was another person.

"You think it's going to work out?" she asked. "That new location for the bakery. Brother Fakir told me you been talking to some people."

"Yes. That's right," he said. "I have to go out for a while, honey. I'll be back later."

"Where you going?"

He didn't answer.

"And who are these people, they have this space for us?"

"Some Italians. They own a place down at the waterfront."

The idea had come to him, how to get Fakir where he needed him when the mule came in. Mancuso wanted Fakir at the warehouse, and Fakir wanted a location for his bakery. All it took was a little talk, a little imagination, and he could get Fakir where he needed him.

"How do you know any Italians?"

"I know plenty of people. No reason to wonder about that."

He slid his hand underneath her muslin dress.

"The kids are watching." She slapped his hand way, but then gave him a big kiss, sloppy as hell, and brushed up close. "And where are you going?"

"Church business."

There was part of him that wanted nothing to do with what lay ahead. He considered taking off, leaving Frisco. Or just doing nothing. But if he were ungrateful in that manner, the powers-that-be would send him back where he came from. Or worse.

Williams walked downstairs and out into the street. He headed toward Bay View, to a little strip joint on the west side of town. There were a couple of sisters on stage. One of them was swirling a white handkerchief while she stripped. She wore a pair of donkey ears and brayed for the crowd.

It was mostly black men here, sitting in the shadows. Then he saw his man, white like a grub. He sat in a vinyl booth with a woman on either side. Laughing like hell. Across from the white man sat a wide-faced Chinese with a black mustache, like in the movies—an ugly man with cruel eyes—and as Williams slid in beside him, something like regret penetrated the coldness, and he wished for a moment they'd left him in jail. But he was who he was. He had no choice but to play along.

TWENTY-NINE

nita Blonde lay in the silt at the bottom of the bay. It was not the deepest water, but she was well weighted and away from the currents. Her corpse moved imperceptibly with the shifting tide. Over time her skin would slough away, and perhaps the bundle would inch slowly landward, and someone walking upon the industrial shore would discover it, the bones inside, the fragments of lycra and silk, the tarnished ear rings, and the bullet that had killed her. Or maybe the bundle would not move at all and the sediment would slowly cover her remains. Meanwhile, though, the tarp had loosened about her head, and her face was exposed. The bottom feeders and the crabs and the scavenger fish had found her. Her eyes were open. The depths above her were murky but not so deep as to exclude all light—and somewhere overhead a container ship passed and her body shifted and settled again in its wake. A pair of mudfish scuttled in closer, drawn by her scent.

Friday morning, Detective Ying drove across the Bay Bridge on his way to Columbus Station. He looked out over the gray water and thought about the depths below, and he did not know if he would be able to glance at the bay again without thinking of that minute when the light had fractured through the open door and he'd fired his gun and watched the woman crumple.

He drove down the Embarcadero and up Kearny to Columbus Station. For years he had been nothing but on time, but today he walked into the skull session late. Angelo was already at the head of the table, Toliveri was to his right, and a half dozen other detectives were gathered around with their files and unsolved cases.

"Traffic," said Ying.

"Yes," said Angelo. "Traffic."

It was the standard excuse. No one argued with it. No one believed it, either.

"We were just turning to the Mancuso murder. You want to run it down?"

Ying started his rundown then, the lab reports and the forensics, the interviews and—

"We've been through this," Angelo interrupted. "Anything new?"

There was plenty new, if Ying wanted to show them the pictures Strehli had taken seven years ago. If he wanted to explain to the gathered detectives his suspicion—logical or not—that the Mancuso murder was connected to the disappearance of Ru Shen. But he was not in the position to make that case.

"No. Nothing new."

"You've been spending a lot of time out of the office lately. Beating the bushes, I assume."

"Yes," said Ying. "Beating the bushes."

"And . . . ?"

"I haven't found anything."

The room was silent. Ying felt the disdain of the other dicks, but he'd felt that on more than one occasion lately.

Angelo pursed his lips. "All right. Given the evidence, we can't move on Dante Mancuso. Meanwhile, I think we need to expand our search. Throw out a wider net."

"There's always the possibility this was a random thing," said Detective Roma. She was a dark-haired woman with dark eyes. "Regina never locks her door. So maybe someone came in— and what we have is a robbery that went bad."

"How about the son?" asked Angelo. "Did you check his alibi?"

His partner was supposed to take the initiative in this regard, but Ying saw in a glance that Toliveri had little to report. Angelo's eyes ran from one to the other, but they ultimately settled on Ying. He was the one leading the case.

"We're working on it," said Ying. "People are reluctant to talk. But we're going out to the warehouse later today, together. To interview the secretary."

Angelo drummed his fingers.

"How about Salvatore's cronies? His old friends?" said Angelo. "Any ideas?"

"George Marinetti," said Detective Roma. "And Ernesto Mollini. Those two, they've been tight with the Mancuso brothers since they were kids. That's what the wife tells me. And they hang around the Serafina Café."

"Toliveri and I can stop by there," said Ying. "This afternoon, when we get back from the warehouse."

"No," said Angelo. "We need to get the ground covered a

little more quickly. Toli, I want you to go talk to the secretary at the warehouse. Get her alone. On her lunch hour. And Ying, you talk to Marinetti and Mollini. Then check back with me, let me know what you've got."

Ying had heard the criticism implicit in Angelo's voice, the suggestion he was not on the ball. He felt the others watching him, wondering if he'd lost it. If all of a sudden he just wasn't any good anymore. It happened, Ying knew. He'd seen it himself.

"All right," said Ying. "I'll see what I can dig up."

The Serafina Café was not the kind of place Ying sought out on his own. It sat in the shadow of the Sam Wong Hotel, off Broadway. It had been there for some thirty years, if not longer, back when the street had been Italian, before Chinatown overgrew its borders. It had a linoleum counter and a tin ceiling and tables with red and white checkered cloths that were not as clean as maybe they had once been. The front window was smudged, and the woman who owned the restaurant, Stella, was known in the neighborhood for berating her Chinese busboys.

Inside, the place was dark. The proprietress stood behind the counter. Stella was a fiery woman, wearing a flower-print dress that was open at the collar. She stood with her hands on her waist and her breasts pushed forward. She was maybe seventy years old.

"I am looking for George Marinetti," said Ying. "And Ernesto Mollini."

Stella said nothing. She pointed at the table in the back, where the two old men sat with cigars burning and a bottle of grappa between them. Ying walked over.

"Mr. Marinetti?"

"Yes."

Marinetti had big eyes that seemed even bigger because of his glasses. He wore a mustache waxed up in a barbershop fashion that had been out of style since the Depression, if not longer, and it was apparent he could not see well despite the glasses. He was extremely friendly, though, and spoke with a certain flair.

"Yes, yes, how can we help you?"

"If you and Mr. Mollini have a few minutes?"

"Certainly," said Marinetti. "Old men like us, we are flattered when anyone comes to talk to us. We have no dignity."

"No teeth, either," said Mollini.

"No. No teeth. No money. But we have time."

"I appreciate it," said Ying, and showed them his badge. "I'd like to speak to you about Salvatore Mancuso."

A palpable melancholy passed over the men.

"You have a drink?"

"No. No, thank you."

"Please. Have some grappa?"

"No."

"No? What part of Italy you from, you don't want any grappa?"

For a second Ying thought maybe Marinetti was even more blind than he thought, then Ernesto let out a guffaw, and Ying realized it was the old rigmarole, a joke at the Chinaman's expense. Marinetti did not seem to mean anything by it, but then they never did.

"You ever visit Salvatore up at his house?"

"On occasion," said Marinetti. "We would have a glass of wine."

"You know his office upstairs?"

"The room where he was killed?"

"Did he keep anything valuable up there that you know about?"

"You think it was a thief who killed him?"

"Money? Jewelry?"

The men shook their heads.

"Did he have any enemies?"

"What do you mean?"

"Business deals, people he owed?"

"He didn't owe anyone."

"Or owed him?"

"He was a respectable man. You going to ask about his love life next?"

"Was there a love life?"

The old man laughed. They snickered and choked a little on their cigars.

"You get our age, you see how funny this is."

"Speak for yourself," said Mollini.

"His brother," said Ying. "Before his brother Giovanni died, there were rumors he thought someone was trying to kill him."

"What rumors?"

"I never hear these rumors."

"Did Giovanni have any enemies?" asked Ying.

"No, no. Everyone loved him. Both of them, the Mancuso brothers. Salvatore and Giovanni."

"Were there any money issues?"

"You already asked that."

"In the Mancuso family—the business. Did he ever talk about how it was doing?"

"The brothers were extremely successful. Especially Salvatore. He knew how to run a business."

Stella approached the table. She had some spaghetti for the men, and put it down with a flourish but did not bother to glance at Ying. Even so, she was not shy about inserting herself in the conversation.

"How can anyone make any money at the docks these days? All the container ships off-load in Oakland," she said, "and the storage warehouses on the waterfront, who needs them?"

"That's not completely so," said Mollini.

"Of course it's so," she said. "You know there's only one way the Mancusos have survived so long."

"Stella," said George. "This isn't the time for that."

"Time for what?" asked Ying.

"No one wants the truth," said Stella, but she still did not look Ying's way. "We had a waterfront once. We had Little Italy. Then they put that son of a bitch Rossi as mayor. Everybody talks like he's a hero now. But him and his friends, the Chinese, the Hong Kongs, the goddamn Sicilians—they made their deals. And you see. You see what you get . . ."

She made a sweeping gesture that included not just Ying but all of Chinatown. Ying had heard this line of thinking before, of course—how Rossi had sold the place out to Hong Kong—but he didn't know what it had to do with the case at hand. Stella threw her hand up in disgust.

"And that boy, Gary Mancuso, he lives like a prince on top of the hill. Everyone else is gone from the waterfront, but not the Mancusos. Tell me how they make all that money out there? You think that warehouse is full of soccer balls? Hah! This was an honest place once, not full of crooks. Secret deals. The Chinese. This, that."

Marinetti shrugged his shoulders and Ernesto shrugged, too, both of them embarrassed, maybe, knowing there was no way to stop Stella once she got going.

"Goddamn Chinese own the police. They own it all. And the only reason they send this one here," she said, pointing at Ying, "is for window dressing. For show. They are not going to catch Salvatore's murderer. This is a dirty business."

There was a clattering in the kitchen, dishes falling to the floor. Stella scurried away, furious. You could hear her scolding the busboy—yelling in Italian though the busboy was Cantonese and didn't understand a lick.

"Salvatore Mancuso was the salt of the earth," said George. "Him and his brother both."

"Yes," said Ernesto.

"I don't know why such an awful thing would happen." Marinetti nodded toward the noise in the kitchen. "The old lady—she is a little crazy."

"Pay no attention."

They started in on their spaghetti. Ying wasn't going to get anything more from them, he knew that. It was all platitudes now. They didn't bother to look up when he left. They were too busy with their noodles and their sauce.

It was possible to reconstruct facial features from the photograph of a decayed corpse, but Ying did not have the equipment or the computer skills. In a sense, he had misrepresented himself to Dante on this issue, intending to get help from an old friend at SI on the photo analysis—but that did not seem wise now. Instead, he did it the hard way. He pulled some file photos of Ru Shen, then went to the Chinatown library where he could examine them unencumbered. While he was there, he pulled some magazine profiles as well.

Ru Shen was a complicated figure, a businessman, Shanghai-born. He had been raised a Buddhist but converted to Christianity. Married an American woman but insisted his children speak Chinese. He dined with the mayor, contributed to downtown development, but objected on spiritual grounds to the materialism of the local Chinese Chamber of Commerce. Ru Shen had made his money as a go-between, helping entrepreneurs in China outfit their factories for U.S. companies—but at some point Ru Shen's religious convictions had prompted him to speak out against the smuggling and kickbacks that permeating the business.

Now Ying studied the photos of Ru Shen and his family alongside Strehli's photos from the container, and he saw the superficial resemblances, particularly in the face of the dead wife, in the size and stature of the children, and in the way Ru Shen's hair was parted, even in death—and though in the end such observations were not definitive, his suspicions were enhanced.

When Ying returned to his office, there was a message from Angelo. The Homicide chief wanted to see him. Angelo was usually pretty hands-off: He had advanced up the ranks in part by knowing how to stay out of the way. Even so, he was taking an interest in this one. The case was all over the newspapers, and it was his old turf after all.

"There's been a break in the case," Angelo said. "Toliveri

met with Gary Mancuso's secretary. And she fell apart on him."

"He cracked the alibi?"

"Partly. It seems Gary wasn't in the warehouse the afternoon of the murder, after all. And he'd been arguing with his father the day before."

"So where was he?"

"An affair, that's what the secretary says. A friend of hers. He lied to us because he was with the other woman. And he didn't want his wife to find out."

"What does the other woman say?"

"We're bringing her in. Her and Gary both. We're going to question them here."

"This afternoon?"

"Detective Roma's with the affair right now. Out at her apartment. Roma's giving her a preliminary, and then she's going to bring her in. Go over it all here while lover boy's in the next room. Compare their stories."

"So you have Gary now?"

Angelo shook his head. "He wasn't at the warehouse. Meeting with his estate lawyer apparently, him and his family. But he's going to be back at the warehouse around three. Toliveri will nab Gary then. And we'll interrogate him here."

"All right," said Ying. "I'll be ready."

Angelo's face had a certain slackness in it all of a sudden, and Ying had a hunch what was coming. "That's another thing."

"What?"

"The way this case is developing, I think it's best for Toliveri and Roma to do the interrogation. We want a woman in the interview room. And Toliveri, he knows these people."

Ying understood the rationale. He'd been brought into cases

in this capacity himself when the suspects were Chinese. Also, he'd had his shot at Mancuso, softening him up, and it was the kind of thing you did sometimes, alternating interrogators until the subject gave forth. He understood, but he didn't like it.

"You're still in charge of the case," Angelo said. "Just drop back. Let Roma and Toliveri do this interrogation."

Angelo left then, and Ying looked out the window. He could see Chinatown from here, the streets where he had walked as a kid, the balustraded pagodas and the crowds coursing their way up Stockton. His world was slipping through his fingers, he thought, everything was getting away. Then his cell rang. It was Grudgeon at UC. He had the ballistics report.

"Negative," he said.

"There's no match?"

"No."

Grudgeon wanted to talk longer—to know what this was all about—but Ying got off the phone. So Blonde's ballistics didn't match, and now Toliveri was bringing in Gary Mancuso. Well, it made things easier, anyway. If he could let it go. If he could drop into the background and let the case run its course. But he kept thinking about Ru Shen. He was all but convinced Ru Shen was the man in Strehli's photographs, but the only way to prove it was to exhume the bodies and perform a DNA analysis. He already knew this wasn't possible from his investigations the year before. He'd been down to the Immigration Authority. According to a man down there, the bodies had been picked up by a local benevolent society, then cremated at the Chinese Cemetery down in Millbrae.

THIRTY

Wiesinski sat in Molly's, an old-timey bar off Union Square. Shamrocks on the wall and the bartender dressed in green. Wiesinski sat in the back where it was dark and he could watch the clientele come and go. After a while the informer strolled in. She was maybe twenty-five years old and wore a blue dress with white polka dots and comported herself with an arrogance that was hard to resist. She wore a string of white pearls and carried a white handbag. And there was a white flower in her hair. A chrysanthemum.

It's an ugly world, Wiesinski thought.

You might look at a woman like her and think otherwise, but the truth was she would betray anyone for a dollar. At the same time she had the kind of looks that made you not care. That made you think, *Go ahead, betray me. Just let me put my hand up your polka-dot dress.*

An ugly, ugly world.

She worked in the Wu Benevolent Society, he knew. A thoughtless job that involved booking passengers to the Far East.

True, it required a certain discretion, considering the nature of some of that travel, but she was paid for that discretion. Trouble was, Miss Lin was an ambitious girl. A little bit greedy. Her employer did not trust her anymore.

So now she was his problem. You would think a metropolis this size could get along without his intervention. That the world could run itself. But it just wasn't so.

Wiesinski studied Miss Lin. She glanced around, looking for her rendezvous. *Looking for me,* he thought. But he let her sit. Let her fidget. She lit a cigarette and ordered herself a drink and when she had finished them both he walked up and said hello.

"I like the chrysanthemum."

"Pardon?"

"I think you understand."

"I am not sure I do."

"I have a place for us back here. Where we can talk."

"Shouldn't we go somewhere more private?"

Wiesinski could not count the number of times he had heard this. But he liked to work out in the open. In a restaurant booth, drink in hand, people said things they didn't say in private. The tongue slipped. Because you felt safe, maybe, in the public space. The bar pretzels, the ashtray, the cocktail glass—these were old friends.

"What is it that you would like to talk to me about?"

"I was told you might be interested in some knowledge I have. That I know something you might want to know."

There were the intricacies only a man like him understood. You worked vice, you knew everyone on every side of the line. People got confused as to your loyalties, but they shouldn't.

Because ultimately you had the same number-one priority as
everyone else.

"And what knowledge is that?"

"A policeman got in touch with me the other day. He asked
me if I would get him some information."

"The policeman got in touch with you?"

"Yes."

"Are you sure that's the way it went? What would cause him
to do such a thing—to choose you?"

"He knows where I work. You know how it is. The police
are everywhere."

The woman batted her eyes. Her smile was coy, very demure.
He felt his dick rise in his pants and he knew she was lying. It
was a sure sign. She had called the cop, he figured, thinking to
sell him something. Then she had changed her mind, figuring
she could do better by turning against him. Despite her coolness, though, he sensed her fear and his dick got harder.

"I told my employer about the policeman. And they said I
should come to you. That you would be interested."

"What was the name of this policeman?"

"Detective Ying."

"Ying?" he repeated.

"Yes."

"And he contacted you?"

"Yes."

"Looking for information?"

"Yes."

"About what?"

"Ru Shen."

Wiesinski contemplated. He knew the avenue Ying's investigation with SI had taken. He knew people at SI, just like he knew people everywhere. And he remembered Ru Shen. A self-righteous man in a business suit who had decided the world should be a sweeter place. Then Ru Shen had vanished, surprise, surprise. Now Ying was back on that trail again. Intelligent but not wise. Dante's influence, no doubt. No wonder Love Wu was worried.

"What else did Ying say?"

"Nothing, just that he wanted to meet me."

"I see."

"What should I do?"

"Go meet him."

"He'll ask me questions. What do I say?"

Wiesinski grinned. "Tell him everything you know."

"I don't know anything."

"Then tell him that."

"He won't give me any money for that."

She smiled then, and Wiesinski understood what she wanted.

"Meet with the man," he said, though in fact he now had something else in mind for her, a different future. But it was best to humor her. Let her feel useful. "See what he wants to know. Try to figure out where he's headed."

"But—he'll want something concrete. Some kind of information."

"I leave that to you. Be inventive. Then come to me—you will be rewarded for your work."

"Nothing in advance?"

He reached under the table and put a hand on her thigh. "Trust me," he said.

She gave him that demure smile and gathered up her purse.

She was haughty but beneath that haughtiness he knew she was afraid. If life was fair, he would come in his pants now, while his hand was still on her thigh, before she slid out of the booth. But life wasn't fair.

It was a hideous business.

He was sorry for the girl. Sorry for himself. The tears welled. Crocodile tears, sure, but tears nonetheless. The burdens were tremendous. So much to mastermind. You could get all twisted up thinking about it. But either way, you had to keep busy. The fucking devil, his work was never done. The girl, handling her would be no problem. Ying, though, and Dante, they would require a little more finesse.

THIRTY-ONE

L ake Bracciano," said Tony Mora. "There's an the old vil-
lage there. From the time of the Renaissance."

Marilyn knew the story surrounding the castle. Paul
Orsini, the duke of Bracciano, had strangled his wife, Isabella de
Medici, throttling her at the dinner table for her infidelity. Shortly
thereafter he'd brought his mistress to live at the castle, and she
was murdered, too.

Nowadays, Bracciano was a popular retreat for newlyweds,
and this was why Tony had brought it up. They were out to
lunch, in a little restaurant in the Marina.

"We should schedule a date," said Tony. "They book out in
advance."

Marilyn knew what she was supposed to do. Lean across the
table. Take his hands between her own.

"Our wedding doesn't have to be a big production," he said.
"But the honeymoon—we could stay in Italy for a while if you
like. Take some time for ourselves."

Tony's eyes were hard and bright. He was a good-looking

man, she had to admit. Unlike other men his age, he hadn't let his body give way. His face was tan, his eyes clear—and there was that lock of black hair that curled and fell over his forehead in a way that was hard to resist. He smiled when he looked at you—as if aware of his looks, his charm. And this bit of self-awareness, too, was hard to resist.

"You want to do this?"

She smiled. The truth was she had been out with Dante the day before and was supposed to meet him on Saturday. The irony was Tony himself would be meeting with Dante later this afternoon. And Gary and Regina Mancuso as well. To discuss the disposition of the Mancuso estate.

"You and me?" Mora smiled. "Off to see the world?"

"Yes," she said. "You and me."

Part of Mora's obsession had to do with her reluctance, she knew. He was drawn to the surface of things. Put on a sheer skirt, a silk blouse, a colorful scarf, and he wanted to make love to you. He wanted to crush you to the wall and touch your expensive clothes.

Marilyn had told him that her family money was all but gone, but she wasn't sure he believed her.

"And there is always the Riviera," he said.

She laughed. She wasn't sure why, exactly—but when she saw a look of self-doubt cross Tony's face, it gave her a fleeting pleasure.

"You're lovely," he said.

His eyes went all smarmy and she could see the boy in him. The boy who worked so hard at being liked. Who hung around the old Italians because he wanted their money, sure, but just as much he wanted a pat on the head. His father had been an estate lawyer, too, and it was his father who had made the connection with Romano's firm, getting him the job in North Beach.

Tony glanced at his watch. "I have to go," he said. "I'm off to see the Mancusos."

Outside the restaurant, they kissed and separated. Marilyn was filled with a sense of loss. Glancing back at Tony, she suspected he had his own intuitions. He had to know this would not last. But as Tony turned the corner, he felt as confident as a man could feel. Swaggering. Glancing sidelong at a passing woman in a print skirt. Catching an eye back, then driving off in his red Alfa, telling himself he had Marilyn by the tits. He had seen her eyes water. And there was a part of him that longed for every woman he saw: the blonde on the corner, the Asian girl back at the office, the anchorwoman on TV, all of them. He ached with desire. He wanted to stick his dick up every ass he saw. He just couldn't help himself. He wanted to fuck the goddamn world.

The legal offices of Romano, DeLillo & Mora were in the Alioto Building, in a little valley below Columbus, on a corner where the streets furcated up from the seawall, then angled back toward the financial district, into Chinatown and the remains of Little Italy. The TransAmerica Pyramid stood across the way—so close you had to crane your head backward to see its crux overhead. The bit of sky over the building's peak was always white, overly pale, as if its presence somehow drained the color from the firmament.

Dante sat in Mora's office alongside Aunt Regina and his cousin Gary. Alice was there, too, his cousin's wife. Alice had short, peach-colored hair and a face full of freckles that made her seem younger and more amiable than she really was.

"We are fortunate," Mora said, "in that Salvatore and Giovanni kept no secrets. My understanding is that you all know pretty much the contents of their testaments—at least as to the disposition of property. But there is an interrelatedness between the estates, as you know. Due to the family business. Some inevitable overlap—which leaves you with some options. Some decisions to make."

"I hear you're on your way to Italy," said Alice suddenly. Gary's wife had a gift for inappropriate remarks, and she seemed to take pleasure in exercising the gift. Her cheeks were wide and her smile cherubic.

"Word gets around." If Mora was nonplussed, he did not show it.

"The Riviera?" asked Alice.

"What's this about?" asked Gary.

"His honeymoon," said Alice, cutting her eyes at Dante, so he understood at a glance that she knew the story of the Mancuso cousins and Marilyn Visconti, and how she had jilted them each in turn. "Tony and Marilyn are making plans."

"Have you set a date for the wedding?" asked Aunt Regina.

"Not yet," said Mora. "But who knows—we may take the honeymoon and skip the formalities."

This got some laughter, and Gary's face went crimson. The business with Marilyn was an old wound, but Alice had opened it.

"Well, congratulations." Her voice lilted and her eyes glinted, but in her posture was a certain meanness. "I know that Marilyn's a hard girl to tie down."

"Thank you." Mora turned his attention to the testaments in

front of him. "I'm going to go through the various codicils, and I'll explain as I go."

The essence of it was this: Dante's father had left everything to him, both the house—which was paid for—and Giovanni's share of the family business. Uncle Salvatore's estate was a bit more elaborate. He had set up a trust for Aunt Regina and another trust for the education of their grandchildren, and he'd given the business to his son. In the will, Uncle Salvatore also forgave the numerous personal loans he had made Gary over the years.

"The question the wills leave open, and deliberately so, is how you want to deal with the family business." Mora addressed Dante now. "As to whether you want to go on as your father had—as a silent partner. Or if you want to become more active—since that's specified as an option. You may become a full working partner."

If Alice and Gary had been at odds before, they were not now. Alice sat up a little more pertly in her chair, and Gary slouched, but it was clear neither of them cared for this prospect. Neither did Dante.

"How about if I simply sell out?" he asked.

"That's an option. You could try to agree on a price. Or you could find an outside buyer—and Gary here would have the option of meeting whatever offer you secured. But that might not be advisable in the current environment."

"I don't understand."

"The way your uncle and father originally envisioned this, if one of you wanted to sell out, the other could take the equity from the building and use it to pay the departing partner. But that equity—"

"We've been running a loss," said Gary.

"What do you mean?"

"I mean we lost all the deepwater shipping years ago— and we borrowed against the property to keep the business going."

Dante thought of Gary's house up on Telegraph, with its marble and its views and its Italian furniture.

"Did my father know about this?"

"He signed the papers."

"So what does this mean?"

"It means there's not much equity. If you want to sell, I can't pay you off. The business will leave the family."

"Why bother to hold on if it's losing money?"

"It's the family business," said Gary. "What else do I know?"

There was something wrong. The business was losing money, but Gary was awash in luxury. The money was coming from some other source. He wondered how long this had been so. And he wondered if his uncle had known, and his father.

Mora interrupted. "There's no reason to decide now," he said. "In fact, this might be the worst time to decide. Given the emotions of the last two weeks."

"Yes," said Aunt Regina.

Mora led them into the lobby. The lawyer took Aunt Regina by the hand, helping her along, and it was apparent to Dante that the old woman enjoyed Mora's attention. She gestured across the lobby toward the old Montgomery Block, where the Pyramid now stood. "Little shops and men in suspenders. They swarmed the streets back then. All those men in suspenders. I remember meeting Salvatore and Giovanni down here for lunch." She laughed, and in the laugh Dante could hear the grief. "They were wearing suspenders, too."

Mora laughed, also, and Dante could not take it anymore. The man was unctuous. He went outside to wave down a taxi.

Alice joined him on the street. They exchanged watery smiles.

"I wonder if Mora knows. He must, of course. How could you marry someone without telling him?"

"I don't understand," he said.

"Marilyn can't have children, you know."

He looked at her then. "I wasn't aware."

"It was the abortion."

"The abortion?"

"Marilyn didn't tell Gary. She didn't tell anyone. She just went off and did it. Whose child was it, that's my question. Gary doesn't like it when I say that, but . . ." Alice glanced about deviously, but did not meet his eyes. "That's what happens. God punishes. He takes away the gifts he gives."

Regina emerged now, flanked by Mora and her son.

"Oh, isn't he a doll," Alice said. "No wonder the women love him."

Whether she was talking about Mora or her husband, he could not be sure. Her voice was full of vitriol.

Dante helped them into the taxi, then went across town on his own errand. He had business coming up any day now, and he still had not replaced the gun the police had confiscated. So he went to a gun shop known in the old days for its willingness to deal beneath the counter. The place had not changed. He bought himself a .40 caliber Glock to replace the one the police had taken, and a small-bore Smith & Wesson for good measure.

Toliveri picked up Gary Mancuso down at the warehouse. At the station, the grilling went on for quite some time. Throughout most of it, Ying hung in the background. He knew the plan: Separate the lovers. Press the notion that Gary Mancuso had killed his father in a moment of rage. Because there were business problems at the warehouse. Because his father had found out about the affair.

But it did not take long to see the plan was not going to bear fruit. Gary and his girlfriend had their stories in sync. More importantly, they had corroboration.

It came from the woman's landlady. She had helped Roma locate the girlfriend's apartment, then volunteered her own testimony as well. Made a trip to the station, not because she liked the young woman, no. Quite the opposite. She had seen her tenant and Gary together many times, making out in the car, on the apartment steps, in the hallway, brazen as could be. The landlady suspected the man was married, and she didn't approve. What's more, her own apartment was right next door; the walls were thin, and she had been forced to listen to them one too many times, all that obscene moaning and thumping at odd hours of the day. And they had been there that day, too, she remembered quite distinctly. The afternoon Salvatore Mancuso was killed. She'd seen them out front and heard them in the apartment, noisy as dogs. She was quite certain because she remembered the news of the murder the next day on TV, and if you didn't believe her memory you could ask her husband. He was as bothered about it as she was, the way the two of them carried on.

At the end Toliveri held his head in his hands—as if he knew he would never make grade before he retired.

Whatever satisfaction Ying felt, it was short-lived. He left the interrogation area and put in a call to Dante. Then he turned off his cell and went out for a walk. He was thinking of Ru Shen, and of the Wus, and of the fact that he was scheduled to meet with Miss Lin tonight, and of the danger in that meeting. But more than that, he was thinking of Anita Blonde. The ballistics had not matched, and he remembered the sound she had made as she lay dying.

THIRTY-TWO

It was just before twilight now, on the other side of the bay, and Ying's wife was leaving the tennis court at El Cerrito. Lei had taken an evening game, a doubles match, and her partner had been Richard Hooper—a man whose wife had died of ovarian cancer a few years back. He was a sweet man whom she suspected had a crush on her, but Lei knew he would never say so. Richard Hooper had a degree of dignity, of self-restraint. He had also met Frank and the kids a time or two here at the club, and the two men seemed to like one another.

Lei got out the cell and called her husband at Columbus Station.

It was warm in the car, pleasantly so. She felt good from the exertion and Richard Hooper had been a good partner.

No answer.

Tied up with the Mancuso investigation. *Better than SI,* she thought, *but he had grown more remote these last few days.*

Richard came out of the club now, emerging from beneath the redwood trellis. He gave her a shy wave and walked to his

Lexus. She watched him and felt the dampness in her blouse and the sweat between her thighs.

She turned the ignition and drove home.

The kids had eaten a pizza dinner at a neighbor's house and would not be back until eight. The house was dark and empty, and for an instant she was gripped by a cold feeling that got hold of her on occasion, a feeling that gripped every cop's wife at some time or the other.

He was going to die.

She shook the feeling off. She put away her racket and took a shower. Inside the shower she wondered what it would be like if Frank died, how she and the kids would get by. She thought of Richard Hooper alone in his house, and let her thoughts drift into a forbidden area. Then she toweled herself off and changed her clothes. When the kids returned, she was clean and composed.

She tried the phone again. Ying still did not answer.

THIRTY-THREE

Ying and Dante were sitting alone in the upstairs room in Winter Alley, where Anita Blonde had died. Downstairs, the old woman was chanting.

It was Friday evening. Outside, an orange moon hung in the sky.

A little while before, Ying had ordered Chinese from some place on Kearny, and a little man with a high collar had delivered it. Now Ying spread out the food. Egg rolls and duck's feet. Broccoli florets. A chicken's bill.

"Why did you ask me here?"

"Eat," Ying said.

"I'm not hungry."

"You're offending me."

Ying pushed a foot at him. It was hard and rubbery. Dante was revolted but he ate it anyway.

"Good?"

"No," said Dante.

Ying shrugged.

"I got Blonde's gun," he said. "And a bullet from your uncle's murder. I sent them down to ballistics."

"Was that wise?"

"I have a friend. Off the force. He did the comparison."

"And?"

"Anita Blonde didn't kill your uncle. Or if she did, she didn't use the same gun she had with her here the other night."

"No?"

"The ballistics don't match."

Dante was not surprised. Anita Blonde was a sneak thief, someone who milled around the edges. She was duplicitous, but he didn't see her as an assassin. Capable of killing, certainly, in the right circumstances—but it wouldn't be her central modus.

"This place was searched once before. When I was with SI."

"What could she have been looking for?"

"The photos," Ying said. "We were in contact, you and I, and maybe they suspected you had passed them along. Also, I visited with your father. Maybe they thought he passed me something. Given my history with SI."

"Did you get an identification on the family in the photos?"

Ying registered the question but did not answer, preoccupied with his own line of thinking. "Or maybe she was looking for something else."

"What could that be?" Dante asked.

"Something we don't have. Or something you're not telling me about."

Ying picked up another webbed foot and offered it to Dante with a certain sadness. When Dante didn't accept, Ying began to eat it himself.

"I killed her for nothing," he said.

"She had her gun out," said Dante.

"It didn't have to happen."

"She made a mistake. It's not your fault."

Despite himself, Dante felt a great indifference. He didn't know if it came from within, or if it was just the recognition of a greater indifference that existed outside himself, an indifference as vast as the night. Blonde was dead. The machinations of the company were part deliberate, part happenstance, and she had gotten caught. Just as he himself would be caught someday.

"Why did you call me here?"

"You want help finding your father's murderer. And me . . ." Ying hesitated. "I want to know who your master is."

"I don't understand."

"Central Intelligence. FBI. ATF. Or is it the Wus?"

"There's times I don't know myself."

"That's not an answer."

"I'm with the good guys. Or that's what I used to think. But there's overlap—and I don't always know where the overlap is. It's the nature of the work."

He knew that Ying wanted a different kind of answer. But there'd been a change in the man since he'd killed Blonde. Maybe it had been there before, underneath the surface—the sense that good and evil were intertwined, that you couldn't take an action without unexpected consequences—but Ying'd kept the idea away from himself. That wasn't possible anymore.

"How's the official investigation going?" Dante asked. "Into my uncle's death."

"Your cousin's changed his story. Toliveri brought him in

today, and his alibi—it seems he wasn't telling the truth."

"He wasn't at the warehouse."

"No."

"Then where?"

"He's having an affair—a woman over in Point Richmond. It seems he was with her, and he didn't want to tell us in front of his mother. Obviously doesn't want the wife to know."

"Did it verify?"

"He's having an affair. That part seems true. As to whether he was with her that afternoon or she's covering for him, we're still looking into it. But it seems their story will check out."

Dante went for the rice. Downstairs, the old woman's chanting had grown a little louder. It was a guttural noise with a vibration at the center of it. He'd heard similar chants in Thailand. In the streets, sometimes, from a beggar lost in meditation. At night, lying in a dragon dream, in the opium house. His last morning in Bangkok, as he'd walked away from the girl on the blood-soaked bed.

"Who do you work for, really?" Ying asked again. "What organization?"

Once again, Dante refrained from answering. "Did you get anything from the photos?"

"Myself, I was with SI for three years," said Ying. "And I earned a lot of enemies. People in the community. Old chums. They called me a lackey. They said I was working for the ghosts."

Dante knew the term. It went back to the old days. The ghosts were white people. Malignant spirits who moved vaporously through the world, but they could not hurt you if you did not acknowledge them. Twenty years ago, when he was a boy, it had seemed silly to him—the Italians so vibrant and full of life. Later he had understood; one night, moving through Chinatown on his own, surrounded by Chinese, the people on the street, they looked right through him. He did not exist. And now, with the Italian neighborhood all but gone, reduced to memory, and that, too, fading . . .

"I was tracking the Wus," said Ying. "So many rumors, so many interconnections. Textiles. The gun trade. Hong Kong companies with links to the mainland. Spies working both sides—and when you got close, when you saw the fabric, you'd be shifted to a new case. Those deaths in the container . . ."

Dante took a sip of the tea. He pushed the rice aside. In it were bits of flesh with a taste he did not recognize. Snake, maybe. Some kind of bird. And at the bottom, a soupy bit of flesh that seemed to have the fur still attached.

"You know the rumors about your family's warehouse," Ying was rambling. His eyes had a glazed look. "Your cousin's money, it's from the smugglers. For turning his head. If it's true, maybe that's what he's hiding, aside from the affair. If your uncle objected, if Gary got himself in a corner . . ."

"I don't think so," said Dante.

"I got forced off SI. They scrawled threats on my wife's car. I'd been looking into the Wus for a while. I'd also been looking into the disappearance of Ru Shen. . . . It was his family in the containers, I'm all but sure."

"Who is he?"

"Who are you?"

Dante regarded Ying. The detective was a good man. It was a mistake to have dragged him into this.

"Go home to your family," said Dante.

"It's too late for that."

"Go home."

Downstairs, the old woman was still chanting. She sat in the front room, on the rattan couch; her back was straight and her hands rested lightly on her lap. She didn't turn her head when Dante entered the room but went on chanting. The sound was too deep and persistent to be coming from the old woman, and indeed her lips seemed to be barely moving. Dante walked in front of her. Her eyes were open, but she did not notice him as he passed through the room and out into the night. Or if she did notice him she gave no sign. She did not blink an eye.

On the staircase wall on Fresno Street, there were pictures of Dante's family going back to the early days: the ancestors in their work blouses and suspenders, their fedoras, their dress coats, and high collars. And there was a daguerreotype from before the end of the nineteenth century, men standing by the old wharf, fishermen and merchants with waxed mustaches similar to old man Marinetti's. What drew his attention, though, were two men on the far right. One of these men had been identified to him as his great-grandfather—a thick-shouldered man who stood with his arms folded. Beside him was a Chinese man dressed incongruously in the European fashion, with a waistcoat and a bowler, but with his pigtails intact. It was a candid shot, relatively speaking, and in the background, moored behind the feluccas, you could see the masts of several Chinese junks. Though the details were fuzzy, it was apparent the junks were in the process of being offloaded, their goods carried to shore.

As a child, he'd wondered more than once about the relationship between his great-grandfather and the Chinese man in the picture. And he'd wondered, too, what was in those boxes the men carried back to shore. It wasn't something you could ever know, it was too far in the past, but Dante could not escape the feeling that events were repeating themselves.

Seven years ago he'd fallen in love with Marilyn. Then Strehli was murdered. Now he was back and three more people were dead.

To keep the ghosts in place, you prayed, you counted the beads, you poured water in the old stump, and you mashed the grapes with your feet in the basement. He was supposed to meet Marilyn tomorrow morning; they would go sailing on the bay. He wondered if he would ask her about the story Gary's wife had told him.

My child?

He lay down on his father's bed. He listened to the house settle and creak; there was a sound like footsteps on the stairs. The hasp on the basement window was still broken, he remembered.

The phone rang. He caught it on the third ring, before the message machine kicked in. It was Joe Williams.

"It's in."

"What's in?" Dante asked, though he knew well enough.

There was a pause on the line.

"Fakir will be there?"

"Both of us," Williams said. "Ten o'clock. Tomorrow morning."

Afterward, Dante called Mason Wu. Then he dialed the number Blonde had given him: the company's man at the DEA, who had been putting things together behind the scenes.

The agent, David Serles, answered on the first ring, and Dante gave him the details.

"I need to meet with you beforehand," said Serles. "Tomorrow morning at seven thirty. We have a plan in place."

Once again, it all seemed too easy. The way Serles picked up right away, as if he'd been waiting for the call. Known it was coming. The truth was, they should have met well in advance. Discussed details of the warehouse layout. The physical barriers. The best places to put a squad. Instead, the company had insisted they work separately.

Then Dante remembered something else. Tomorrow was Saturday, and the warehouse crew would be off. His cousin Gary, though—like his father and Dante's father as well—had a habit of coming down to the office Saturday mornings to catch up on the paperwork. At least it had been his habit in the old days. Either way, he could not take the risk that Gary would show up tomorrow. Things could get out of hand, and he did not want his cousin on the scene.

THIRTY-FOUR

Ying lingered in the room where Anita Blonde had died. His grandmother had gone into a silent meditation, and Ying took comfort in the silence. The little house on Winter Alley had seen a lot of family history over the years. His grandmother had a shrine to the ancestors in her bedroom, and he could feel their presence in the house, a stillness like the stillness of a pond on a winter night. Anita Blonde was there as well, at the center of their silence, dying on the bedroom floor.

He checked his cell and saw that he had missed two calls, both from his wife. He called her now, and as he spoke he imagined the sound of his voice vibrating the air, traveling along the old pine floorboards to the place where the old woman kneeled. Inside the old walls, the pipes let out a small moan.

Everything vibrated with everything else. A butterfly flapped its wings in Qingdao and the trade winds shifted.

"Where are you?" Lei asked. She had a rose petal voice laced with suspicion.

"I'm with Grandmother Ying," he said. "But I have an appointment."

"This late?"

"The Mancuso case—there's a big push on to get it solved."

It was partly true, but he could not help feeling as if he were lying. Because his appointment was with his informer in a lounge down in South City. The one time he had met her before, his heart had raced with illicit feelings, made more intense by the danger, by the feeling that he was about to penetrate the mystery of the Wus, and by the knowledge that informers often played both sides and he was placing himself at risk.

"The kids missed you this morning, you were gone so early."

"I know," he said. "I miss them. I miss you."

There was a pause in which he noticed again the silence of his grandmother's house.

"All right," she said.

"Did you play today?"

"Yes."

"How did you do?"

"Very well. It was a close match."

"Was it doubles?"

"Yes."

"Who was your partner?"

"Richard Hooper."

He was jealous. Inappropriately so, perhaps. Richard Hooper was a nice man, still suffering over the death of his wife. He could not say anything without looking foolish. *But it should be me up at the club with my wife,* Ying thought. *It should be the two of us driving volleys across the net, our bodies taut, reaching, straining one toward the other.*

"All right," she said. "I'll be in bed when you get here."

"I won't wake you up."

Downstairs, his grandmother sat all but motionless. Her eyes were open, glimmering in the half dark. Her skin was dark and leathery. If you looked closely, you could see her chest move, the slow in-and-out. Ying pressed his cheek against hers and felt a vague shudder pass through her body and then his own. In this trance, her body temperature had dropped. He kissed her. Then he got in his car and headed south on 101, toward the New Asia Restaurant and Lounge.

The place had been built back in the sixties. There was a domed ceiling inside and a hanging glass ball. Onstage a Thai woman sang a pop song of indeterminate origin to a crowd that was more interested in their drinks and their chatter. It was a mixed group, Asian locals and airport businessmen. An illicit couple went after one another in one of the booths nearby.

The informer was not here.

He had a drink, even though he was not much of a drinker. The drink came with a little parasol. Then he had another drink and ordered some appetizers.

He studied the crowd around him, careful of the fact that this could be a trap. No one seemed to pay him any mind. On the way to the door, a big man in an oversized business suit stopped at his booth. He had a bulbous nose and warm eyes and a disarming smile. He peered at Ying intently.

"Can you tell me the time? My watch—it seems to have stopped." The man showed his watch, and it indeed appeared to have stopped.

"Eleven thirty."

"Thank you."

The appetizers came. Ordinarily Ying was a man of moderation who seldom drank. He watched his diet and exercised every other day. He had a measured routine. These last few days, though, since Anita Blonde's death, things had been different. He finished his appetizers greedily and ordered another drink.

An hour went by, and still the woman did not show.

The Thai singer went on break. A business party at a nearby table called it quits and the illicit couple started arguing. Ying took another taste of his drink, and as he did so he felt the effects of the alcohol, the buzz just catching up to him.

He pushed the drink away and paid his bill.

The woman wasn't coming. Something had happened. Maybe she couldn't get away; it wasn't safe.

Outside in the lobby he saw the man in the oversized suit talking on a cell phone over in the corner. The man gave him the briefest of glances and turned his back. Ying started to go out the main entrance but then changed his mind. Instead he went out the way he had come and circled around to his car. The night sky seemed very black above the cadmium lamps, and suddenly he was gripped with fear. On the way home, he checked the rearview mirror. He engaged in the customary maneuvers, but there was no one following, at least as far as he could tell.

At home, he checked in on his children. He watched them sleeping. Then he got in bed next to Lei—who lay with her hair splayed in the moonlight. By the time he fell asleep it was close to two. At six o-clock, four hours later, his cell went off.

The voice on other end belonged to a man by the name of

Bill James. Ying was surprised to hear from him. They had worked together at SI, and James had helped with the security arrangements when Ying was being harassed. More than once, James had shared his disgruntlement with the bureaucracy.

"Sorry to wake you," he said now.

"What's up?"

The last time Ying had seen Bill James had been on the day he'd cleaned out his desk, and the agent had expressed envy and his own desire to get the hell out. Even so, James had been promoted a few weeks later, and he was in administration now. The truth was, Ying had never quite trusted him.

James's voice was apologetic, as if he did not want to be making this call. "I have a request for your presence."

"What's this about?"

"Grove Street," he said. "The county building. Room sixty-seven. You need to be there at seven thirty."

"Is this SI business?"

Lei was up on her elbows, still half-asleep. He got the impression that she did not really see him—as if she were looking at him through a veil.

"It's a DEA office, in the basement."

"Can you give me details?"

"The DEA guy is Serles. David Serles."

The name wasn't familiar.

"You can't tell me more?"

"Serles will detail you," said James. "To be honest, I don't know much more."

Lei had rolled away from him, back to sleep. It was Saturday morning. He could roll over, too, he thought. There was nothing stopping him. He could cling to his wife, ignore the call.

Instead Ying climbed out of bed and got himself ready.

As he put on his shoes, he thought briefly of Miss Lin. He could not know, of course, that the police coroner had the body of an Asian woman, midtwenties, on a slab down in the morgue. Suicide, maybe, it was hard to tell. Fell from her bedroom window the previous evening, ten stories above Geary. Face disfigured by the fall, dress bloodied. Chrysanthemum in her hair.

THIRTY-FIVE

The evening before—as Ying sat sipping his umbrella drink in the New Asia Restaurant and Lounge—Dante had climbed the Filbert Stairs to his cousin's house up on the promontory. It was closing in on eleven, late for an unannounced visit, but Dante rang anyway. He came because he didn't want his cousin at the warehouse in the morning, but Gary could be stubborn, Dante knew; and he and his cousin were not on the best of terms. So keeping him away would require persuasion—and in the end, it might not be persuasion of the gentlest form that would be the most effective.

Alice answered the door. She wore a simple frock with a lace neckline. Her face was pale and maybe a little swollen. Her expression was vulnerable at first, then the smirk took over. If she knew Gary had spent the afternoon with the police, she didn't show it.

"I'm afraid my husband is out."

"Where can I find him?"

"He went to his mother's," said Alice. "Regina's back at her house, and Gary's helping her settle in."

Her eyes were moist, and her head tilted and wavered. He suspected she'd been drinking. She did not care for him, he knew, but something in her posture suggested she was considering inviting him inside; then her eyes skittered away.

"I'll walk over and see if I can catch him," said Dante.

It did not take Dante long to figure out that Gary was not at his mother's house either. The lights were dim, and the place was quiet. Dante cupped his hands to the front window—and after a moment or two he saw his Aunt Regina lying on the couch. The living room was dark, but the light from the kitchen fell through the archway and illuminated her features. Her mouth was open and she was lying in her clothes, asleep.

Gary wasn't here. Dante knew the cops had called him down to the station earlier. Probably he and his lover were off somewhere licking their wounds.

Even if Alice didn't know Gary had been hauled in for questioning, she knew about the other woman, Dante suspected. Probably she'd known for a while. It explained her foul humor, at least in part. But she shouldn't have been surprised; he'd cheated on his first wife, too. Alice should have known because she'd been the object of desire the first time around. But Dante did not think Gary would stay out all night. Even if Alice knew about the affair, she wouldn't like it thrown in her face. Besides, Dante knew his cousin. He was a sneak. Gary would fuck around, but he would have some kind of excuse. Out with the boys. Working late. Waiting on a late-night delivery.

So Dante walked up the hill to Montgomery Street, and his

hunch proved right. Just after midnight, his cousin pulled up in his BMW; he triggered the garage door with his remote, and Dante strolled into the garage behind him, before the automatic had a chance to close.

"What are you doing here?" Gary's eyes were wide with surprise. "If you want to talk about the will—the money—"

"Enjoy your conversation with the police?"

"That's none of your business."

"Cheating on your wife."

"Listen—"

"I don't want you going into the office tomorrow."

"Fuck you."

Gary tried to push past him then, but Dante wouldn't let him. He backed his cousin against the wall. There were garden tools nearby. A rake. A shovel.

"You want me to tell Alice what's been going on?"

"You have no right."

"I have every right."

There was a noise out on the street, a dog, maybe, or a raccoon, something inconsequential, but in that instant Dante turned and Gary reached for the shovel. It was a foolish thing to do. Dante hit him in the stomach. It was a quick jab, hard and without restraint. Dante hit him again, then grabbed him by the collar and pushed him to the wall. If Gary knew how to fight Dante might have been vulnerable, but Gary knew nothing. Dante would tear off his cousin's testicles if need be.

"This is the story. There is going to be a bust down at the warehouse tomorrow. You stay away, and I can help you stay clean. Otherwise, this crap you been pulling, whatever's been doing down at the warehouse, I can't save you."

"I don't need you to save me."

"What were you arguing about, you and Uncle Salvatore?"

"You," he said. "I didn't want you in the goddamn business."

"You've got something else going on."

"Don't be so self-righteous. Your father was no innocent."

"What are you talking about?"

"You think you're some kind of goddamn saint. You and them. The Brothers Mancuso. They turn their heads, act like it's all on the up-and-up. Me, just because I'm a little more proactive—"

About this time Alice showed up at the door that led from the garage into the house. She was in her night robe now. It was a frilly, frumpy thing, and she held it closed at the neck.

"Gary," she said. "What's going on here?"

Dante let him go. Gary was bleeding from the lip, and he was bent over, but he didn't look at his wife.

"How do I know there's going to be a sting?" Gary asked him. "Why should I believe anything you say?"

"Because you don't have any choice."

"What are you two doing?"

Gary turned on her. "Shut up, God damn you."

Dante studied the pair of them, eyes moving from one to the next. "You're husband's taking the day off tomorrow," he said.

Alice looked as if she found them both offensive. "It doesn't matter to me. I have an hair appointment." Then she went inside.

"See what I have to deal with?" Gary said.

"Don't come in tomorrow."

Dante started away. He got maybe halfway to the garage door before his cousin hissed out at him.

"Dante?"

Dante turned.

"I fucked Marilyn," Gary smiled. "You thought you were the only one, but I fucked her, too."

Gary stood with his back to the wall. His fists were clenched. It would have been a pleasure to beat him to a pulp. But instead Dante turned away and headed down the hill.

He had to get up early tomorrow. He needed his sleep.

THIRTY-SIX

At 7:30, hungover and sleep-starved, Detective Ying walked through the front doors of the Grove Street building. Inside was a collection of state offices, where birth documents and other records were stored. Ying found the inside stairs and descended into the lower regions of the building, into the labyrinths belowground, looking for Room 67. As the room was not easily found, he had to circle the floor a second time.

Meanwhile, Dante had entered another way, as directed, through the delivery area and down an iron staircase, so he was the one to arrive first. The man who greeted him had an oversized jaw and the practiced handshake of a government dick. He had his jacket off and wore his gun in a leather shoulder strap, out where you could see it.

"Agent Serles. DEA."

"This all seems to be coming down a bit quickly."

"It always does."

There was a knock on the door and Ying entered. Dante and

the Chinese Homicide detective regarded each other with surprise, each wondering how the other had come to be there, neither knowing how much the other was tied to this man in front of them, or if they were all being played by some unseen hand.

"I understand you two have already met," said Serles.

"He brought me in for questioning. After my uncle was murdered."

Ying nodded tightly.

"Well, that's the kind of coincidence that happens in our line of work." Serles sounded oddly cheerful. "Let me give you some background, Detective Ying. I'm with Drug Enforcement, as you know, and Dante here is with another agency." Serles cracked a thin smile, as if they were all comrades in this business. "He works in a unique capacity—and he came to San Francisco to help with the arrest of two drug traffickers. One of them— Mason Wu—is someone whom you yourself pursued when you were with SI."

The office in which they stood had a thrown-together look. It was a grim little room in the bowels of the building. There was a window that looked out onto an air shaft but it didn't let in any light. Someone had put a clean coffee cup on the desk and some fresh sheets of paper, but there was a patina of dust over the desk itself as well as on the folding chairs and a bookshelf in the corner.

"The thing is, Detective Ying," Serles said, "the DEA would like your help on this."

"*My* help?"

"During your time with SI, you gathered information on the Wu family. Our intention is to take Mason Wu today, and possibly others. We want you there to help us with the interrogation."

"After you have them in custody, I'll give you all the help you need."

Serles shook his head. "No, we'd like you on-site when we take them in."

"May I ask why?"

"We're taking them to a secure location. And we want you on hand. It's not without risk, I admit. But we'll keep you out of the line of fire until the apprehension has been made."

Ying walked over to the window and looked out. The bottom of the shaft was littered with debris. He stared through the smudged glass as if the answer to Serles's question lay there in that debris.

"All right," he said. "I'll come along."

Dante didn't know if this was a such great idea. Things got messy when you crossed company lines. Serles presented himself as DEA, but the company had a way of operating in two worlds at once, the official and the unofficial, so that it was hard to differentiate between the two or know precisely what their true intentions were.

Serles produced a map of the warehouse. "We have two parties coming to meet with Dante at the Mancuso warehouse. One is headed up by Mason Wu. And the other by an ex-convict affiliated with the Nation of Islam."

"Yusef Fakir," said Dante.

Ying nodded. He knew the name.

"We are going to arrest Fakir as well today, and this is how it will happen," said Serles. "The Wus will come in by boat, dock-ing at the east end of the building. Fakir and one of his cronies will come in the front entrance. The two groups will meet in Salvatore Mancuso's old office with Dante. That's where the transaction will take place. We've already wired it for sound and video.

"When they leave, each group will go out the way they came in. We'll have video of them exchanging drugs for money. And then our people will step in and arrest them. We'll take Fakir and his sidekick in the parking lot. Our agents will be concealed and ready to move."

"And on the dock?" Ying said.

"We'll have our men there as well. When the Wus leave their speedboat behind, we'll commandeer it—and we'll block their departure on the dock."

"And me?" asked Ying.

"We have a role for you. We'll give you a clipboard and embed you with a loading crew, out of harm's way."

Dante had gone over all this with Blonde, but he still wondered at what point the warehouse had been wired—and if everything had been arranged as precisely as Serles explained. There was always something hidden. Even if everything was as it seemed, there were always flaws, little details that went askew.

"One thing," said Dante.

"Yes?"

"I don't want my cousin implicated. Whatever you have against him, you let it go. That was part of the deal."

"We're not interested in your cousin."

"And me—this is the last time. I want out clean."

The man's smile twisted. "That's not really under my control."

"Just pass it along," Dante said. "This is the last goddamn stunt I'm pulling."

Outside, Dante and Ying found themselves together.

"I suppose I should thank you," Ying said, though he didn't look very grateful. "For telling them to bring me onboard. Giving me a chance to go after the Wus."

"Don't thank me," said Dante. "I had nothing to do with it."

THIRTY-SEVEN

Later that morning, Marilyn Visconti left her apartment to meet Dante at his grandfather's boat—down a gangway in the older part of the North Beach Marina. It would be a pleasant walk, down Mason and across Bay, especially on a day like this, with the sun so brilliant and the sky so blue. The weather had changed all of a sudden, an offshore breeze kept the fog away, and you could sense the heat starting to build. It would be pleasant to have a picnic on the boat. So on the way she stopped at Scalia's Grocery.

The sign said Scalia & Sons, but Dominic Scalia had passed on, and neither of his sons were in the business anymore. One was a dentist and lived in the South Bay. The other had died in Vietnam. That left Mama Scalia to run the store, and she was almost always there, lounging behind the counter in her black smock.

"Ah, the goat girl," she said.

Mama Scalia had seen Marilyn some twenty years before,

leading a goat down the street at the Italian day parade. So Marilyn was forever the "goat girl."

Scalia's Grocery was not what it had been. The deli counter had been taken out and restocked with factory-made sandwiches. Mama Scalia still carried the old hard salami, though, and Marilyn found some cheese and crackers in the back. It was too early in the day for wine, but then—feeling reckless—she bought it anyway.

"You going on a picnic?"

"Yes."

"That is the thing about North Beach. It is always beautiful. It is always a good day for a picnic. You say hello to that good-looking father of yours, too. Tell your mother I will steal him if she's not careful. I always had my eyes on that big house of yours."

Mama Scalia had put the same tagline on the end of their conversations since Marilyn could remember, apparently unaware that her mother was dead and her father lodged at St. Vincent's. Unaware, too, that her family no longer owned the big house at the top of Vallejo.

"I will," she said. "I'll tell them both. And I'll tell my mother to lock the door."

Mama Scalia laughed. "She better," she said. "She better."

Marilyn headed through Lombard flats—the old tule land that had once teemed with the families of fishermen and dockhands and cannery workers. The old shanty town was long gone, of course, replaced by row houses of pink stucco. The day was warming quickly. Ahead of her, she could see the sheen of the bay.

She found the boat docked behind Scoma's Grill, exactly where it had been seven years ago. Some old fishermen sat on a bench nearby. Old Italians who did not go to sea anymore, but remembered how it had been back in the day. The fisherman sat on the seagull-splattered bench with the wizened faces of their grandfathers, speaking in Italian and somewhere in that stream she heard her family's name. She knew the kind of talk that went on. *Think they're better than the rest, her and her Genoese parents. . . . That mother, half Italian, half German, but still a Jew, no matter she sent her daughter to the church. . . . You know the story, the daughter and the Mancuso boys, she was leading them both around by the prick.* She headed away from the old men, toward the tourist pier. The bulk of the fishing fleet had been moored here once upon a time. In the old days, the Italians would reenact the discovery of America. Hundreds of people crammed the docks, the bishop waving his hand over the whole business, blessing the fleet. When it was over they'd dragged the statue of the Virgin up the street. Always the Virgin.

The gossip was partly true. Her mother had regarded herself as superior; she'd grown weary of the Italians and their endless preening. And maybe herself, she had taken up with Gary Mancuso on a lark. But she'd fallen in love with Dante, and she'd paid the price. Because after Gary found out, he had come over to her apartment. She'd been unable to stop what happened next. Or maybe she was lying to herself. Maybe she could have stopped him. Maybe she had felt sorry for him. Maybe she'd loved him a little. So when Gary pushed her against the wall, she put her hand in his curly hair, trying to calm him, and he misread that gesture. Because then he'd lifted her skirt and she had been unable to push him away.

She had not told Dante. She did not know a way to explain such a thing. And so she had run off.

At the end of the pier, the seals were making a god-awful noise. The tourists were tossing bread. A little girl hollered at her mother. The seagulls skimmed along the water, looking for food, something to scavenge.

Dante should be to the boat by now.

She headed back. The old men were still there. And a couple of women. One of them she recognized.

Mrs. Romero.

"I hear you're going to Italy on your honeymoon," said Mrs. Romero. "Your mother would be proud. Such a nice boy."

"Oh, so this is Marilyn Visconti. We saw her walk by a few minutes ago," said one of the old men. "We wondered who she might be."

"It is such a wonderful thing, marriage."

"And Tony Mora is such a charming man," said Mrs. Romero. "Quite a catch."

"What does she have in that bag?" said one of the others. Mussolino, maybe, or Scarpetti. She had a hard time telling the old men one from the other, and anyway they talked as if she wasn't there. "Looks like she's going on a picnic."

The old woman smiled. It was not so sincere. The old men sat there with their Italian smirks. They'd seen her hanging near the Mancuso boat. Knew the stories. Knew who she was waiting for. These old Italians, they knew it all.

She walked away. Felt them watching. Glanced one last time over her shoulder at the boat. An hour late now. He wasn't going to show. Dante's revenge. Her lips turned in a hard smile. *Slut.* She kept on walking. *Whore.* Swinging her bag. *Goat girl, no one will marry you.* And the sound of the old ones was like the cawing of the gulls, miserable birds scrabbling with each other over some small bit of debris—a piece of flesh to tear apart and devour.

THIRTY-EIGHT

The Mancuso warehouse was out past Third Street, at the east end of the city. It sat at the front end of the Potrero Pier, and you could hear the water whisper as it brushed against the pilings. Railroad tracks ran up to the pier—old tracks, no longer in use—but if you put your ear to the steel you could nonetheless hear the moaning of the rails. Across the bay you could see Oakland, the giant container ships and the towering cranes, and you could hear the white noise of the freight trucks on the Nimitz Freeway.

In the concrete pipe across from the warehouse a homeless man sat, gumming an apple, and the wind whistled through his toothless head. On the bench, a couple of fishermen cast their lines into the contaminated water. They coughed and hacked and spit, and the sound of their talk filtered across the water. But the sounds of those individual men were lost in the white noise, in the slap of the water, in the moan of the rails and the traffic on Third Street. All the sounds blurred together to become one sound, and that was the sound of the dying waterfront. It was

the old song, the familiar complaint. How the people downtown had sold out the working man. How the Port Authority
had got together with Hong Kong and the New York Jews and
Alioto's Sicilian buddies to sell the waterfront down the tubes.
After that it was the hippies and the faggots and those sons of
bitches with their computers. But these complaints were nothing new. The big-chested Irish and the unionist Harry Bridges
and the anarchist Carlo Tresca had seen it coming, the industrial
conspiracy that would take away all the jobs and replace everyone with machines. But they were silenced by the war, by the
navy and General DeWitt and his operations to move all unnat-
uralized aliens away from the waterfront, to round up the Japs
and the Wops and the Krauts and in the process shut up anyone
else who dared to speak. Sons of bitches had been at it from the
beginning. Once it had been little coves and beaches and hol-
lows all along here, finger piers that extended out to Chinese
junks filled with silk and tea and opium. Then came the seawall,
all around the city. The coves and inlets were backfilled with
mud, with debris, with the corpses of Indians and Negroes—
and with the rotting hulks of abandoned ships. They filled up
the wet lands between the seawall and bedrock with anything
they could find, then crisscrossed the whole business with roads
that ran helter-skelter to the docks. It was all cemented over
now, but you could know the truth of things if you only lay
upon the ground and listened to what lay beneath the concrete.

Or maybe there was no way to know at all. Maybe the past
had just vanished and all you got was what you saw. Still, something stirred Dante as he set foot onto the family pier. And Ying,
too, as he headed toward the loading dock with his clipboard.
And Williams and Fakir, heading down the Embarcadero. And

those three Chinese on the speedboat, descendents of the Wu clan, ancient smugglers. Maybe they all sensed for a moment that which lay unexpressed in the land as they converged toward the Mancuso warehouse. Or maybe they heard only the superficial sounds, the slap of the waves, the cries of the gulls, the groan of abandoned machinery. Maybe there were no secrets. Just noise and cacophony. Like the blare of that foghorn in the distance, sounding for no apparent reason on this clear and sunny day.

THIRTY-NINE

It was fifteen minutes before ten when Ying saw the speed-boat. It was a modern craft, very low and sleek, and it moved like a knife through the water. The boat cut its speed and turned toward the pier. There were three men on board, dressed for a pleasure outing, though nothing in their demeanor suggested they were enjoying themselves. The boat eased closer. Then it moved out of view, under the pier.

Ying stood with a clipboard in hand. He stood alongside another man with a clipboard who was verifying the particulars of a shipment of restaurant supplies as it was transferred from the dock onto a waiting truck. Ying's apparent role was to double-check the shipment on behalf of the warehouse, and neither the other clerk nor the crew paid him much attention.

Now two men from the speedboat appeared on the dock, and a dockworker came forward to lead them toward the main building. The dockworker was a very big man who wore a black sweatshirt with two words printed on the back: MANCUSO STORAGE.

Ying recognized the two men from the boat: Mason Wu and Charlie Yi.

He knew them from his days with SI, because he had studied their faces in photographs and once ran a stakeout outside Wu's house. Wu was the money man, the higher-up. Yi provided the muscle. Together they pretty much ran the Wu family's drug trade.

A third man had stayed behind on the speedboat at the landing beneath the pier. The wheel man, as the expression went. He would watch the craft and keep it idling, waiting for Yi and Wu to return.

Meanwhile, the crew had done loading and they were backing the truck off the dock, so now Ying stood out in plain view, alone with his clipboard. A tactical squad was embedded here, Ying had been told, but he had not been told where or which group it might be, only to take inventory with the loading crew. But now the loading crew was gone, the dock empty.

He had no cover.

Wu and Yi paused. The man in the Mancuso sweatshirt turned and gave a look in Ying's direction. There was a brief conversation, then Wu nodded his head and the men all disappeared inside the warehouse.

Ying had the vague feeling they had been discussing him. The hackles rose on his neck.

Now the man in the black sweatshirt reemerged. He strolled toward Ying. Something about the man seemed vaguely familiar—his gait, maybe, his smile. He was with the tact squad, Ying determined. And he's on his way to direct me out of harm's way. To tell me to get the hell off this dock.

⌐⊙⌐

For the last half hour, Dante had been sitting in the front office: an odd, sprawling room shared until recently by his cousin Gary and his Uncle Salvatore. Before that his uncle and his father had inhabited these quarters for some forty years, and the walls still bore the marks of their presence. Pictures everywhere.

Grandfather Pellicano, in his fishing gear, out on the pier.

Dante's grandmother in her black shawl.

His mother—before she'd gone mad.

His father.

Himself.

The Pelican—back when he was still with the force. When everything had been his, the streets and the people and the wild smell of the city. The whole goddamn business.

The office was an oversized room, very wide, with doors at either end and an open stairwell dead center. The stairwell led to a storage room below, and from there to a landing beneath the dock: a platform that hovered over the water. He remembered going down there when he was a kid, and sometimes his father and his uncle used to bring down their rods and go fishing in the shallows under the pier.

Dante hit the stairwell switch, and the surge blew the bare bulb that hung over the bottom of the steps. It always happened with that light, ever since he could remember; the circuit was faulty. He turned the corner. It was darker still and the door onto the platform would not open. He could hear the gulls outside and a speedboat idling in the water.

Dante went back upstairs. A little after ten, the door opened and in came three men. Dante recognized Wu and Yi. The third man Dante hadn't seen before: He was a big man in a company sweatshirt. One of Serles's undercover operatives, maybe, posing as an employee at the family warehouse. The big man delivered Wu and Yi then went back out the way he had come.

"Where's the product?" said Wu.

Dante looked out his window toward the parking lot. An old Nova had just pulled in, one of the big models from the early seventies, battered, painted the original chartreuse. Williams was driving.

"Coming," said Dante.

Fakir had his misgivings. Brother Williams had told him about the Mancuso warehouse, and how the owners were interested in renting out part of the space to the bakery. He'd been skeptical, and as Williams wheeled the ancient Nova into the lot, his skepticism returned. Fakir had grown up in the city, his mother had worked swabbing bowls in North Beach, and he'd never known the Italians to do anyone any special favors. But the bakery needed new quarters, and Brother Williams insisted the owners were sympathetic. More importantly, they were willing to cut a deal.

Brother Williams had changed these last weeks. He'd always had a darkness in him, a quiet place you couldn't penetrate, but now Fakir sensed a certain urgency. He'd seen it before when men got out of prison, and it wasn't always a good sign.

"Ready?" said Williams.

"Yes," said Fakir. "We will see."

They headed toward the building. Fakir had a memory of coming down to this area when he was a young man, looking for a job—but the landscape had changed. The cannery across the way had been razed, and there were weeds growing in the lot.

Williams held his leather case by the handle, and he walked with his eyes forward and his back straight.

"What do you have in the case?"

"Information about the bakery. Some pamphlets."

Fakir nodded.

"Also some baked goods. Sister Lakeesha's cookies. You know—something sweet to pave the way."

Fakir nodded. "Wise," he said. "But in my experience, they take the sweets either way. We should be careful about anything we negotiate here."

"Today's just about talk," said Williams. "We take a look around at the facilities. We don't sign anything."

They were at the door now and Fakir felt in his gut the same wariness he felt anytime he did business with the man.

"Another thing," said Williams. "The partners will be here."

"Partners?"

"A couple of Chinese."

They were in the lobby now. "What else haven't you told me?" Fakir asked.

"The orange door," said Williams. "We just knock and walk in."

Williams led the way. There were three men inside. An Italian stood next to a stairwell. And two Chinese. One of the Chinese wore khakis, and the other had a black mustache of the type painted on samurai dolls. The man in the khakis smiled and shook his hand, but Fakir didn't believe the smile. There was something up. Some kind of bullshit.

"What do you have for us?"

Williams stepped forward and put the case on the desk.

"What is this?" Fakir asked.

No one answered.

Williams stepped away, behind Fakir. The man in the khakis snapped open the case. As he did so, the other Chinese reached into his pocket, and in that instant Fakir caught a glimpse of the Italian—and the Italian's eyes bore into his own, then flitted away, sizing each man there even as he, too, reached beneath his jacket. And Fakir knew then that he had been had, and he understood that the instrument of his betrayal was the man behind him: Williams. He swung around, knowing it was too late. The mechanism had clicked and the barrel was pointed at his head.

O utside, Ying watched the man in the black sweatshirt coming across the dock. He was a big man, but he moved quickly. He had a wide, pugnacious face and a quick smile and very bright eyes, and once again Ying had the feeling he'd seen the man before but could not pin it down.

"Detective Ying?"

"Yes."

"Back this way."

He followed the man back between a couple rows of pallets stacked high with wooden crates. The sun was overhead and Ying could hear some wind chimes coming from across the water somewhere, and their sound was mixed with the calling of the gulls.

When the man turned, he held a gun in his hand. Ying recognized him now. The man leaned forward in the same manner he had that night at the New Asia Restaurant and Lounge, when he'd asked Ying for the time. He smiled now just as he'd done then. Ying saw the wristwatch on his gun hand. The same watch. The second hand made its sweep.

"Detective Ying, you have been betrayed."

The man gave it an instant to sink in, then he fired. Ying lurched back. He might have fallen immediately but the stacked goods broke his backward momentum, and he stood remarkably straight for a long moment, leaning against the pallets.

"Who?" Ying said, or tried to say. He wanted to know who had betrayed him. Dante, he wondered. Or the informer. Or Bill James, down at SI.

He heard the wind chimes, and the sound was like that of the small pagoda chimes he had heard as a child, hanging on his mother's porch.

He touched his wound. His legs failed him and he slid down the box. He sat on the ground, legs splayed, head against the box. The man stood watching. He smiled as before.

"Who?"

The man leaned over and whispered in Ying's ear. *Nothing happens that Master Wu does not want to happen.* The man arched himself up now, regarding him with both curiosity and pleasure. *Maybe he will not shoot me again,* Ying thought, *maybe I won't die—* and for the briefest of moments he thought of his wife, standing by the window in her tennis shorts. The blood was thick now, and a great yearning passed though him—a wave of darkness, and in that darkness he heard the chimes again. This was not a mystery he was going to solve. Too many loose ends, all unraveling. Though there was another part of him still piecing things together. A frayed bit of consciousness, fast dissolving. Miss Lin had told the Wus he was pursuing Ru Shen. But Agent James had told him to come here. . . . Under whose instruction . . . ? Someone with connections to SI . . . Someone with connections to the Wus . . . Someone who wanted him to die here, on this dock . . .

Who?

The man in the black sweatshirt watched. Then Ying's eyes opened all of the sudden, his body moved with an unusual vehemence, and the man fired into Ying's torso. The man studied Ying for another instant. He could have killed him last night, but they had wanted his corpse here. Just as they had wanted the woman in the polka-dot dress to fall from her bedroom window. He did not ask the reasons. He did his job. Now he fired a final shot, just for good measure. Then he went to wait for his colleagues down at the boat.

D ante had seen the way Fakir's face fell into confusion at the sight of the heroin. And he saw Williams reaching for his gun, and Yi, too—and he realized that the company's stated intention was not their intention at all, and this was not a sting so much as an execution. The company wanted Fakir, and Williams had brought him here. And judging from the quick look that had fallen between Williams and Yi, he guessed that Fakir was not the only one they meant to kill.

There were no videotapes recording the transaction for prosecution later on. No tactical crew waiting to make arrests outside. It was just Yi and Williams, recruited as murderers. And afterward, the company would distance themselves—a drug deal gone bad.

He saw all this in an instant, realizing it before he had time to think out the details. In the same instant, he went for his gun, heading toward that stairway that dropped toward the nether regions beneath the dock.

Just then Fakir swung around, sensing Williams behind him. But Williams shot Fakir in the back. Yi and Dante exchanged fire but Fakir staggered into the way and was hit once more. Meanwhile Mason Wu had dropped to his knees behind the desk.

Dante clambered sideways across the floor. He pitched himself down the stairwell, his body spinning in midair then plummeting downward. He landed at the bottom of the stairs. Williams then appeared at the top, firing wildly into the hole, and Dante was shot. Williams fired again and Dante tried to steady himself. Then he turned the corner and fell face forward into the blackness.

Williams stood at the top of the stairs.

"Did you kill him?" asked Yi.

"I think so."

"What the hell's going on?" asked Mason Wu.

Wu emerged from behind the desk. He held a chrome-plated shooter but the action seemed to have died down and he pointed the barrel toward the floor. His eyes were on the heroin.

"You're dead," said Yi.

"Huh?"

Wu glanced up from the heroin. He understood then, but it was too late. Yi shot him in the face. Wu twitched about on his feet, then collapsed to the floor. The twitching went on for a while. Yi shot him again. There was blood everywhere.

"We were supposed to kill the Italian first," Yi said to Williams. "He was the only one who knew how to use a gun."

"Fakir got in my way."

Williams glanced at Brother Fakir laying there. He felt something like remorse feathering at the inside of his chest, but then it passed away. Maybe he would feel more later on, when he thought of how Fakir had taken him in, and how the loss of Fakir would tear Cole Valley asunder, but he had never felt such remorse in the past and there was no reason why he should feel it now.

"Go down there and make sure."

"There's no light."

"I get the drugs. You take the money. Then we go our separate ways."

"All right."

Williams remembered the plan. They were to kill Fakir and Mason Wu, too. And to make things neat and clean, this Italian as well. Yi got some kind of reward of his own—something to do with the local drug business. He himself got a new identity. Free to roam with a trunk full of cash.

Williams headed down the stairs. He looked into the darkness with some foreboding. The truth was he didn't know if he had wounded Dante or killed him or even hit him at all. He did know that he didn't much want to turn the corner into the room where the Italian had vanished. *Because the Italian's eyes will be adjusted to the darkness,* he thought. *Because the Italian knows every bit of this building and I know nothing. Because if I turn that corner and he is still alive, then he will shoot me dead.* And as these thoughts went through his head, Williams considered the idea of not turning the corner at all, just firing into the darkness at the bottom of the landing, pretending he had finished the job. Occupied as he was with his thoughts and his fears, he sighed, not realizing he had done so. Then he heard a little scratching noise around the corner, like mice scuttling, or fingers tapping on the floor. He fired blindly into the darkness, then fired again. The noise stopped. "That finishes him," he said.

"Are you sure?" Yi asked from above.

Williams was not sure at all. He only knew he wasn't going around the corner.

"Absolutely," he said. "He's dead."

He peered a moment longer into the darkness. He did not notice that Yi had taken position at the top of the stairs behind him, gun arm extended, waiting for just that answer.

D ante lay with his cheek pressed onto the floor. After he had fallen, he had blacked out. Now he was awake again, but the bullet had torn through his shoulder, and the pain made him grit his teeth. He scuttled his good hand over the floor, looking for his gun. He had heard the men talking and Williams coming down the stairs, and then two shots had rung out in the stairwell. Even if Dante could find his gun now, he did not know how much it would help. He would to have twist himself around somehow, firing upward, and accomplish that movement without giving away his position.

After the gunfire, he sat as still as he could. The men exchanged a few words. He heard Williams in the stairway, pronouncing him dead. And then there was another shot and he heard Williams stumble down the stairs, slamming into the cabinet at the bottom. Dante twisted about, looking for the gun, but the noise he made scampering was lost because just then there was a fusillade of shots from up above. Williams pitched around the corner. Dante saw the man's shadow. Then he collapsed onto the spot Dante had been only a moment before.

Dante listened to the man die, and he waited.

Meanwhile the pain was wild in his shoulder. He heard Yi moving up above and then the pain became too much and he drifted under. He drifted back again, then away, and somewhere in this drifting, before he slipped into the blackness, he heard the speedboat outside roar back to life. Then that sound, too, diminished.

PART FOUR

FORTY

D ante was high. He lay in bed, in the trauma wing of San Francisco General. It was a busy night in the trauma ward, as Saturday nights often were, but the medic had wrapped his shoulder and given him a painkiller. Morphine, maybe. Demerol. It didn't matter. He was high and it felt good. When he closed his eyes, he saw the dream-dark streets and the long sweep of the bay and the city lights glimmering just as he had seen them from the jet window the evening he'd descended into San Francisco.

He opened his eyes and Angelo was by his bedside, his ex-partner. The Homicide chief stood there with a dour expression and his hands in his pockets. Though it would have been nice to think so, Dante didn't guess Angelo was here for old time's sake. Alongside him was a woman whose face he didn't know, but everything else about her was familiar. The blue jacket. The hard eyes. The lips that never turned a smile.

"What happened out there?" asked Angelo.

They had come in a moment or two ago, not long after the

nurse had administered the shot. If he shuttered his eyes, it wasn't hard to imagine they were not here at all.

"Why don't we start from the top?" Dante said. His tongue was thick and he needed something to drink. "If you could pour me some juice. My shoulder, as you can see . . ."

The woman gave him a look that said she wasn't going to pour him any goddamn juice.

"This is Special Agent Waldorf. FBI," said Angelo. "She has a few questions for you. And I do as well."

There would be jurisdictional issues, Dante thought. City cops and FBI did not necessarily work so well together. Angelo poured the juice and handed it to him. The taste was so cold and wonderful that Dante managed for the moment to forget everything he disliked about his ex-partner.

"Ying?" asked Dante. "How is Detective Ying?"

Angelo sucked in his cheeks and let out his breath and looked away. Then the chief's gray eyes settled back on him, and Dante knew the answer.

"Not so lucky as you," said Angelo. "Gutshot. Bled to death out there on your dock. His wife . . . It wasn't easy to tell her."

Angelo played the good cop. Now as always. Back then, too, he'd been the one to call on the loved ones, to knock on the door and tell the folks the news. Angelo enjoyed it, Dante thought. Enjoyed examining the bodies, sifting through the personal effects. Seeing the grief on the relatives' faces. Going over it later, alone, as you lay in bed at night. It was a weird kind of pleasure, as Dante knew. But after a while it wore you down.

Angelo had grown a notch or two heavier since Dante had seen him last—a soft-spoken man, out of shape and overweight—

a man without much of a physical presence who nonetheless was fierce beneath the surface and full of ambition. His hair was steel-gray and his eyes were milky. Though they had been a good team once, best of buddies, Angelo had distanced himself as soon as he saw Dante going down over the Strehli business.

"We'd like to know the details." said Special Agent Waldorf. "What happened out there at the warehouse?"

The woman had frizzy hair and wore a blazer over her print dress. She might have been attractive if not for the way she carried herself. Her shoulders were square, and she wore a perfume that smelled like aftershave.

"They way it looks," Angelo said. "There was a drug deal going down at your place—and it went bad. I want to know what Ying was doing there."

"I don't think I need to explain to you how serious this is," said Waldorf. "A policeman is dead."

Dante closed his eyes. He saw the streets again, the smear of dark and light, the sky overhead all bruised up with beautiful colors. He would disappear into that beauty if he only he could keep his eyes closed. If only he could go there and never come back.

"You don't talk to us, I'll return later with three more agents," said Agent Waldorf. "We'll keep you up all goddamn night. You can forget your pain medicine. Forget the juice and the hospital bed. We'll take you into federal custody."

Dante kept his eyes closed. He did not want to talk to these people, but sooner or later he would have to. Sometimes it was best to take the initiative.

"It was a DEA operation," he said at last. "Or that's what I was told. I was working with them on assignment."

"You're with DEA?"

"I was on assignment," he said. "And Ying was brought in at the last minute because of his connections with SI. The DEA was supposed to provide backup. They were supposed to make arrests. Instead, they left us in the lurch."

"This sounds like so much bullshit," said Agent Waldorf.

"Give me your cell. I'll call someone—give you everything you want."

The number he dialed was forbidden but he dialed it anyway. The voice on the other end was the voice of the insect. Maybe not the same insect—but the species shared a certain consciousness.

"This is Dante Mancuso."

The insect said nothing.

"You left me hanging. And I'm thinking it wasn't an accident."

"Where are you?" the insect asked.

"I've got the FBI with me. Explain it before I do. Get these pricks off me. Either you tell them what's going on here, or I'll tell them myself. And then I'll go to the goddamn media. Blow every whistle I can."

"That wouldn't be wise."

"Why don't you talk to Agent Waldorf?"

Agent Waldorf put her pale lips to the receiver. She listened for a while but she did not say much and she was not on the phone long. Then she turned to Angelo. "My suggestion is we continue this later." The pair of them left, Angelo trailing behind. It was pretty apparent which of them was in charge.

Dante slept. When he woke up, the uniformed cop outside his door was gone. The Bureau had pulled rank on Angelo and the guard had been taken away. Agent Waldorf had talked to somebody down at the company, he figured, and the company had told them to back off.

The sting was successful in the ways the company had wanted, he guessed. It had never been about capturing Fakir and Wu—at least not alive. Instead they'd gotten rid of Fakir and discredited him in the process, linking him to the drug trade in a fiery death. And Mason Wu was dead, too. Rumor said that Love Wu had wanted to remove his grand-nephew, and apparently that's what the company wanted as well. They'd gotten Yi to pull the trigger. Given him a higher post, no doubt. At least temporarily.

In the process, they went after me, too, Dante thought. Part of him understood. For the convenience of it, just to get rid of him. And that's the way it had gone, almost. Charles Yi had taken the money and the drugs—and left him for dead.

But Ying? Why kill him?

The only answer he could come up with was that Ying had been with SI once upon a time, and Ying's fingers, like his own, had touched the Strehli business.

Still, he could not quite link it all together. The Wus. The company. The dead family in the shipping container. The intersection of Hong Kong and San Francisco and the criminal underground, the place where government overlapped with druglords, with smugglers, with legitimate commerce. It was an old business, all these interconnections, as old as the city, and their exact nature shifted on you, just like the nature of the company itself.

What all this had to do with his father's death, or his uncle's, he did not know. But there was one place where he hadn't yet had the opportunity to look.

Il Libro di Vita Segreta.

There was an orderlies' closet down the hall. He would wait until the next break. Then he would grab himself some street clothes and visit the rectory down at Washington Square.

FORTY-ONE

Father Campanella's apartment was in the back of the rectory on the second floor, overlooking the schoolyard. There was a rear entrance on the ground floor, but it was well bolted and there were bars over the window. The bars had been inset with the tamperproof screws, so Dante climbed onto the retaining wall, same as he had done as a kid. It was difficult maneuvering with his shoulder in a bandage, but the drugs helped keep the pain at bay. He found the fire escape and worked his way onto the roof. The skylight over Campanella's quarters was open just enough to where he could get a grip beneath the edge, and with his good hand he pulled until the hinge popped. The plastic slid loose from the frame, and he dropped himself through.

He drew the curtain, then turned on the lights. A crucifix hung on the wall over the man's bed, and there was a picture of Mary and of the church's patron saints, and another picture of the souls tormented in hell, circling one another as they fell through the various levels of torment. To Dante, the souls seemed almost ecstatic in their misery, swirling through the vortex toward the waiting demon. The devil was scabrous and fiery-eyed. He crouched in anticipation, excrement at his feet, and in the excrement were the bones of the damned.

The priest's desk had been stacked high with correspondence, and Dante went through it looking for his father's *Il Libro*. Letters from fellow priests. Pamphlets and newsletters. Brochures for religious statues, for vestments and chalices and holy objects. Bank statements mixed in with correspondence from the penitentiary.

At length, he found what he was a looking for on a nearby bookshelf: a thick manila envelope with the name MANCUSO scrawled on the outside. Before he could examine it, though, he heard a noise behind him.

Father Campanella stood in the threshold.

"You couldn't wait till morning?"

Dante didn't know what to say. It was as if he and the priest had stepped back thirty years, to when Father Campanella caught Dante and his buddies on the school roof with a crucifix they'd stolen from the nunnery.

"There's more going on here then meets the eye," said Dante.

"Apparently so. Why don't you sit down?"

"I thought you were out of town—and . . ."

"I returned this evening. I was in the chapel just now."

"Oh."

"Is there something you want to talk about?"

Another man might have expressed alarm, or outrage, at this invasion of his quarters. Or called the police. Campanella, though, whatever his flaws was not inclined toward unmediated action.

Dante gestured at the skylight. "I'll make good on the damages."

"Your arm . . ."

"A little accident. I slipped and fell."

If the priest doubted him, he said nothing.

"I just need to look at what's in here. At my father's *Il Libro*."

"Take your time."

Father Campanella motioned to the armchair and Dante sat down. He feared the priest might come and look over his shoulder—Campanella could be nosey, and cloying, especially when it came to matters of the spirit—but instead he merely sat in the armchair opposite Dante, under the crucifix, and folded his hands.

Inside the book was a collection of articles and papers. Put together not by his father, Dante quickly realized, but by Strehli. A packet of photographs—the same ones his uncle had had the negatives for. A newspaper article about the discovery of the corpses in the container. A magazine biography of Ru Shen.

Also there was a journal, written in Chinese. Dante found a letter, tucked inside its bindings. Unlike the journal, the letter was in English, written in a quavering hand.

I am the businessman Ru Shen, placed under house arrest some months ago, after my most recent visit to China. I had thought to use my influence and money to buy passage back to America, but it now seems that neither my influence nor my money was great enough. Because here, in this darkening container, we are running short on pro-

visions, and it seems the cylinder that provided us with the flow of fresh air has been sabotaged. We are slowly suffocating.

My wife and daughters lay quietly, using as little air as possible. Even the slightest exertion shortens the breath, dwindling our supply, and the lamp by which I write grows dimmer by the moment.

So I must summarize.

Before arranging this passage, my family and I were held for the better part of the spring in our quarters in the Beijing Hotel. I feared the whole while we would be dragged off to prison, but I now understand this betrayal was what they had in mind. For myself and my family to die anonymously, in steerage, in the guise of immigrant stowaways.

The reason has to do with public statements I have made and testimony I have promised, suggesting that the smuggling of guns and drugs and other contraband into the United States was going on with joint cooperation between the two governments. They turn a blind eye because China wants the business, and the U.S. companies want the cheap labor, and there is money that goes to officials on both sides, including their respective intelligence communities.

Some time ago, I began keeping a journal: a history of transactions and those agents who facilitated them. This information I intended to use in testimony, when the time came—and thus I took this journal with me when we fled China, even as I left documents and identification behind.

I must stop, because even this small exertion is draining me, and the lamp is all but out. Whoever finds us, you will find my journal here upon my person. I hope it will be less of a curse for you than it has been upon myself and family.

Respectfully,
Ru Shen

Dante felt the priest regarding him. Father Campanella had led the parish for some thirty years. Every day he took an afternoon stroll down Columbus and in the evening you could find him at Enrico's having a drink. He was an effeminate man, with blue eyes and delicate hands, and people made the type of jokes you might expect.

"You talked to my father before he died."

"Yes. He wanted me to give the *Libro* to you. He wanted to be sure you took possession."

"Did you read this?"

"No. As you see, the package was sealed."

"At the end, my father thought someone was trying to kill him. Did he mention this to you?"

"I believe he was having delusions. When a man dies, what a man feels guilty for, and what he has actually done . . ." Campanella paused, stumbling for the words. "What I am trying to say, the demons are often more grandiose than the crime."

"What else did he say to you?"

"I'm afraid I have to claim silence on those things. I took a vow. But he died at peace, I assure you."

"I'm not so sure."

The priest's eyes went soft and his lip quivered. Once upon a time Dante had been an altar boy. He had rung the Eucharist bells, three bells, three times, each. Then he had walked up to the altar with the wine and water, ten steps, and afterward rang the bells again. Meanwhile, Campanella had raised his hands and muttered the words of the transubstantiation, and Dante had rung the bells yet again: once for the Father, once for the Son, once for the Holy Spirit. Then he'd followed the priest, assisting

with the communion, holding the paten beneath the parish-
ioners' throats as they took the host. More than once, when they
were walking back to the altar, he'd seen the same weariness pass
across Father Campanella's face. The same softness, the same
quiver of doubt.

"There was one thing I can pass along. Your father, he
wanted you to forgive him."

"For what?"

"He said he kept some things from you. But he only did so
to protect you. He was worried, though, that he had made a
mistake."

"Who else visited with him before he died?"

"Your uncle, of course. And the doctor."

"Anyone else?"

"The mayor. A number of his friends, but especially him.
They were close, you know, from the old days. And Mayor
Rossi—he came over more than once. To give him comfort."

"Was it a comfort to him?"

"At such times, the Lord always finds a way."

There was the same softness, though, the same quiver in the
eyes. Dante didn't know. Maybe the priest was right, and his
father had died a natural death. But somebody had broken into
his father's house. Somebody had torn up his uncle's office as
well.

The journal, Dante guessed. *That's what they'd been looking for.*

Dante stood up to leave. He had another call to make. Father
Campanella smiled then, extending his hand as he rose from the
chair, and Dante realized what was coming.

"Would you like to pray with me?"

It was the double trap. If you turned down the priest at a

time like this, at the closing of *Il Libro di Vita Segreta,* you were accursed. You betrayed the memories of the deceased. But if you prayed and pretended to believe when you had no faith, you were accursed twice over. In the end, there was little choice.

"All right," Dante said.

He and the priest got down on their knees.

Our Father . . .

FORTY-TWO

Things had gone full circle. Seven years earlier, Dante had stood in the vestibule of Mayor Rossi's house, high up on Russian Hill, and asked him to use his influence to set up a special investigation into the Strehli murder. The mayor had put his hand on Dante's shoulder, affable as hell. He'd smiled and shrugged and given Dante a little talk on the separation of powers, and how he could not influence the shape of the judicial process even if he wanted.

"I'm only the mayor," he had said. "Not the king. That's the rub."

Now Dante climbed the hill again. When Rossi opened the door, he saw the same blustery grin, the same glistening eyes, though there was also a certain wariness there, and the mayor's face seemed worn from all the years of ingratiating smiles.

"What happened?"

The bandage on Dante's shoulder had begun to leak, and the pain was returning—but Dante brushed the question aside. In his good hand, Dante held the packet he'd gotten from Father Campanella.

"*La Vita Segreta*," Dante said. "My father's last words."

"I don't understand."

"You knew there was something else behind the Strehli murder. You knew that seven years ago."

The mayor shook his head. He glanced again at Dante's shoulder.

"I understand you're upset," he said. "Your father's death. Your uncle. But this obsession with Strehli—it's ruining you."

"Caselli was paid to confess. He didn't kill Strehli."

"You're a bit single-minded, this time of the evening—"

"Strehli was killed because he'd discovered something in that shipping container. Before he was murdered, he sent this packet to my father. But I think you already know that."

The mayor said nothing.

"My father came to you, didn't he?" said Dante. "My father came to you seven years ago, looking for advice."

"Your arm—"

"Tell me."

Rossi took a nervous glance up the staircase behind him, as if afraid someone might hear. It was an elegant staircase and you could hear music coming from the rooms beyond, the swell of violins.

"My wife," Rossi nodded toward the music. "Please, let's talk in my den."

Dante had been in the den, too, that evening seven years ago, and it was pretty much as he remembered it: a high-ceilinged room with sheer curtains, darkly furnished—a masculine room

that smelled of mahogany and leather. On the wall hung
mementos from Rossi's years in public office. Honorary degrees.
Medals of honor. Pictures of himself with dignitaries. News
clippings telling the familiar story, the one every immigrant likes
to tell: about the climb out of poverty, out of the mud and dirt,
to this elegant room in this elegant house, with these remembrances on the wall. To this elegant room where pictures of his
daughters, dark-haired and beautiful, sat on the rolltop desk. The
mayor's eyes glistened sadly.

"Your father did come to me seven years ago, yes. What happened, before Strehli died, he sent those photographs to your
father. Your father looked at those photographs, and he was
frightened of what might happen. Frightened for himself. And
for you."

"For me?"

"After Strehli was killed, you were dead set on finding out
what was up. He was worried that if you investigated further,
whoever killed Strehli, they would kill you, too. We talked about
it a long time. In the end, I suggested he give me what Strehli
had sent him. Then I would pass it along to the powers-that-be.
And I would protect his identity. I would say it had all been
passed to me anonymously. And that's what happened. He gave
me the file—the same one you have there, I assume. A few photos, a newspaper article, a letter allegedly written by Mr. Shen.
But I see now—your father must have made copies."

"And then?"

"I did as I said. I turned it all over to the appropriate author-
ities."

"Who?"

The mayor held up a hand. It was the same hand he'd held

up seven years ago. The same smile. The same shrug. "You know as a government official—even as a mayor—you brush up against security issues. I'm afraid I can't tell you that. My suggestion is that you let this go. Your father's concern—it was that you survive. The Strehli case was not your jurisdiction—and if you had pursued it . . ."

"You may have explained it to my father that way, but you had your own reasons."

"That's not fair."

"And you let them set me up. You fed me to the lions."

"Why would I do such a thing?"

"To protect yourself. Because you were afraid of what the Strehli investigation might uncover."

"I'm going to tell you what I told your father back then, and what I told him again before he died," the mayor said. "If you look at the information Strehli assembled—it says nothing concrete. It's a tissue of conspiracy theory with nothing behind it. There's nothing identifying the people in that container. And there's nothing verifying the authenticity of that letter."

"But what about the journal?"

"There is no journal," said the Mayor, but his voice lacked conviction, and his eyes were on the packet in Dante's hand. "No one ever found a journal."

Dante took a last look around the room, and saw again the mayor's beautiful daughters. He felt a sadness for the girls, and sadness for the mayor, and for the crab fishermen who had come before him and spent their lives pulling the harvest out of the ocean.

"You get started, you'll get a witch hunt going. And your family, they're not innocent. That warehouse—how do you think they got the contracts they did, the deals? Everyone else is going broke, and they survive. No one is pure in this world, and you should stop and think—"

"What do you mean?"

"I mean your father, your uncle, they had their dealings, too. How do you think they survived?"

Dante had taken a step forward, and Rossi backed toward the wall. The younger man still had one good hand and there was a certain fury in his hard features, in the dark eyes and drawn cheeks.

"I loved your father and your uncle both. You know that. I wouldn't have done anything to hurt them."

Dante loomed over the mayor. He watched the man cower and felt an ugliness pass through his own heart, the desire to push Rossi against the wall and kick him into submission.

"What are you going to do?"

The mayor's voice was high now. The man trembled, and this made Dante want to kick him all the more, but he saw in the old man's face all the old men he had even known. He wanted to kick them to death, all those old men. A man like Rossi, though, he would not pull the trigger. Not personally, anyway. There was someone else behind this. Rossi might know, but to get it out of him, he feared, he would have to be merciless. He would have to kick and not stop kicking. Dante took a glance at the wall, at the beautiful daughters. Then he turned and went out into the street.

Mayor Rossi stood in his den, looking through the gauze curtains. The sheers made a kind of film over the glass so that light from the street was filtered. Then a car went by, and Dante was illuminated from behind. His shadow grew large and fell across the glass, and then dwindled again. Then he was gone.

What was in that journal? Rossi wondered. *Maybe nothing at all. Maybe it has nothing to do with me.*

I have nothing to be ashamed of, he told himself. In this day and age, though, he knew how it was. One thing led to another, and the next thing you knew, the story was out, it got larger, it twisted this way and that, and all of a sudden you were responsible for all the sinister doings of the world.

It had a been a joint decision, he wanted to tell Dante. Your old man as much as me. I explained to him the situation, the risks in coming forward, and he had agreed to hide it away.

But he didn't tell me he had kept the copies. And he didn't tell me about the goddamn journal. Not at first, anyway. Not till years later, when he was in his death throes, babbling.

For myself, I would never have betrayed him.

But I have my wife, my daughters, grandchildren. They are vulnerable.

All I wanted was for this city to be a beautiful place.

There are people more powerful than us to whom we must all bend. Ideas. Institutions. The fabric of the times.

Man is by his nature corrupt. And things in this world do not happen without the touch of man.

He glanced once again at the photos, his life spread out on the wall.

Upstairs, his wife was playing Rossini. Mussolini's favorite. It had been on the Victrola the day Il Duce had his son-in-law executed.

Rossi closed his eyes. He didn't like what he had to do, but there was no choice.

He picked up the phone. He dialed the same number he'd dialed seven years ago, when Strehli had started talking about what he'd found in that container, back when all this fuss had started.

FORTY-THREE

Dante stood on Vallejo Street, overlooking the Barbary Coast. He was on the far end of his high now, the rush gone, fading—but despite everything there was still a kind of contentment, a sense of coasting, of imminent arrival. At the sametime he felt the old desire—the ache returning. There was a small hole in his heart that he knew would grow larger sooner enough, and there would be nothing to fill it.

It was a hospital high, without the ugly jerk and punch of street dope. Pure and uncut.

Dope like this, even on the downslide, there were moments when you felt the boundaries between yourself and the rest of the world slip away. The kind of moments his grandmother used to talk about, more or less.

God sees it all. He sees every thing. He knows what's in everyone's heart. And when you die, you will know, too.

The kind of moments aesthetics had. And lunatics. And people on their deathbeds.

Below him, at the bottom of the Kearny Stairs, a prostitute

was weaving her way out of the Hungry I and toward Chinatown. Up the street a tourist turned his head to watch, and a flock of parrots burst from the belfry of the Cathedral of Saints Peter and Paul. Love Wu was sitting in his wheelchair on his tenth-floor balcony, his oxygen tanks beside him. Below him relatives were mourning his great-nephew, Mason, but Love Wu was thinking only of the travels of his youth. The streets of Shanghai. Of Rome. Remembering a brown-eyed Italian girl with whom he had exchanged the briefest of glances, her face suddenly coming very clear to him, not knowing then or now that the same girl had turned down the bedsheets of the room where Salvatore and Regina Mancuso stayed when they adopted Gary. The memory vanished in a blink. Up the hill, Marilyn Visconti rolled in her bed, unable to sleep, and Mayor Rossi put down the phone, and Ying's grandmother stood on the fire balcony, eyes closed, and let out a low moan that was lost in the sound of the parrots winging by, and Dante watched shadows emerge from shadows down on the Barbary Coast, thinking for an instant he saw all the connections, he understood every goddamn thing—then, just as quickly, his omniscience disappeared, the knowledge temporary, fading from memory as soon as it was grasped, lost in the instant between one reverie and the next, scattered by the force of his desire and the pain that had just now returned, burning like a flame in his shoulder.

FORTY-FOUR

O n Fresno Street, a cat crouched in a window box, and the alley echoed with rickshaw music, emanating it seemed from several apartments at once. A fresh patina of broken glass littered the alley—a beer bottle smashed and scattered like the *I Ching*. Grandmother Pellicano would have found significance in such things. A reason for saying a prayer. For crossing herself. But these were portents Dante could not read. In his enhanced state, though, he found the alley reassuring in its solidity. It was home, at least. The porch light shone dim as ever. The key stuck in the same clumsy way.

He would not be able to stay long. The police guard had been removed from his hospital room, but he did not know why. He could not trust the company's intentions.

Inside, the house was quiet and dark, and the air carried—as it did everywhere in The Beach—the faint smell of mold, a fungus flowering deep in the timbers. The place was tidy, though. Dante had gotten his father's house back in order, straightening out the mess the police had made. So now there was something like serenity here, and the pictures of his relatives looked down with equanimity. He went upstairs to the bedroom to get himself into some fresh clothes. To strap on a holster and load his gun.

A light flashed on the phone machine, but when he played it, there was no message.

He would not stay here tonight. He would go around the corner to the Basque Hotel. He was exhausted, though, and he settled himself for a moment in the big chair that had been his father's favorite. His father had spent an infinite amount of time in the chair, so the imprint of his body was deep in the cushions, his smell in the fabric, and Dante remembered wandering by the room, seeing his father with his head back while Dante's mother, downstairs in the kitchen, sang in that high, beautiful voice that was hers alone. She sang those quavering arias of the female nobility: women forsaken, women at the edge of madness—and sometimes his father, too, would raise his voice, answering his mother's, and their voices would carry up and down the stairs.

He realized now what his father had done. How he had held quiet about Strehli's photographs and Ru Shen's journal. Held quiet because he feared what would happen to Dante if he were stubborn enough to push the investigation. And for another reason not quite so altruistic, if the mayor was to be believed. If so, his father must have been tempted at times to destroy that journal, or to translate it, but instead he'd done neither. Nonetheless he must have wondered about its secrets as he grew old, as he padded from room to room, drinking his grappa and eating his meatball sandwiches.

What was in these pages? Dante wondered.

The accounts of a businessman turned activist. A man who

knew the smuggling routes, the backdoor deals, the connections between Hong Kong money and the Chinese and the San Franciscans on the other side of the Pacific.

Something like a plan was forming in Dante's head. A way of insulating himself. Of using the journal to his own advantage.

He thought of his moment with Marilyn, and how she had pressed against him in the doorway of the abandoned storefront. He thought of Jake Cicero, and the offer he had made to bring Dante on as a detective if he stayed in town. He thought of his inheritance, and how his father had paid off the mortgage before he died. And he told himself he could stay here if he wanted. He could put behind him all those lonely nights, sheets bunched beneath his middle. He could forget the Ninth Ward, with its cockroaches the size of mice scuttling along the hardwood. Forget, too, the image of the woman on her bed in Bangkok. He could stay here in North Beach. He could make it up with Marilyn. He could look outside over the kiltered rooftops to see the old Calabrese on the street, all dressed in black, hunched over like crows on the wire.

He was tired, exhausted. The pain in his shoulder had worsened and he remembered the Vicodin in his father's medicine cabinet. He should get up, grab the Vicodin, go down to the Basque, but there was a puzzle in his head, something he was on the verge of solving, here in his father's chair.

The journal . . .

Who had the mayor talked to seven years ago? To whom had he given the Strehli file back then?

The company was an amorphous thing, personal intentions collided with the other intentions, not quite visible, and a plan that had started out became something else and emerged with a life of its own. So maybe in the beginning the sting's purpose had been to get rid of Fakir. To punish him for crimes past, real or imagined, and discredit him in the eyes of his own community. At some point it was decided that they might as well get Mason Wu, too. The way it had gone down, it suggested that there was an intersection of interest. The company and Love Wu.

Fakir was right about one thing: The company had its hands in the drug business. They'd wanted Fakir dead and Mason Wu, too. Then, as the plan came together and Dante started looking into the Strehli business, they'd decided to get rid of Dante and Ying, as well.

The reason had to do with the journal, Dante figured. There was a corrupt operative behind it all somewhere. Working with the sanction of the company, maybe or maybe not, but either way that operative had things he did not want revealed.

Who?

The answer had been hovering before him after he left the mayor's house and stood at the top of the Kearny stairs, staring down at the Barbary Coast. It hovered again before him now. The answer could be in the journal, but at the moment it seemed as if it were in front of him, in the dream images that tantalized him, in the phantasmagoria between sleep and consciousness, in the carnival parade of masked creatures that moved just beyond seeing in the land of shadows. And as he headed deeper into that world he remembered the basement window, the broken hasp, and he told himself he would get up in a moment, leave his father's house, but he didn't. His exhaustion was too strong.

FORTY-FIVE

What woke him up, exactly, he didn't know. Maybe it was the pain flaring in his shoulder. Or the sound of the house settling. Something unusual in the sound. Not quiet right. Dante sat in the utter silence, looking across the room at the bed where his father had died.

Then the phone rang.

The machine clicked over to take a message, then filled with the sound of the wire. Whoever it was, they had rung off.

The medication was fading, and the pain sliced through. Dante groped down the hall and rummaged the medicine cabinet and shook out a pair of his father's Vicodins.

Then the phone rang again. He heard his father's voice on the outgoing message, speaking in a mix of English and Italian. And a creaking noise. Not quite like the usual settling.

"Dante, this is Marilyn."

He might have picked up the phone then—but in the mirror, down the stairs, he saw movement. A shadow, a barest ripple, a quivering in the surface of the glass that suggested someone at the bottom of the stairs. Dante slid his revolver from its holster.

On the phone, Marilyn continued.

"I went to the Marina, to the boat, and you weren't there. . . . And so I thought . . ." She paused, sounding flustered. "I don't know what I thought . . . but there's a rumor going around today. About a shooting at the warehouse. And then on the news . . ."

It was one of those moments when things hung in the balance. Marilyn was on the other end, and if he picked up now there was a chance of reconciliation. Such moments could pass; you could miss them. He kept his eyes on the mirror.

"If you get this, call me," she said.

Even so he heard the chill in her voice, there at the end: worry mixed with the suspicion he had abandoned her again.

Dante wondered if he had imagined the movement downstairs, but at the same time he was going over the geography of the living room in his head. There were too many places for a person to conceal himself. If Dante went downstairs to investigate, the advantage went to the intruder. No, he wanted the intruder to come to him. Dante wanted the visitor to think he had not noticed his presence.

Dante sat down beside the phone, remembering the elaborate games he'd played as a kid. Staging phone calls in a voice loud enough for his parents to hear. So they would think he was on his way to the library, to church, to the movies, when in fact he had other things in mind.

He dialed the number of the meteorological society, same as he had done when he was young, then put his finger down on the receiver, killing the connection. All the time with his eye on the mirror.

"Marilyn," he said.

He paused then, trying to play it like there was someone else on the line, so his visitor would believe he was carrying on a conversation. He remembered his grandmother in the last days of her life, and his mother in her madness, talking to dead relatives, people you could not see. He knew how the phone echoed in the little house, how the mutterings and smallest noises carried everywhere.

"No, I'm fine," he said. "I was just dozing, and I couldn't get to the phone."

The ruse was absurd but he went on with it, quiet now—as if listening to Marilyn on the other end. He sat poised, gun in his hand, watching the mirror. He doubted his visitor would charge the stairs. This was someone who took no chances. Who killed old men in their sleep.

"No, no. Listen—I was there at the dock when the police made the arrests—but it's okay." He went on for a while, then, giving his imaginary listener a truncated, tumbled version of events. "I want to tell you more, but I just took a couple of Vicodin. I hurt my arm. . . . No, no. It's not serious. But I need to sleep. So I took something to knock me out."

He waited a long second.

"I love you, too."

He felt a stirring in his gut, a wash of foolishness at his performance. Then he returned to his father's bedroom. He took some pillows and laid them end to end, covering them with the quilt, fashioning things so in the darkness it would look like there was someone lying on the bed. Then he positioned himself in the closet.

He waited.

There was a mirror on the wall opposite the bed—a companion to the one at the top of the stairs, with the same frame and the same elaborate fluting. The way it was positioned would give him an instant of warning before the killer entered the bedroom—an instant when the intruder's shape would be illuminated in the mirror, backlit by the light coming through the window at the end of the hall.

Time passed. Twenty minutes. Thirty. An hour. Outside a blues guitar at the corner saloon hit a discordant note. The white noise on Columbus fell and rose and fell again. A drunk shouted out she'd been stabbed—and the rickshaw music faded away. There was the thin sound of something breaking, over and over, as if someone were throwing cocktail glasses from a high window. A throttled laugh. Sometime past final call, a garbage truck hit the alley—the sound of Latino men talking, rolling the cans, the hiss and clatter of the truck's hydraulic gate.

Through all this Dante listened to the house. The shifting, the bend and creak of the building at its middle. Then—a new sound, at the bottom of the stairs: floorboards responding to pressure. A footstep. The sound moved. On the staircase now. A man with a gun, his hand on the banister. Dante tried to visualize where the intruder might be. The creaking shifted, lower, not where it had been before. When the killer reached the top of the stairs, he would see his darkened reflection in the mirror.

The Vicodin had taken effect. It eased the pain, and as Dante nodded back into narcosis, the image of the man of the top of the stairs became more vivid, the shadow approaching the vanity, walking through the mirror, into the world on the other side—then he realized with a panic he was dreaming, on the verge of crossing over, and he shook himself awake.

It was too late.

The intruder had made it to the top of the stairs, but he had not stopped, he had not lingered. He had stepped quickly down the hall and now Dante saw him in the bedroom doorway, already entering, moving with a swiftness that was surprising, extending his arm in the shooter's motion towards the cushions Dante had formed on the bed. The shooter fired—a small blast of blue—and in that same instant seemed to understand his error: it was not a man on the bed, but pillows, bedclothes—and he glanced up, jerking his arm toward the closet just as Dante himself fired, just as the bedroom mirror caught the reflection of gunfire, sparks of starlight, blue and white in the glass, and the doorjamb shattered by Dante's head, and the shadow over the bed hovered a moment, then fell forward. Dante emptied his gun into the prone figure, then flipped on the lights.

It was Wiesinski.

The Big Why.

Once upon a time death had been a surprise, but it didn't surprise Dante anymore. It made a certain sense to him now, this corpse splayed out on his father's bed, bleeding into the mattress. It tied things together—and there was a kind of dark pleasure in that, as if some secret had been revealed, even though he knew such revelations were short-lived, quickly obscured. Wiesinski. The man responsible for Strehli's death. Who framed Dante when he tried to investigate seven years ago. Who'd shown up in New Orleans, during Mardi Gras, and fingered him for recruitment. Wiesinski, the company man. Who'd stalked Dante's father during his final days, who'd killed his uncle. Who'd set up the Fakir sting and sent Anita Blonde to rummage his bedroom, and Ying's place as well. The Big Why, with his twisted logic, his insatiable desires. The man who didn't want Ru Shen's journal revealed, because to reveal it was to show his hand behind the scenes.

But now the journal is in my possession, Dante thought, *and I can use it to my advantage. To guarantee myself safe passage, another life. Or to keep the company at bay. To stay here.* And for the moment— sitting on the bed, leaning his head against the backboard—he imagined such a scheme might work. He would call Marilyn in the morning. He would live here in his father's house and stroll with his hands behind his back, and the people in the neighborhood would pat him on the back, and he would be the man he had been destined to be. And he could live safe from the fear that a company man would visit him someday and put a bullet in the back of his head.

He glanced at the dead man, and something else occurred to him.

No one knows.

He struggled to get up, but his head was heavy. He closed his eyes—only for a minute, he told himself—but then the exhaustion, the Vicodin, they came at him in waves. He fought for a minute, trying to lift his head, but gave up. Sleep was not so bad, no. The darkness was refreshing. Out to sea. The wind in his face, the spray of the black water. Marilyn by his side.

The dead man lay in his father's bed, and Dante woke up beside him. It was late, well into the afternoon. Dante was hungry, and his mouth was dry. He went downstairs to his father's kitchen. He fixed himself a meatball sandwich and poured himself some grappa. And he took another Vicodin.

No one had come for Dante. And he did not think they would. The police had waived jurisdiction on the warehouse sting to the Feds, and the Feds had backed off after talking to the insect.

After dark, he would have to take another trip out to the bay.

In the meantime there was cleanup to do. He dug the bullets out of the wall. Mopped the floors. Scrubbed the walls. Searched the room for scattered bits of flesh. Fortunately, Wiesinski had done most of his bleeding directly on the mattress. It took a while, it took patience—especially with his bandaged arm—but Dante dragged the mattress down to the basement. Then he dragged Wiesinski down there, as well. He loaded Wiesinski into the back of his father's truck and put the mattress on top of the body, threw in his ruined clothes, and covered it all with a tarp.

Later that night, he took his grandfather's boat. The night was windy but clear. He dumped Wiesinski into the blackest part of the bay.

He weighted the mattress and sunk that, too.

No one knows.

He approached the shore. He held the journal in his hand now. His passport, his protection from the company's revenge. It had occurred to him the company might not know about the journal. Wiesinski would not have said anything because he would not have wanted the exposure. He would have wanted to handle it on his own.

The mayor knew, but the mayor had done whatever damage he could do. He could not call Wiesinski anymore. He would have to shiver it out on his own. *I am safe,* Dante told himself. (Though there was another part of him that suspected otherwise, that knew safety was not permanent. And there would be another visitor someday, climbing those stairs as he lay sleeping.)

Dante held the journal and looked out at the shoreline, at the jagged piers and the old tower on Telegraph Hill. His father had told him that when you went after things bigger than you, it was a form of arrogance. There were things you could not expect to change. Evils you could not erase. And his grandmother, with her superstitions, waving her hands, muttering, had essentially believed the same.

Say your prayers. Invoke the gods. Hope for the best.

There was no action you could take that did not unleash another action, no meting of justice that did not bring, by way of happenstance, punishment for the innocent as well as the guilty. Because there were others behind Wiesinski, no doubt, and still others behind them.

The water was calm and black. For a moment Dante was overcome by hunger, by desire. For what, he wasn't sure. For the old restaurants with the family around the table. For Joe DiMaggio with his arm around a big blonde. For the big-muscled fisherman wrestling a netload of fish. For the old ladies in the canneries. He saw the lights of Chinatown, serpentine, snaking over the crest, into Little Italy. Who was there to punish? Only the mayor, or men like him. Old men and their kids. Meanwhile, there was a song in the air, the crying of the gulls, the brown pelicans swooping down. There were the colored lights of pleasure crafts moored over the stumps of the old finger piers, out where the junks had used to linger. Crates of opium and perfume. It was a tangled business, the secret life of the Barbary Coast, the commerce you could not see. The commerce that made the other commerce possible. And who was to blame?

He turned to the back of the journal. The Chinese did it that way, starting at the back and writing from right to left. So he turned the book upside down and he tore out that last page, or the first, whichever it was supposed to be. He examined the torn page in his hand. He looked at the carefully brushed Chinese characters and guessed at the mystery between the lines. The secret life of Chinese laborers. Guns and drugs smuggled in container ships. A presidential candidate taking money from across the sea to turn his head the other way. A family warehouse where the shipping clerks signed off without examining the contents. Where you made a little extra money for closing your eyes. He took the page then and threw it into the sea. Then he tore out another. There was so little left of the old days, how could he betray them? The old men in the park. The hateful old woman at Serafina's Cafe. His cousin. Grandmother Ying. He tore out another page and another. The pages swirled and disappeared into the wake. Overhead, a pelican flew high in the morning light and then dove into the water. It was a beautiful bird. Dante turned off the motor and waited for it to resurface.

An Asian steamer came through the Golden Gate. The morning ferry headed out past Alcatraz. The tourists gathered on the wharf. Dante stayed out there for a long time, becalmed, waiting—but the bird did not surface. Then he turned on the motor and brought the old felucca into port.